THE SAMURAI'S SECRET

A TALE OF FORBIDDEN LOVE

REI KIMURA

For more information contact:
Riverdale Avenue Books/Magnus Lit Imprint
5676 Riverdale Avenue
Riverdale, NY 10471
www.riverdaleavebooks.com

Design by www.formatting4U.com
Cover design by Scott Carpenter

Digital ISBN: 9781626016743
Trade ISBN: 9781626016750

First edition, March 2024

Dedication:

"To those who dare to live a life different from others
To walk a path less travelled
Fearlessly and with great strength"

This story is dedicated to you!

Acknowledgements

To the family member who gave me access to the centuries old forgotten diaries and papers that inspired this book, thank you!

Chapter One

Fusao waited till his mother had retired into her room for the night. He had to be sure that she had fallen into a deep sleep from the soft flurry of snores that penetrated through the thin walls separating their rooms before he could put his plans into action. Ever since he was a boy, Fusao found his mother's snores strangely comforting, soft and musical, they reminded him of the first flurry of snowflakes in winter, scurrying gently down from the sky.

And yet, tonight, nothing felt comforting. He was weighed down by the heavy knowledge that this could very well be the last time he would see her. For all intents and purposes, it wasn't any special or memorable night, just an ordinary one for almost everyone around except for Fusao it was a night of nervous energy and desperation.

After so many years of living in the shadows of a fake life and the ultimate betrayal, he had reached the end of his road and just couldn't tolerate any more pain or humiliation. None of the things that mattered so much before, like maintaining a correct face to the outside world, his place and honor within the family and society and above all, trying so hard to suppress the shame of being a Doseiai, one who loves his own kind, and the source of his mother's despair and embarrassment, bothered him tonight.

A gleaming hocho, or kitchen knife, lay on the low table in front of him, the very hocho his mother had used to clean and cut the fish for their dinner together barely a few hours ago. It lay, clean and sharpened, ready for their next meal, totally oblivious to its sinister mission in the hours to come.

"Funny how a common kitchen tool used to prepare food to feed and nourish life can also become the instrument in which to take it away," Fusao thought and for the first time since he had made the decision to carry out this deadly mission, a thin film of nervous sweat started to form

1

on his brow as he thought of the daring and gruesome task ahead. As the minutes ticked by, the sweat started to trickle down his face in tiny glistening drops of fear and panic.

"It's not too late, there's still time to stop," his palpitating heart hammered out the unflinching rhythm of these restraining words over and over again, trying to weaken a resolve which had taken almost a month to build up.

"No! No! Be quiet!" that steely resolve screamed back. "Tonight it must be done and I'm ready!"

The night deepened and as if to challenge its darkness, the moon rose higher and higher in the sky, forming an eerie silver backdrop for the stark, black silhouette of the small but majestic castle perched high up on the hill that lorded it over the whole village and county of Minamimoto. Although it was getting late, a few houses were still awash with lights from the flickering oil lamps inside and in the distance came the muffled but unmistakable sounds of a family celebrating an occasion, maybe a birthday, a baby boy's birth or a father's promotion.

"Family harmony and contentment, how much we take it for granted," Fusao thought as he stopped for a moment to listen to the laughter and clinking of sake cups floating out of the lighted windows of a cluster of farming houses before moving swiftly and silently towards the castle gates, his dark yukata flapping soundlessly in the light breeze.

As he had expected, the main entrance to the castle was well guarded by a small army of heavily armed night sentinels, and at least two more hiding in the shadows, ready to spring into action against any intruders. Fusao didn't even know whether he could get in or not, it all depended on Destiny and the worst that could happen to him was that he would be seized for trying to sneak into the castle. He didn't care one way or the other because at the end of the night, he would be seized anyway.

The chief guard recognized Fusao as the special "protégé" of the samurai and signaled to the rest to let him enter without any questions.

"But, Sir, isn't this Fusao who left the castle under a cloud? Should we really let him in?" a more cautious guard protested.

In the shadows, Fusao held his breath; if he was refused entry fate would have stepped in to take the agonizing question of whether he was doing the right thing out of his hands. But it was late and freezing and the chief guard didn't want the trouble of checking their nocturnal visitor's credentials with the castle administrator and risk the samurai's displeasure if he turned away a favored protégé so he took the chance and waved Fusao on.

Hardly able to believe that it had been easier to enter the castle than he had expected, Fusao crept up the familiar path to the eastern wing where a magnificent set of low buildings housed the living quarters of Lord Okimoto. The new grand samurai of the Minamimoto province had assumed power and control since the passing of his father, the revered Lord Nobunaga who had started unwittingly this whole circle of tragedy in the twilight and some say senile years of his life.

"Okimoto," Fusao whispered, his tongue rolling tenderly over that name.

"Apart from his family, only I have the privilege of calling him that!"

Anyone else who dared to address him other than "My Lord Nobunaga" would get a taste of that famous Nobunaga temper! The arrogance and beauty of that magnificent body and aristocratic face sent a tingle down Fusao's spine as he made his way to the passage that connected the samurai's private rooms with the guardhouse.

The young samurai's mother, Lady Momoe, was obsessed with the idea that his life was always in danger and the passage allowed the guards quick access to his rooms in the event of any emergencies. By a stroke of luck, he had been allowed into the castle by the chief guard who had carelessly presumed that he was still the samurai's favored protégé.

But Fusao knew that soon, very soon, these very same guards who had let him in would be the ones to burst into Lord Okimoto's private chambers, their faces contorted with disbelief at what lay before their eyes and a wailing would reverberate round the room because they had failed to protect their lord, Nobunaga. Fusao could feel that horrifying scene unfolding before him even as he glided soundlessly down the passage, already seeing himself as a lonely specter wandering aimlessly for all eternity in the dim, cold passages of the Minamimoto Castle.

A couple of lamps swayed gently in the breeze that floated in through the tiny cracks on the wooden walls and they threw some light into the dim, twisted maze of passages but Fusao didn't need any light because he knew his way around only too well. The third door was the one which opened into Lord Okimoto's rooms. As he gently fingered the soft carvings on its wooden frames, Fusao thought of the many times he had crept through that door to meet his lover in a secret and forbidden union that knew no bounds and no self-restraint.

But it was over. Tonight was the moment he had chosen to finish with this forbidden love that not even the highest birth and the most powerful place in society could sanction. His own life was worthless..

Fusao was no hero, he knew he was afraid to die but to live in secrecy the way he had been his whole life was to suffer a life worse than death and after the baby's birth, he could take his lover with him without feeling any qualms because now the Nobunaga family had a successor and assured continuation of their bloodline. The Lady Momoe, mother of Lord Okimoto finally had the grandson she had burnt many joss sticks at the Shinto temples to have, so it was their time now.

The door of the inner chamber glided open with a mere whisper. There under the moon light streaming into the room, Fusao could see the bulge under the futons that covered and warmed his lover as he lay in a deep sleep. He drank in the beauty of that sleeping face with its chiseled features and marveled at how, even in repose, his beloved one had the arrogant confidence of his high breeding and power that both awed and excited Fusao. Even in this most tense moments of his life, Fusao felt his loins stirring at the memory of the unbridled passion they had once shared on those very futons.

There were at least a dozen other rooms connected to this one in a maze of secret passages and hidden doors, each one a tribute to Lady Momoe's obsessive fear of assassination. How ironic, then, that a once faithful servant, so familiar with the inner workings of the castle through sneaking around through those very same tunnels to lie intimately with her son would now sneak through them to assassinate him. Fusao's resolve hardened as he thought of how his lover had discarded him so easily, so cruelly. Yes, today would be the day that everything had to finish because he could no longer bear the pain of that love.

With the silence and stealth of a fox, Fusao moved to a crouching position beside the futon of his sleeping lover and, throwing all resolve to the wind, he reached out to gently stroke a strong muscular arm that was flung across the futon as he had done countless times before. For a few long seconds, Fusao hesitated, wondering how he could snuff the life out of the beautiful man before him and his heart constricted with pain. Was there a way, any way out? Was this the only way they could be together for all eternity?

In a small pouch hidden deep inside his yukata was a bundle of beautiful poems they had written to each other glorifying their forbidden love that would never have a chance to come out of its shadows and be celebrated with all the joy it deserved. Fusao had written a last poem to his lover a few days ago and it lay now inside his yukata close to his wounded heart, the rough parchment paper scraping his skin.

A hand reached out to stroke his thigh and the man on the futon whispered, his voice still hazy with sleep, "Is that you, Fusao? It's been so long without you…"

Fusao turned away from that trusting face and, with a small cry, plunged the honcho he held in his trembling hands deep into the chest of his lover. He did not stop till the honcho had gone into the chest that was still flooded with love and desire for him.

The tears gushed down his ashen face as he plunged the hocho deeper and deeper, ignoring the muffled cries of shock that cried out his name, "Why, Fusao? Why?" as Okimoto's blood trickled down out from the body Fusao had grown to know so intimately.

The whispers gave way to searing screams of pain. Fusao flung himself across the room with the shock of what he had done as his lover, Lord Okimoto, grand samurai of the great Nobunaga dynasty lay gasping before him, his face a death mask of pain, betrayal and disbelief.

A fierce thundering of feet shook the room as the guards raced down the passage towards them and there was a smile on Fusao's lips as he surrendered himself to their merciless assaults. He would be dead soon and their souls would find each other in a union of uninhibited love at last.

Chapter Two

In her tiny office in one of the back streets of Shibuya, investigative historian, Mayumi Onodera had just started a slow after lunch mid-week afternoon at her desk, flipping through the usual articles in the latest issue of the Non-no magazine, nothing very heavy or important, just some whimsical magazine for women and young girls on the all-time favorite issues of love, beauty tips, celebrity gossip and haute couture. But the pull and promise of the exotic glossy covers was so irresistible that even a down to earth and pragmatic historian like Mayumi could succumb to their frivolous contents once in a while just to disconnect from the heaviness of her line of work.

The room was dominated by a large ornate working table with its usual clutter of papers, newspaper cuttings and scattered stationary, except that today, it also hosted an additional uninvited guest. Miki, the lofty oversized ginger cat Mayumi brought to the office on most days, had decided to add to the clutter by settling down on the soft fleecy scarf his owner had finally thrown across the table to protect her papers, for his afternoon nap. Mayumi sighed, no matter how hard she tried to sort out her table, it always ended up in this glorious mess by early afternoon and Miki's recent acquisition of it as his territory didn't help. But he looked so comfortable, snuggled into her scarf, she didn't have the heart to forcibly return him to his rightful places, the window ledge or a large wicker basket in a corner next to an artificial money plant.

Fortunately, her last assignment, a few months ago, had given Mayumi a big financial break. Her assignment had taken her to Singapore, a city-state of some strange sentimental significance to her mother that she had never expected to visit quite so soon. On top of that, the job had led to new contacts with a number of wealthy families in Tokyo who had joined the current trend of ancestor tracing in the high society and retained her services especially as she came highly recommended by revered Japanese American DNA entrepreneur, Tetsuyo Akinicho.

Compared to her other assignments, these minor ancestor tracings had been very easy, all she had to do was live in the right museums, heritage libraries and Gen Nihon (the very exclusive lineage tracing center) for a few days and she had everything she needed to wrap up her work and receive a flat fee for it.

Her change of professional fortunes had brought Mayumi some respite, for the moment at least, from her skeptical family's anxious demands for answers to the question of "how can a historian, whatever that may be, ever earn a decent living?" But it wasn't long before her resourceful mother found a new cause to champion, she simply substituted that with another more bothersome question of when Mayumi was ready to find a nice boy and settle down.

At 28 years old, Mayumi thought she was doing very well without a man to restrict and mess up her life! She was still recovering from the aftershocks of her last boyfriend a year ago, the super-clingy type who had already decided how many children they would have and even their names, barely three months into their relationship and everywhere she turned, Nobu was there.

Her mother had welcomed Nobu with open arms as the solid family man who would have a steadying influence on her eccentric daughter and curb those wild spurts. God, that had been irritating and if her mother loved Nobu so much, let her marry him then! For a woman who had travelled all the way to Singapore by herself on what she would only say was a personal mission, Kyoko was surprisingly traditional in her insistence that the usual package of marriage, kids and a life of domestic bliss should be upheld by her daughter.

It didn't help that most of Mayumi's best friends from the university were already well launched on the marriage pad with at least a kid or two in tow. In fact, Mayumi was the last one of the group of five who was still single and not fretting about it at all. Some called women like her cakes that had passed their expiration dates but Mayumi couldn't care less. She knew she would succumb to the institution of marriage only if she found a man who could take her independent and eccentric ways, including sleeping with a temperamental cat and her extraordinary line of work.

But until then, she was content to live alone in her small but comfortable apartment near the Shibuya station with the office just a 10 minute walk away. Of course she still enjoyed the company of men and didn't mind the occasional party and sleep over with some attractive guy, but no, she wasn't ready for commitment. She loved herself and her work too much to let any long-term relationship get in the way in a society that demanded that a woman surrender herself and her career to the doubtful bliss of marriage!

The phone rang and Mayumi knew by the personalized ring tone she recently downloaded into her mobile phone that it was her mother. She groaned, Good God, knowing her Mother was going to ask the same questions about her lack of a boyfriend to drape herself around because a cousin's daughter had just got hitched over the weekend. Maybe she should tell her mother she was gay and not interested in men! Better not, then her mother would only pester her more about meeting a woman and settling down. She knew she was in a no-win situation. Mayumi figured it was best to simply allow her mother to voice her opinions regarding her daughter's life and try to change the conversation.

Five minutes after she put down the phone on her mother, with the usual hurried promises to date more or face a matchmaking agency and an arranged marriage, the shiny new doorbell of her office, compliments of her last lucrative case, rang. Then the door opened abruptly to admit an elderly couple accompanied by a younger man.

Crap! Mayumi groaned inwardly. *Couldn't they have just waited a couple of minutes before charging in like that!*

The old man looked around the cluttered room pointedly before directing his eyes to the magazine laden chairs, obviously deciding which chair he should clear to get a seat.

"Sorry it's a bit untidy round here because we are kind of reorganizing ourselves at the moment," Mayumi muttered embarrassedly and began to hastily remove the papers and magazines from the chairs and clear a corner of the table, including Miki, for their consultation. The old couple sat down on the chairs helped by the young man of exceptionally good looks, possibly their grandson.

When everyone had settled down, Mayumi returned to her seat behind her desk, brought out a few sheets of paper and pen and asked the standard question that was supposed to start a consultation.

"How can I help you?"

Her clients remained silent for quite a while but Mayumi made no attempts to hurry them. In her line of work, sometimes people came with very unusual requests and delicate family secrets and they naturally needed time to warm up before telling their stories. She was very used to such awkward pre consultation moments and it was her job to wait until her clients were ready to talk.

The old woman glared at her faltering husband and motioned firmly for him to start the ball rolling. After swallowing a few times, he began to speak at last, stiffly as if he were uncomfortable with the subject.

"My name is Daisuke Fujita. We come from Minamimoto and this is my wife Harumi and the young man here is my grandson, Toyoki."

Mayumi bowed in acknowledgement, handed the old man her name card and waited while he scrutinized her credentials.

Satisfied at last, Mr. Fujita nodded and continued, "We came to Tokyo because an old Tokyo University friend of mine who lives in USA told me that you can help us clear up a family mystery that has been hanging over my wife's family for decades and recently resurfaced when we found some very old papers."

The friend must be Tetsuyo Akinicho, Mayumi thought, *bless him for pushing so many clients her way!*

There was a rustle as his wife, Harumi, fumbled in her bag and drew out what looked like a brown wooden file which she opened to disclose a bundle of old papers protected and sealed in a plastic case. She placed it on the table. Through the thin clear plastic cover Mayumi could make out some words written in very old Japanese characters. In her second year at the university the faculty had offered some optional courses and one of them was old Edo period Japanese language and writing interpretation, and although she couldn't bring herself to endure and complete the dry and boring course for one whole semester, two months of deciphering and translating were enough for her to have learnt something quite substantial. And now she was grateful for those two months because at least she felt sufficiently confident of her old language interpretation skills to accept the job.

As Mayumi took the papers out of their plastic case and started going through them, she noticed the old woman looking at her anxiously, pleading with her eyes that she handle the priceless papers with care so they would not fall to pieces.

"These are very old papers about one of our ancestors which have been passed from one generation to another and are considered a very precious family heirloom," she said at last, unable to contain herself. "But for decades no one has bothered to find out what they say and now I think it's time one of us takes it up."

"Perhaps, for a start, you should tell me everything you know about these papers and we'll go from there," Mayumi suggested.

"These papers belong to one of my direct ancestors," the old lady, Harumi, said. "I'm descended from a distinguished family of Samurai who served the shoguns of this country for generations. We can go as far back, I think, as the 11th century and trace my lineage to the Grand Samurai, the Lord Oda Nobunaga. After the war, as you know, the Allied Forces took away all our lands and distributed it to the farmers and everything was gone just like that." The old woman seemed to trail off for a moment as if lost in the past. Suddenly she shook her head and began to speak again.

"My father couldn't take our sudden change of fortunes and committed suicide in the only noble way, by cutting himself up in the hara-kiri ritual. But before he died, he gave me a box filled with pictures and these papers he had kept hidden because he didn't trust anyone after the war and was obsessed with the fear that someone, especially a foreigner would steal them."

Mayumi glanced down at the papers wondering what could have been so important to the old man for him to go to such lengths to conceal them.

"Well, according to my father, these papers have been in the family for centuries but until now, no one has tried to have them deciphered or translated and as you can see, they are falling to pieces. My father made me promise to try and unravel the mystery that lies behind these papers before the writings really faded away and this family story is lost forever. I am ashamed to admit that I never got around to doing anything until now because of my grandson's persistent reminders."

Mayumi looked up at the handsome young man wondering what role he had to play in the mystery. He stared back unsmilingly.

"From some of the symbols and old calligraphy I recognize only very vaguely, I think that most of them are love poems or a kind of personal diary centered around a dark forbidden dalliance of one of my ancestors, because the word love appears everywhere in the papers. We just want to know what it all means and if you can translate them into modern Japanese language, it would recreate a piece of our history for us."

10

A dark forbidden dalliance? Mayumi thought to herself. This could be interesting for a change. Not like the usual boring family lineage search.

"There is of course a deep mystery surrounding this ancestor, some of us in the family know of it but no one wants to discuss the subject simply because it's easier to let sleeping dogs lie, especially those as mysterious as this," Harumi san continued. "But it was my father's wish that I get to the bottom of these papers, and I must honor that wish."

"May I ask why you think a mystery lies within these papers? Love letters from a samurai to his ladylove was not that unusual. I've seen them in the historical archives before."

"In the 18th century there was an attempted assassination in this samurai branch of my family," said the old woman. "One of the samurai was stabbed almost to death one night and no one was ever caught or blamed for it. A powerful samurai had been brutally attacked and no one was made accountable for that? it seems unbelievable as if they knew who the attacker was, and everything had to be covered up to protect the family honor. I started to search the family registers and old samurai history of our family's town and my research confirmed that there was indeed such a horrific attack on this ancestor, and still I couldn't figure out who had committed the crime. I believe these papers hold the key to this attack and the mystery of his connection to my ancestor." The elderly woman paused a moment as if to catch her breath. Mayumi could see it was exhausting for her to tell such an emotional story that she had kept to herself for so long.

The story captivated Mayumi. The mystery and the death, it was all so intriguing. She felt the familiar adrenaline charge of challenging another new case as she gently put the pieces of centuries old papers back into their plastic casing under the watchful eyes of Harumi san.

"Will you take on this case and find out what story these old papers have been trying to tell us for centuries?" Harumi san asked.

Chapter Three

Mayumi waited until her clients had left the office before taking out the papers for a more detailed examination. The old lady, Harumi, had seemed reluctant to leave such precious family heirlooms with a stranger but Mayumi assured her they would be safe.

"Please take care of these papers because they are originals," Harumi san said as she threw a last worried glance around the cluttered office with its untidy piles before going to the door. Mayumi made a mental note to clean up her act. It seemed her office didn't make her clients feel comfortable about leaving priceless documents behind and she couldn't blame them!

But she forgot about her embarrassment and resolution as soon as the door closed on the little group and she felt the familiar surge of a historian's excitement and awe of actually touching such rare literary masterpieces of Japan's Edo period outside a museum showcase and the anticipation of unravelling the secrets they held.

On closer scrutiny, Mayumi ascertained that the papers were arranged in some kind of system, divided into a few bundles each bound with a string that had become frayed and faded with time. What caught her immediate attention was the red seal of a magnolia blossom marking each bundle, did that have any special meaning? But of course, it was probably the seal or family crest of the samurai, was it Nobunaga that Harumi san had mentioned? The color of the red seals had run over the hundreds of years since they had been stamped by someone on the papers and the blurry images looked like blotches of blood.

A shiver ran down Mayumi's spine as she felt the lives of the writer and his subjects whispering through those frail, yellowed pages and once again, she had to remind herself to keep focused, stay detached and dissect it just like any other case.

But it was never easy to stay impersonal and detached because history was an emotional subject with her and sometimes the lives and events of her ancestor tracing assignments really entered into her bloodstream and the older the period, the more they got to her.

Her mother had never been comfortable with Mayumi's chosen career and had only recently given up telling her that a young pretty woman should be in some happy, more refreshing job instead of being locked up in the dark, musty pages of history books, dead people and historical events. Mayumi long ago resigned herself to the fact her family would never understand her passion for history and what one of her professors had once said after reading a particularly passionate thesis, that she was born a historian.

As soon as she started to work on the papers, she forgot about everything else. The first page had stuck to its special plastic casing and Mayumi was terrified that she would tear it as she slowly drew out the dry crackling paper inch by inch. It appeared to be the oldest piece judging by the date the writer had penned on the top right hand corner, the 10th year of the Edo dynasty. It was written in the style of that period and Mayumi's trained eyes could see that the characters were uneven and amateurish, obviously written by someone who was not well schooled in calligraphy or even someone from the lower class.

A frown creased Mayumi's brow as she tried to make sense of that interesting discovery. Hadn't Harumi san mention that the letters belonged to her samurai ancestor and not some semi educated person from the village? These letters could not have been written by a samurai because a samurai would be much better schooled and his lettering more refined. What was the connection then between a high-ranking Samurai of the Nobunaga clan and the writer of such badly penned letters that they would end up in his possession?

Although most of the characters were too blurred to be deciphered without her special magnifying glass, Mayumi could feel the power of those words leaping out at her, crafted by some ancient hand long dead, and she felt the fine hairs at the back of her neck rise. It was as if they had remained silent too long and now they wanted to be released. She had left her magnifying glass at home and, with frenzied energy, Mayumi squinted at the blur lines and squiggles, trying to make out enough words on the first page to know what the writer wanted to say.

The shrill scream of an alarm on her desk broke the electrifying silence and energy of intense concentration and it made her jump.

"Great, I needed just that to complete the whole sinister picture," Mayumi thought wryly, "an alarm that wails like a spirit in distress as indeed there seems to be one in these creepy papers!"

But it was only the electronic schedule she had bought in an electronic mall in Singapore on her last assignment there, it was a useful tool to keep her appointments up to date but now that she was onto this eerie new case, she must remember to change its alarm tone! Its present wailing tone was just too unnerving and she was glad for the warm, living and breathing presence of her cat.

Then Mayumi groaned as she remembered why she had set the alarm. Today was the day she had promised to make the 90 minute train ride to Matsudo in the Chiba area to have dinner with her mother and spend the night there. Usually, she found these occasional overnight rituals complete with delicious home cooked meals and all the motherly pampering a girl could ask for rejuvenating, but today Mayumi just wanted to be alone to start work on those deep dark papers. But it was a special day for her mother and she couldn't just back out, not today.

As a compromise between her work and her mother, she decided to bring copies of some of the papers with her to study. She hastily took the first few pages of the earliest bundle in terms of date down to the convenience store to photocopy. It was better to leave the original documents in the small safe in her office.

For the umpteenth time, Mayumi felt a strange electric current flowing into her from the papers in her hands and she tried to shake away the insane feeling that the characters were, in some strange psychic way, reaching out to her, crying for help and for release. Jeez, what was it with those papers? She had to get a grip on herself if she wanted to dissect the case and solve it with a cool historian's eye.

It was a weekday and just before the start of the evening rush hour so Mayumi managed to get a good corner seat on the train, all the better to have some privacy to study the documents. She started with the earliest letter according to the barely legible date scrawled on the top, always the right-hand corner, the 10th year of the Emperor Nakamikado. Mayumi consulted her organizer where she kept a list of all the emperors of Japan for just such an event.

"Emperor Nakamikado ruled from 1709 to 1735, during the Edo period," she muttered to herself. "So, 10th year of his reign places the writer at around 1719, just about 300 years ago."

The characters were badly written in the old style of that era and difficult to read. To make any sense of the jerky squiggles without a magnifying glass, which would have attracted unwanted attention on the commuter train, Mayumi had to draw on all her knowledge from the laborious and agonizing hours she had devoted to the study of ancient writing at the university and never thought to use again outside a library.

"Today, the master gave me this paper and ink and asked me to write" was the first sentence.

"So I was right!" Mayumi thought triumphantly. "These letters were penned by someone in a lower social position and he had a "master" meaning a feudal lord or even someone connected to the samurai."

Interesting… And yet still perplexing. Feudal lords didn't mix socially with peasants and certainly weren't in the habit of giving paper and ink to one. And who was this peasant who obviously knew how to read and write? Why, the working-class farmers and peasants of that period weren't even allowed to have surnames, let alone any opportunities of learning to read and write! This wasn't some modern classless society she was looking at but a period in the history of Japan, where class was defined and dissected with the precision of the best timepiece! And God helped anyone who tried to break those rules!

"Yotsuya!" the serious voice blared out through the train's PA system. Mayumi groaned, more out of habit than any real distress. In her absorption with the letters, she had missed her station, Shinjuku, and would have to double back to catch the connecting train to Chiba which she would probably miss now. Like most Japanese, normally, Mayumi hated to have a planned time schedule derailed but today, she welcomed the half an hour or so extra time this would give her to continue reading and translating the first paper.

"My father is tired out from his day at the fields and right now, Mother is preparing our dinner, natto and miso shiro soup tonight."

The writing was stilted and uncertain about simple, unremarkable things. It was as if the writer had been given ink and paper for the first time and didn't know what he should write about! None of the sinister or steamy sex stuff Mayumi had been expecting because of Harumi san´s reference to the word "äi" or "love" that she said seemed to be written all over the papers.

Deep in thought, Mayumi managed to make it to Kanda station and transfer to the super express Joban Line to Matsudo.

15

Then she sobered as she settled into her seat in the half full train as it raced out of Tokyo city. The late afternoon spring sky had already darkened to a fuzzy grey and the dazzling lights of hundreds of advertisements were coming alive with amazing uniformity as if someone had switched on the lights of a Christmas tree. Mayumi thought of the writer of the letters in her purse. Long dead, he would never know the bright lights and wonderful technology of modern Japan and yet his memory and legacy lived on in those few pieces of papers! How awesome and undefeatable by time History was!

Chapter Four

Most of the humble houses of the farmers in Minamimoto were dimly lit but perched high up on top of a small hill, the lights of the samurai's majestic castle shone, bright and fearless, boasting of the power and strength of the Nobunaga family who lived there. Only they had the right to such bright lights and all the other houses had to be dimmer in deference to their feudal lord and master because no star could shine brighter than his. The wide sweep of subdued lights at the foot of the hill looked uncannily like the deep bow of a whole community of subjects before their master and it was awesome.

But in the last few years, as the fiercely arrogant Lord Nobunaga grew older, he began to wind down and behave very strangely, becoming more humble and almost human, in his interaction with people. Then he started going down personally to inspect his vast rice fields and actually taking an interest in them. Usually, he went alone with just a couple of his most personal guards, heavily armed and always ready to protect their master, but without any of the fuss and protocol that surrounded the samurai wherever he went down to the village in his heydays.

Although his presence in their midst was more of a hindrance to the simple farming folk of the area more accustomed to an aloof and distant feudal master than one who walked around them and took an interest in their work, no one dared say anything. The Lord Nobunaga was lord and master of them all and he could do anything he wanted. It was his birthright to be eccentric and arrogant and if it amused him to have a passing fancy for peasants, his subjects had to live with that and pray that it would not last very long.

The great Lord Nobunaga was the one who had taken an unusual interest in Fusao and given him his first paper and ink with lofty orders to write. For a boy of his humble position, it was overwhelming to be noticed by a powerful samurai who seemed to know that among the village boys, Fusao was the only one who could write, courtesy of an old uncle who had lived and worked in the Edo capital as an official to the Shogun before returning to his native Matsumoto to retire.

As a young boy, Fusao had sometimes gone to spend the summer with his uncle and helped him craft the traditional wooden dolls that gave the old man both a modest living and something to do after his retirement. Unknown to Fusao's parents, uncle and nephew also spent many an evening writing on whatever scraps of paper they could find and sometimes even with sticks on the ground while the former reminisced about his days in the Shogun's office. If Fusao's parents had known about these after work activities of their son, they would have stopped him from going to Matsumoto because they believed a peasant would always be a peasant with no way up the social ladder of feudal Japan. It didn't do any good to give a boy any ideas above his station and dislodge his focus on his destiny in life, laboring and farming for his samurai overlords.

But his parents never found out until it was too late. Fusao's summer visits to Matsumoto continued until he was old enough to join his father in the rice fields to start what he had been born for, service to his feudal lords.

Fusao was always grateful to his uncle for teaching him the spiritual joys and possibilities of being able to write and although it did make him different and a little better respected than the other village boys who couldn't even read or write their own names, he was realistic and had no other greater expectations in life. His father, grandfather and all their forefathers before him had been farmers in service and bondage all their lives to their feudal lords and that was what Fusao knew he had to be from the time he was born, a farmer and nothing more. When his father, Naoki, finally discovered what his son had been up to in Matsumoto apart from crafting wooden dolls, he proceeded to relentlessly drum into the boy's head that being able to read and write didn't mean he could go and have fancy ideas about himself.

The first time Lord Nobunaga wandered into their humble home at the end of a street that was caked with dried mud in summer and slushy with melted ice in winter, Yuko, Fusao's mother was so shocked that she just stood frozen to the same spot before remembering her station in life and falling almost on her knees in a deep bow of respect.

What was the grand samurai, Lord Nobunaga doing in their home?

The bowl of rice she had been holding fell from her shaking hands and she watched in horror as the rice grains spattered against Lord Nobunaga's feet.

"I am so sorry, my Lord, for being so clumsy," she whispered, kneeling down to wipe the rice grains away from the feet of a person most people regarded as second only to God. She braced herself for the heavy hand of a soldier on her head for daring to soil the samurai's shoes.

When Lord Nobunaga motioned for the trembling Yuko to get up and asked for her son instead, it was Fusao's turn to be petrified. He didn't know why a powerful samurai would want to have anything to do with him and, flanked by two fully armed soldiers and a handsome young man whom Fusao later discovered was the samurai's son and heir, the awesome group was enough to set any young peasant boy's limbs shaking with apprehension.

Fusao could tell by the way her face had turned white that his mother also was anxious about the Lord Nobunaga's interest in him but she could not disobey a samurai's request and pointed to where her son was sitting on the floor, cutting up some vegetables for dinner. Fusao was just 15 years old. That day Fusao was at home because his father had decided to go into the town to settle some business and did not need him for the rice fields. The boy had hoped for a quiet day at home and the last thing he expected was to be the object of interest to the most powerful man of the prefecture and it terrified him.

"Get up, Fusao, and bow." His mother whispered. "You must show respect to our lord and master."

Before Fusao could do her bidding and scramble to his feet, the old samurai came over and motioned for him to remain seated. Dumbstruck and with his eyes respectfully averted, he watched as the most powerful man in the region placed a few pieces of paper, an ink pot and a brush on the low table in front of him. The two soldiers moved protectively to their master's side and glared at the white faced peasant boy with a ferocity that made him shrivel up inside and Fusao could tell that they were disgusted he had made their master come to him, a mere peasant boy. The impropriety and reversal of protocol was just unbearable to them!

At their master's command, one of the soldiers appeared with a torch and filled the dark room with the brightest light Fusao had ever seen. It was fascinating, turning murky darkness into warm golden fluid and he was mesmerized by that light, the brightest their house had ever seen.

"Write!" the Lord Nobunaga said peremptorily and once again, he reminded them that he was the samurai issuing an order.

His authoritative voice made the nervous boy jump and the inkpot rattled precariously on the scuffed wooden table. The young peasant was too petrified to steady it.

As he continued to hesitate, Fusao felt a tiny, but impatient, prod from the sword of one of the soldiers on his back and he bowed his head swiftly over the paper and held it reverently as if it was the most sacred thing he had ever touched. With trembling hands and a heart beating rapidly with the nervousness of being watched by so many distinguished visitors, Fusao put the paper on the table and tried to write. His uncle had always given him only old bits of paper to write and practice on but the beautiful scented paper before him was the whitest and purest he had ever seen.

Reluctant to mar the white perfectness of the paper before him with his ungainly scribbles, Fusao hesitated. Once again, he felt another prod from the tip of a soldier's sword. Since his uncle's death two years ago, Fusao hadn't picked up a single brush and his heart was hammering as he tried to remember the characters he had learnt. But they were all dancing in front of him, elusive and out of reach. He tried but he couldn't seem to catch any of them.

"Write!" the samurai commanded again and this time his voice held a hint of impatience.

Petrified, Fusao's hand refused to move and then Lord Okimoto, the samurai's son and heir took the brush from him, their fingers brushing, and wrote something on the upper right-hand corner of the paper, all the while watching him with a strange intensity.

"This is today's date," he said, handing the brush back to Fusao. "Now it will all come back to you and you can start writing."

Fusao took the brush from his noble rescuer, feeling himself drowning in the beauty of his fluid dark eyes and brilliant smile and began to write with a sudden rush of energy and confidence. "Today, my Lord Nobunaga honored our humble house with his visit and gave me the whitest paper and the blackest ink I ever saw."

The old samurai watched Fusao penning line after line for a while and when he had seen enough, he gave a signal to his guards and the whole group left without a single word, as swiftly as they had arrived, without explanation or accountability, taking away the brilliant illumination they had brought with them. Once again the house was plunged into the dimness of its single oil lamp. But the magic of their visit and Lord Okimoto's smoldering dark eyes lingered on in the young boy's mind and he continued to write, not stopping until he had filled that piece of white paper with line after line of words from his heart.

Naoki returned a few hours later and although it was very late, Fusao had stayed up to show him the paper and tell him the incredible story of the grand samurai's visit. Although Naoki wasn't interested in some fantasy stories about samurai paying house calls on peasants, he decided to humor Fusao and hear him out because he had important news for his son.

"You know I'm getting old, son," Naoki began as soon as he could get a word in. "And you are already 15 years old, and it's time we start arranging a suitable girl for you. Others younger than you have had their betrothals already settled and that's why I went to Matsumoto town this morning to visit a distant branch of this family."

"Today is a happy day for us because I managed to arrange your marriage with a nice and beautiful girl called Aiko. She is 13 years old and after a two years' betrothal, she will move here to marry you. It will certainly be good for your mother to have a girl around to help her with the chores."

Fusao stopped short in his feverish account about the samurai's visit and heard his father for the first time. What had Naoki just said? He had arranged marriage with a distant cousin for him? The very words made Fusao's blood curdle, and he cringed from the blow his father had unwittingly inflicted on him. Naoki could just as well have physically taken a rope and whipped Fusao senseless for the impact those words made on him.

"No, no," his whole body recoiled against his father's proposal but he knew that when the time came, he would not be able to fight the inevitable because a father's word was law in any family and no child could go against it. So he bit back the words of protest and kept quiet.

Before he went to sleep that night, Fusao took out the wooden case of papers he had hidden deep in the oshire and wrote the character "marriage" and after looking at it for a long moment, he added the sad, ineffective word of protest "No" under it.

The magic was gone and the fire of the samurai's visit had died down into ashes, Fusao did not feel inspired to write anymore and he put his wooden case of papers back into the oshire and buried himself in his futon.

21

Chapter Five

The dinner had gone better than Mayumi had expected mainly because no one mentioned a word about her lack of matrimonial prospects or her strange choice of career. Whatever Kyoko Tanaka was, there was no denial that she was an excellent cook and whenever her daughter, whom she was sure was living on fast food and instant noodles, came home, she would cook with the full force of her culinary skills. Her mother had gone to extra trouble this time and Mayumi was replete with the very best home cooked food and energized, her mind was clearer and sharper than the day before.

They had talked mostly about old times and her mother seemed in a somber mood that night. Then Mayumi remembered it was April 1st. For as long as she could remember, every year, on April 1st Kyoko Tanaka would go into some kind of meditation and light joss sticks on the small ancestor tablet she kept in a discreet corner of her room. Mayumi had never understood the significance of this day for her mother but she swore, someday she would ask her mother about the subject. But tonight, because Kyoko had left her alone, she decided not to ply her with the usual questions of April 1st but to her surprise, this year, her mother ventured to open the door of her heart just a crack for Mayumi.

"You know of course that the Awa Maru, a war time Japanese hospital ship, sank on April 1st, 1945, so I pray for the victims every year," she said. "Someday when I'm ready, I'll tell you about our family's involvement in this horrible tragedy."

On the train going back to her modest apartment in Shibuya, Mayumi could not stop thinking of her mother's words about the Awa Maru and wondering how her family was somehow connected. Maybe some close member had been one of the victims and that was why her mother was so blue on April 1st every year and insisted Mayumi come home for dinner wherever she was. Mayumi's education on the Awa

Maru had started long before she hit the history books because her mother had taken her to the Zojoji Temple a few times to lay huge bouquets of white flowers beside the black marble plaque which honored the victims whose names were engraved on its two adjoining walls.

To divert herself from the annual frustration she always felt against her mother for refusing to share such an important piece of history with her, Mayumi took out the old papers she had been looking at on the trip out.

"The master gave me this paper and ink to write," Mayumi read the first line again, she still wasn't able to find an explanation as to why a person from the working class who had a "master" was able to write although not in the best of penmanship or why a samurai would consort with one of his subjects from the peasant class. Of course, Harumi san had naturally assumed that these papers belonged to the samurai or members of his family or elite retainers at the castle, because only they had the privilege of education but the "word" master had proved that assumption wrong. The writer of the letters haunted Mayumi and she couldn't stop thinking about him and his strange alliance with the grand Samurai and his family. There was definitely something here that didn't quite fit into the scheme of things.

She changed to the local train almost automatically like a sleepwalker and as soon as she got a seat on the train, Mayumi went back to the small stack of photocopied papers again.

The second page was neatly divided into columns, four columns in all. But one paragraph in particular, the last one on the left, caught her eye. There on the paper written bold and firm was a very clear "no." She was not left wondering what the word "no" was associated with because further down the column, another word leapt out of the page, "marriage" again written in a bold hand for emphasis.

Despite herself, Mayumi couldn't help smiling at the age old conflicts associated with that word "marriage" because although centuries separated her and the writer of these letters, the same problems over that word plagued them both. She was at the receiving end of that conflict aplenty from her over anxious mother so she understood perfectly the frustration with which the writer had scrawled the word "No." There was a tiny hole where his brush had cut into the paper and broken it with the force of his frustration.

But unlike her, the writer's frustration must have been tenfold because he could not fight his family's decision to arrange a marriage for him, one that was carefully matched to unite families, even among the peasant class. Mayumi could feel the burning anguish of the writer expressed in those two words. His family had arranged a marriage for him and he was torn between duty to obey and his own aversion to the whole idea. Mayumi felt that she had hit on something. Did he have a secret and forbidden lover then?

"Poor guy," she thought and across the chasm of the centuries that separated them, she could feel his desperation and his pain.

It had been a long and tiring day and as soon as she arrived at her apartment, Mayumi headed to the tiny bathroom to stand under a hot invigorating shower and feel the warm water washing out the stress from her tense body. The hot shower revived her and she felt like having some life and 21st century J pop music around her to chase away the blues of the 18th century so she loaded a new CD she had just bought into her laptop and let the "cute boy" voice of J pop's current squeeze, Takuya Kimura fill her apartment with his youth and vitality.

Fully alert now, Mayumi took out the original papers and placed them carefully on the small table next to her dictionary after making sure that her cat was fast asleep in his special place, among the folded futons in the oshire and was not likely to make sudden moves like jumping on the table and scratching the precious letters to bits. It was getting late and Mayumi knew she should leave the deciphering work till the next day but she just couldn't wait. The letters were burning a hole in her brain and she knew that unless she got something done tonight, she would not be able to sleep anyway.

She started by slowly writing out her interpretation of each symbol in the contemporary Japanese kanji. A number of characters turned out to be quite similar making her work easier but some were so badly written and blurred by age and fading Edo period ink that she couldn't even make out the strokes, much less decipher them. But in the end, with the help of her special high power historian's magnifying glass, she was able to slowly reconstruct the characters, stroke by stroke.

* * * * *

The sky was a brilliant blue and a couple of white clouds were so still and so clearly etched into it that they looked as if they had been painted onto that blue perfection. There was a thundering of hooves and a man appeared, racing his magnificent horse towards her. She had chosen her best kimono that day and she knew she was a vision of swishing blue silk against a backdrop of breath taking pink cherry trees flanking that little lane and plunging the whole area into the glorious pink and white explosion of the cherry blossoms in full bloom. She caught her breath as the horse stopped abruptly in front of her and a man dressed in an ash grey yukata leapt from the horse. She squinted in the bright sunlight but she couldn't see his face, only the dazzling white paper in his left hand and his soft voice crooning the words of the love poem he had penned in that paper.

The beautiful girl was crying from the beauty of that love song and she wanted to break through the shadows that hid the handsome face of the young man from her. She knew she had to be quick before this vision of male perfection leapt back onto his horse and rode away forever but something was wrong. She couldn't move her head and her body with its usual agility, it was ridiculous but it felt like a time span of one year to make each move and each time she got a little closer, a new chasm opened up to distance them.

The young man continued his crooning and she lunged forward, desperate to reach him but her feet had turned to stone. The girl knew she was going to lose her young man because some evil spirit stood between them, denying them their unity of body and soul. And her sorrows exploded in a wail of anguish that echoed through the dim corridors of the valleys and mountains through all eternity.

Mayumi woke up with a start and the luminous dials of her bedside clock showed 2:24 a.m. She shivered as she realized it had all been a dream! Thank God, there had not been a tragic beautiful girl and a handsome young man with a shadowy face crooning love songs. A dream, that was all it had been! She must have fallen asleep at her desk while doing her work and she felt a tiny pin prick of pain on her right cheek where her face had fallen onto the sharp tip of her pen.

Her body was still heavy with sleep and Mayumi decided there would not be any more work done. With an effort, she shifted from her desk and collapsed onto the small sofa-bed convertible just behind. A love poem and a handsome young man in an ash grey kimono… these were Mayumi's last thoughts as she sank into a deep sleep.

Chapter Six

It had been a terrible night dominated by a very bad dream. Fusao's head pounded with the pain of the unnatural position he had slept in. In that dream his father had called him into his room and informed him that his betrothed, a girl from a distant branch of the family was arriving that day and they would be married in two years' time when she reached her 15th birthday.

Fusao moved his head. Something rustled just next to his pillow. It was the paper the old samurai of the castle had given him, and then everything came rushing back to him. Yes, that had been real, the visit of the Lord Nobunaga with his entourage, the sheet of pure white papers, the brush and the ink and the order to write something. None of it had been a dream. Two words leapt out from the paper and invaded his sleep-befuddled head with the sharpness of their reality. "Marriage... No!" they screamed.

Oh God, that other thing too, it wasn't a dream! Then he remembered how he had tried to sleep and after an hour of restless turning and tossing, he had got up to feel his precious stationary and the soothing touch of the pure white papers had finally sent him into a slumber.

For a long moment, Fusao lay on the straw filled futon with the beans of his pillow moving and rustling beneath his head as he watched the first rays of sunlight filtering through the thin paper screen of the only window in the room. They danced merrily on the floor making a mockery of his throbbing head and bleary eyes. One thing bothered him greatly in the light of day, that his father had arranged marriage with a girl for him and there was no way he could ever object.

But over and above that, Fusao was disturbed by the question of why he should recoil with such great violence from an arranged marriage, something that was completely natural to every young man his age.

In the next room, he could hear the familiar sounds of Naoki, the object of his distress, calmly getting dressed for another hard day in the fields and from the tiny kitchen at the back of the house, the wonderful aroma of his mother new cooking rice for their breakfast of nori (seaweed), natto (fermented beans) and two different kinds of tsukemono (pickles) wafted into the room. The smell of food was warm, comfortable and wholesome, like his mother, without any of the stern authority of Naoki that allowed no concessions and no opposition in the family.

The day was starting like any other normal day, and after a hearty breakfast, Fusao´s mother waved husband and son off to the fields. Naoki had started to plant onions in a small adjoining field a few months ago and discovered that he seemed to have a flair for producing the finest crops of juicy tasty onions that everyone in the town jostled each other for.

Naoki's onions were the talk of the town and apart from the revenue they brought, being good at something also gave him the only sense of pride and importance that a peasant could ever have so these days, he was slowly expanding the onion field and spending more time in it. Fusao didn't have any objections to that because, if the truth be known, he found the sharp pungent smell of the onions more exciting and stimulating than the dull, silent and odorless rice fields. And besides, the work was much easier and less back breaking.

He stole a furtive look at his father as they plodded silently to their destination but Naoki´s stern profile yielded nothing and he didn't mention anything about his son´s impending marriage.

"Maybe he had just mentioned the subject in jest and after one cup of sake too many?" Fusao thought hopefully. "But no, that cannot be because father never jokes, not even when he is drunk."

The day passed without any memorable remark or incident and when Naoki remained silent on the subject of his son´s proposed marriage, it dawned on Fusao that in his father's opinion, there was no need for any discussion because he had already made a decision that was expected to be obeyed and the matter was considered closed.

It was like a death sentence to him. Fusao resolutely pushed this "decree" aside and willed his mind back to happier and more exciting events like the awesome visit of the Lord Nobunaga and his gorgeous son. He was shocked at the audacity of his own dark secret thoughts and ashamed of himself, but Fusao could not stop thinking of the young Lord Okimoto and how a strange energy had flowed between them the instant their eyes met for one brief unforgettable moment.

27

"I am shameless, worse than the harlots in the brothel," he chided himself. "And father would kill me with his bare hands if he knew the kind of filth that is going through my mind and body."

But on the way back to the house, Fusao's spirits rose a little and he got really excited about going through the pieces of exquisite stationary from the great Lord Nobunaga himself, the first things he could really call his own in a country where doors had no locks and the paper thin walls ensured that no member of the family ever had any privacy. But the stationary and writing was his own private world because only he in the whole house, and perhaps even in the whole village, could use those tools of culture and education.

"Amazing," he thought happily. "I can write anything I want about father and he wouldn't be the wiser even if I placed the paper right before him! He would have to beg me to read it for him!"

This was the only area where Fusao felt he could gain say or assert some kind of control over his father, this ability to read and write and the thought of even this tiny victory brought a smile to his lips.

* * * * *

Naoki saw the smile on his son's face and gave a sigh of relief. Naoki had been disturbed, far more than he could admit to anyone, by the distress he seemed to have caused his son with his order to marry. He couldn't understand why Fusao would object so strongly to an arranged marriage. After all, it was the natural course every young man's life took as soon as he reached the age of 17.

As they approached their home, a thin spiral of smoke sailed towards them like a snake from the back of the house. The familiar smell of soya sauce told them that Yuko was stirring a boiling pot of stew in the outhouse, the one that filled their bellies with an extraordinary warmth and gave them energy even on the coldest winter days.

Dinner was the usual subdued affair with muted conversation on the day's events and the routine for the next day. It was always the same, nothing exciting ever happened in the five hundred or so peasant homes in Minamimoto. The lights came on and went off at exactly the same time most nights, usually early because farmers, like Naoki, had to wake at the crack of dawn.

* * * * *

But that night, Fusao was nursing an exciting secret and as soon as he had finished putting away the bowls and chopsticks, he rushed over to the oshire in his room where the samurai's stationary lay safely stored away and started to clean the brushes carefully, bristle by bristle.

He was so engrossed that he did not see his father watching him from a crack in the sliding door and when he realized that he was being watched, Fusao hastily put away the brushes. Naoki must have already been informed by Yuko that his son's earlier ramblings about the samurai's visit to their house had been real but he didn't ask Fusao anything because he didn't consider it an event to be happy about. Like every other peasant, he would rather not be noticed by the samurai at all.

Although Fusao knew his father would never dare to destroy or confiscate a gift from their great feudal lord, he wasn't going to take any chances. The sheets of paper and brushes were the most precious things to the young peasant boy because they linked him to Lord Nobunaga's son who had taken a brush and helped him write his first character. Fusao hid his gifts in a flat wooden file under a loose piece of tatami in his room.

The rest of the week went by without any particular incident and father and son walked to the rice fields every day, autumn was approaching and they needed to prepare the soil for the next season. It was serious business and there was no time now for toying with onion fields because they had to harvest enough rice to pay their dues to their feudal lord at the end of the year.

But after a few days of relative calm, the following week brought "an incident." In Minamimoto where life was divided into rigid routines of eat, sleep and work, any single departure from this daily path was "an incident." It arrived in the form of a well-dressed man who shouted out his presence to Fusao and his father as they worked silently in the rice fields, knee deep in water and slosh.

The stranger's impeccable clothes looked so glaringly out of place amidst the mud and grimy work yukatas of their peasant world that Naoki and Fusao stood for a moment frozen into a kind of silent protest at this intrusion. Decades of submission to heartless feudal lords had taught Naoki that when a well-groomed emissary from the samurai came calling, the news was never good. His heart sank. What now? Had they unknowingly offended anyone from the castle?

The stranger motioned Naoki over and Fusao watched the uneasiness on his father's face as he hastily obeyed that command, a well-dressed man like that could be an emissary of some standing from the samurai and not to be taken lightly. As Fusao watched the two men in deep conversation and as the stranger directed a couple of nods in his direction, it was his turn to feel uneasy. he slight breeze that had sprung up lifted the hairs at the back of his neck. The young peasant boy couldn't understand what was happening and why the Lord Nobunaga was paying so much attention to his family as of recently. They were, after all, just peasants, no better than work horses to their Feudal lords and mother was right, it did not bode well to be singled out for attention.

The euphoria of the last few days had started to wear off and he too was beginning to question what the samurai could possibly want from him apart from the services and loyalty he already commanded from everyone in the prefecture.

Fusao thought about his mother's words and, shuddering a little from the rising wind that was sending a chill through his sodden work clothes, he went back to work. But the vision of the two men conversing in the distance and his father's deferential bows stayed within sight and he couldn't concentrate.

After what seemed like an eternity, the man left, and Naoki called out to his son to continue working. Fusao sighed. His father wasn't going to tell him what the commotion had been all about after all but perhaps, Fusao thought, he would open up on their way home? He could only hope for that because the absolute authority of his father did not allow a son to question or make any demands on him.

But as Fusao bent down to resume the back breaking task of pushing the rice plants into the soft waterlogged soil, he felt the first stirrings of discontent. Would anything ever change in his lifetime, that a son could have a say about his own life and his destiny?

A huge black magpie cruised over his head and, with a nasty cackle, unloaded its feces on his head. Fusao shook his head sadly, "A bad omen so I guess not!"

Naoki didn't say anything on the way home, stopping only to exchange small pleasantries with the other peasants making the same evening pilgrimage home from their respective rice fields. Fusao started to breathe normally again, maybe there was really nothing significant to say and the man was just a rich rice trader came to look their rice fields over. But a tense muscle moving on Naoki's left jaw put Fusao on edge throughout dinner and he groaned inwardly, "What's up now? Is there never going to be peace in this family again?"

It was obvious from his mother's white resigned face that she too thought the same thing but neither of them said a word. they had to wait for Naoki to speak when he was ready.

"Tomorrow Lord Nobunaga of the castle is coming to our house, and he wants to see you again, "Fusao's father said suddenly, his words drawing sharp intakes of breath from his son and wife as the unexpected announcement broke at last the brittle tension that had been gripping them the whole evening. The chopsticks in Fusao's hands slithered slowly down. He watched, in a kind of fixated horror, as the sticky rice grains littered the tatami mat in front of him.

All kinds of wild thoughts were chasing through Fusao's mind as he heard his father saying, "It's against correct protocol and absolutely improper for a samurai to visit the home of peasants like us. It just isn't right, and I feel very uncomfortable about this."

"When I was young, everyone was afraid even to look in the direction of the castle and the only time we could catch a glimpse of the samurai and his entourage was during the summer festival when he swept by us in his carriage and even then, we had to bow our heads so that we did not look him in the eye."

Fusao knew what his father meant, the air of royalty, pomp and inaccessibility surrounding the samurai and his family and close circles was what kept the peasants in awe of them and in line with the huge social gulf that separated them from the upper classes in Japan. The peasants had great illusions and fantasies about their feudal lords who should stay there in their high pedestals, godly figures that were beyond the reach of common people, to be worshipped and feared. It was unlike the grand samurai to deal with such lowly peasants. so yes, Fusao understood perfectly his father's distress and disapproval.

But beyond that, he was plagued by another anxiety, why him? And that night, it was especially difficult to fall into the deep sleep he needed to prepare his body for another day of hard labor.

"Damn the samurai and his son," Fusao thought angrily. "They should really just leave us alone."

Chapter Seven

Toyoki Fujita had escaped to his bedroom straight after dinner and lately it seemed to be the only place that he could find some peace. It was a room that lived out the fantasies of every young man, the latest electronic gadgets strewn haphazardly all over the room as if the owner had bought them on impulse and tossed them aside when he became bored with them.

"I'm disgustingly self-indulgent," Toyoki thought as he ran his eyes over the electronic clutter in his room. Strange, though, that despite being surrounded by this treasure trove of electronic toys, his favorite was a really old and totally outdated Walkman. Toyoki remembered the day he found it he was 22 and, to ease the pain over his father's sudden and unexpected death, he had thrown himself into clearing out his father's room after the funeral. Stashed away in a corner of an old antique writing bureau, Toyoki found the Walkman and a few tapes that he had never stopped listening to since.

A few years ago, his mother had died in a freak accident, run over by a car as she crossed the road to a funeral parlor to attend an old schoolmate's funeral wake. Toyoki, who had been very close to her, was inconsolable and had only recently accepted her death and moved on. But he knew he was still horribly messed up and had a lot of issues in his life to sort out.

After his mother's death, Toyoki moved in with his grandparents who doted on him and denied him nothing, the best education that money could buy, a wardrobe filled with the latest fashions in clothes and when the iPod became the rage, his grandmother, who still lived in a prewar world of technology, actually presented him with one! But it was still his father's old Walkman with its four precious tapes of therapeutic music that he turned to when he was troubled.

Toyoki's eyes wandered to the expanse of wall beside the door where an old painting hung. It represented his whole heritage, a long family history of blue-blooded nobles and samurai fiercely loyal to the emperor and shoguns for whom they had fought many bloody wars of honor. Besides, this painting was a picture of one of the most prominent of his ancestors, his great grandfather. It showed him commanding a large squadron of pre-war soldiers. Sometimes Toyoki would shudder at that cruel face with eyes narrowed into ice-cold granite slits. It was hard to believe that the same blood ran in his veins. Sometimes when he gazed at the faded pictures of his ancestors on the painting, ridiculous thoughts ran through his mind, that he was so restless because he was an 18th century warrior trapped in the body of a 21st century man. Maybe that was why he was never satisfied with the life and things or even the family, he had. It was insane, but Toyoki often felt that he was in the wrong place and the wrong time! Damn, he was a sicko all right, thinking of samurai and bloody wars instead of enjoying his privileged 21st century life!

He never liked the way such thoughts went, so Toyoki was relieved when the phone in the sitting room rang. instinctively he turned off the Walkman. It wasn't that he was snoopy, but he always needed to know what was going on in the house. The whispering sounds of his grandmother's slippers told him that his she had beat him to answering the phone. After the usual exchange of telephone pleasantries, Toyoki heard the name Mayumi mentioned. It was the lady historian they had gone to consult in Tokyo the previous week. For the first time that day, he came alive, maybe she had some news for them at last!

The big somewhat draughty two-story house had been a gift from a powerful Shogun to his great, great grandfather for his loyalty and services and was the only property they were allowed to keep after the war. It was a typical traditional Japanese house, big with landscaped gardens befitting the status of its occupants. As a child, Toyoki had loved sliding across the highly polished wooden floors at breakneck speed and the interesting history surrounding their home, like how it was said that the Matsu tree hanging languidly over the wooden fence was at least 500 years old!

Toyoki loved that tree. When he was growing up, he used to press his ears against its gnarled trunk and whisper, "Talk to me and tell me all the things you have seen and heard for the past 500 years, tell me about the people who lived, loved and even died under your spreading branches!"

But it remained resolutely silent, giving nothing away.

His grandmother often told him stories of the family's fabulous wealth from rice trading before the war and the grand parties that were held in these very grounds under the spreading branches of the Matsu tree.

"All of it gone," her eyes always reddened with the intensity of emotions whenever she spoke of their lost fortunes. "After the war, all confiscated by the Allied forces, our lands, everything except this house, even the goods and cash we couldn't hide in time. One day we were samurai class and feudal lords and the next we had nothing, just thrown to the bottom of society to start all over again." She paused for a moment, regaining her composure.

"Do you know after the war our lands were distributed to the peasants and farmers and we had to sell all our kimonos and fine tableware to the very people we once "owned" for the rice that were planted on land that belonged to us? In the beginning, I would wake up in cold sweat, willing this horrible reversal of fortunes to be just a dream but it was no dream. It was as real as our post war poverty was. From a princess with the finest kimonos, to a servant forced to scrub floors and do all the work that was done by our large stable of servants before. Luckily your grandfather was able to get a post through an old family connection at the Mainichi Newspapers and worked his way to Executive managing director which is why we are what we are today!"

Sometimes when Toyoki thought of the struggle his grandparents had endured after the war, he was ashamed of the self-absorbed lifestyle they allowed him to lead. His grandmother once said that she felt they had to make up to their descendants for losing all the family's lands and social status after the war, although they had done nothing wrong, except for being in the generation that fought and lost a war.

A branch of the Matsu tree rattled against Toyoki's window, snapping him out of his reverie. The sound reminded Toyoki that he had been about to go downstairs.. He sprinted down the creaking wooden stairs.

His grandmother saw him and said, "The girl from Tokyo called and asked whether we can make a trip to her office, to discuss some preliminary results of her research into our documents."

"Oh ok, you fix it up and I'll go along," Toyoki replied, abruptly making an about turn to return to his room when he saw that particular glint in the old lady's eyes whenever any lady of marriageable age called.

"I wish you'd show a bit more interest in her," his grandmother called predictably after his retreating back and Toyoki knew she was referring to his limited interest in girls. "Who knows, she can be a good partner for you!"

Toyoki was laughing as he closed his bedroom door firmly behind him and lowered himself onto his bed again, shaking his head. Poor Grandma, she must be pretty desperate to foist a total stranger on him! How could she be so clueless? How could she not know?

His mind wandered again, this time back to the bittersweet years when he did his undergraduate studies at the upper crust University of Michigan in Arbor, USA. When he left Japan, his grandmother had given him an envelope containing two million yen and a list of what he should achieve. One of those achievements was to find a nice rich girlfriend and have lots of children. It was almost pathetic the way Grandma never got over the reversal of her family fortunes and was always trying by whatever means to recover their pre-war wealth and status.

Life in the USA had been a rollercoaster of good days and some very bad days. All he did was study very hard to get his degree and return to Japan as soon as possible. Grandma had never been to the USA and like most Japanese idolized the country and the American Dream. She never knew, and Toyoki saw no reason to enlighten her on how difficult it was for a Japanese student to get much of a social life in the university. Asian men were not exactly in demand with the blonde, blue-eyed set. But he had found someone special to pass the lonely nights with. Even though the affair was just for sex it allowed him a small amount of comfort.

After spending three years in the US, Toyoki returned to Japan but found himself a little out of place and realized that he had become used to the concept of individualism in the US and found the community above the individual philosophy of Japan stifling and a suppression of individual expression and growth.

But eventually he managed to get back on track with the support of a few very good friends. But before he plunged headlong into the merciless Japanese corporate world, Toyoki decided to do what he had always wanted, explore what he called his family's "unfinished business."

Toyoki had grown up on a diet of fascinating stories about his famous samurai ancestors, but there always seemed to be a way grandma danced around certain topics which piqued Toyoki's curiosity. But although greatly interested, he had procrastinated in pursuing his family's mysteries any further. Then two months ago, while clearing out a cupboard in an old disused building on their property, Toyoki had found a badly scuffed brown wooden file filled with bundles of old, yellow stained papers.

He had rushed back to the main house to ask his grandmother about it.

"Oh, Toyoki, you've found it at last!" Harumi cried, running her fingers over the dusty surface of the wooden file. "Do you know I've been searching for these for years? About 15 years ago, my father passed it to me and told me it contained papers from one of our samurai ancestors. He made me promise to try and find out what they were but then your father died, and I was so distraught I just couldn't look at them. Later, when I remembered my promise to him, I tried to look for it, but my search was in vain. How on earth did it get to that cupboard in the old building?"

His hands were shaking as he untied the first bundle carefully, but when he unraveled them fully and scanned his eyes over the papers, he couldn't understand read them in the slightest! Damn it, they're mine, I want to know what they say! Suddenly a realization dawned on him.

"Of course," he said, taking a breath and calming himself. "They are written in old characters of that era, and we need to find someone who can decipher them. "That had started the whole process of searching for the right person for the job and finally his grandparents had settled on a strong recommendation from an old family friend, Tetsuyo Akinicho who now lived in the US and appointed Mayumi Onodera, an up-and-coming historian in Japan.

Toyoki sighed as he put the papers reverently back into its plastic casing the night before they went to see the historian. His only regret was that his father did not live to see them finally taking action to unravel a family secret that had been kept under wraps for too long.

"Father would have loved to be around for this," he thought sadly as he invoked a childhood habit and made a silent vow under the ancient Matsu tree that soon the mysteries his grandmother kept of their family would finally be revealed.

Chapter Eight

After putting down the phone, it hit upon Mayumi that instead of sending a fax or email reporting her latest findings, she could perhaps take the train to Minamimoto and deliver the news to her clients in person. Her line of work involved some very emotional and personal issues and sometimes the sensitive information she uncovered was better received in person than just a cold formal written report in a brown impersonal envelope. Of course, it depended on the client and the circumstances, corporate clients preferred to stay impersonal and professional and asked for written reports all the way, but individuals sometimes needed personal interaction with her. They needed to know all the details of her findings and sometimes it became emotional and hard for her to handle.

A few cases took a few bizarre turns and touched even her stoic historian's heart, especially the case of Tomi Suzuki a year ago. Tomi had been adopted at birth and after living with the need to trace her biological parents for decades, finally decided to take the plunge and engaged a historian's services. Armed with just a blurry photo and a name, it took Mayumi almost two weeks to track down an elderly couple eking out a living on a small farm in the remote hills of Shikoku island.

Fortunately for her, the couple were friendly and very ready to talk. Even when Mayumi asked for a strand of hair for possible DNA testing, they were completely trusting and willing to oblige. What became even more exciting was the discovery that they had had another son who was given away at birth together with their daughter but to another family in Hokkaido, North Japan.

On the way back to Tokyo, Mayumi had gone through the personal file of her client just to while away the two-hour train journey and been disturbed by the fact that Tomi and her husband, Nobu shared the same year and date of birth and that he came from Chitose in Hokkaido. Like Tomi, he too had been adopted at birth. That was what had drawn them

37

together in the first place, the similar circumstances of their lives. Mayumi had felt the hair at the back of her neck rising wondering whether there was any remote possibility that Tomi could be connected to Nobu in more ways than by marriage. She told herself a hundred times that no, there was no possibility that her clients could be related to each other in any other way than by marriage. It was just one of those freak coincidences, but something made her send them for DNA testing.

The result came out a few days later and Mayumi's simple case of biological parents tracing took a bizarre twist, Nobu and Tomi were a set of twins who had been given away at birth by the elderly couple in Shikoku.

For two days she kept her findings to herself, then on the third day she took a train to her clients' apartment and broke the news that shattered their lives. Through the tears of shock and disbelief, Mayumi recommended a second DNA testing to be sure beyond reasonable doubt and prayed that the first DNA testing would come out a mistake. Instead, the second testing proved beyond reasonable doubt that Nobu and Tomi were the set of twins her investigations had turned up and it was time to face reality.

Although Mayumi made it a very strict professional policy not to get personally involved with any of her clients, this particular case moved her so much that she found herself actually counselling the couple. Eventually, they decided to stay married but to avoid having children and it was the only case where Mayumi actually became friends with her clients.

She was thinking of this case as she went through, for the umpteenth time, the first few pages of the papers. It was strange and she couldn't get over her initial findings that the letters had not been written by someone in the family but instead by a peasant who appeared for some unexplainable reason to have been favored by the samurai and taught to write. Why would a samurai mingle so closely with a peasant in an era when it was almost indecent for any such interaction?

Mayumi could sense the nervousness of the peasant when he first started to write through the first few pages where random words like food, castle, lord, marriage, were written. It just didn't make sense. She could almost smell the raw fear of the peasant as she imagined him scribbling haphazardly under the watchful and nerve wrecking eye of his lord and master.

The part that still didn't fit this puzzle was why a samurai would want to go near a peasant, much less watch him write! Whatever the reason for this strange union, it became clear that as the peasant continued to write, he became less inhibited and more comfortable with the samurai and beautiful poems and daily accounts were beginning to appear.

The Fujitas had suggested a meeting on Wednesday which left her only two days to organize her deciphering and related findings into a professional report, but Mayumi was used to even more hair-raising deadlines so two days wasn't really considered a challenge. With the cases promise of mystery and intrigue, the case had caught Mayumi's attention fully

Chapter Nine

Three times a week, Fusao woke up at the crack of dawn and went down to the river to fetch water for his mother. He liked to be there early, before the usual clusters of women gathered to wash their clothes, gossip or fill their buckets. In particular he hated Naomi san, a middle-aged woman who threw spiteful looks at him and whispered that he was "doseiai" to the other village women. Damn, how Fusao often wished to get his hands around that scrawny neck!

But, in general, he didn't have anything against women although since he started filling out, the giggly young girls of the village had been throwing surreptitious looks in his direction which unnerved and worried him more because he couldn't seem to feel any response to such flattering attention as any young man his age should. The boys he grew up and played with had long since transferred their interest to these young girls and having reached marriageable age, readily agreed to their families' attempts to matchmake them.

Recently, in the darkness of night and under cover of his futon, Fusao had started to touch himself and agonize over whether he was really doseiai as Naomi san suggested because he never fantasized about women the way all his friends confessed, they did almost every day. He wanted to ask his father why he didn't share the fervent pre-occupation with girls of the other pimply young men his age but Naoki's stern, judgmental face didn't encourage any personal discussions of this nature.

Once a group of young men organized a trip to another village known for its "sake" house, a polite term for the area's most popular brothel, reputed to be excellent at "breaking in" any fumbling young man. Fusao had allowed Yoshi, his childhood playmate, to persuade him to go along, more to prove to himself that he was no different from the other boys with their sexual needs than for any real desire to be "broken in."

40

That trip had proved a humiliating disaster and demoralized him even more. Fusao had never seen anything like the dimly lit "sake house" with its giggly groups of girls showing more thigh and shoulders than he had ever seen in any woman. The girls didn't stay in groups for long and soon they were paired off with Yoshi and the other men under the sharp, hustling eyes of an older woman who seemed more concerned about a faster turnover rate than the quality of service.

A pretty young girl came over to Fusao and began to play with his long black hair and ears, whispering seductively that she wanted to take care of him. As the girl who called herself Kiko started to touch him in earnest, Fusao felt his body stiffen up and he knew at that moment that he would never like women. Disgusted with himself and with Kiko's bold advances, he pushed her away and ran out of the brothel, never stopping until he reached the edge of a stream and vomited into it.

That night, he cried himself to sleep like a baby, smothering his bewildered sobs with his pillow and the frightening question drummed in his head "Why can't I feel anything? Why can't my body react to a woman's touch as it is supposed to?"

The beans in his pillow whispered back, "Because you're a doseiai like Naomi san says! You like boys such as yourself." and Fusao threw the pillow across the room as far away from him as possible. The thought of touching a woman's body made him feel nauseous again. And then he thought of the Samurai's son, Lord Okimoto's body, and the way his hand had brushed against Fusao's when he had helped the body steady his hand to write. The thought set his loins on fire and he never failed to harden. Fusao knew he was facing a problem.

Just after sunrise the next morning, four soldiers arrived at their home to announce the imminent arrival of Lord Nobunaga and his entourage which sent Fusao's mother into a frenzy of trying to put the house in order and pleading with her husband not to go to work and leave her alone to cope with their terrifying visitors of unpredictable intentions.

The samurai took his time. It was only two hours later that the sound of the guards outside springing into action and a horse carriage screeching to a stop outside the house announced his arrival. A young man, of about Fusao's age, probably a servant or page boy, entered the house carrying a package and he was followed closely by the samurai's son, Lord Okimoto, resplendent in a heavy dark kimono with a gold encased sword slung across his waist. His long black hair was tied up, held by golden threads. Lord Nobunaga came last, flanked by two attendants who existed only to attend to his every need.

It was a sight awesome enough to send Fusao and his family falling on their knees and keeping their heads bowed till they were given permission to get up. Out of the corner of his eyes, Fusao saw the young servant opening up the parcel and laying out more stationary on the only low table in the room and his heart began to beat faster. The Lord Nobunaga was here to order him to write again which, for some strange reason, seemed to satisfy a whim in him, for the moment, at least.

A stray beam of sunlight caught the gold casing of Lord Okimoto's sword and dazzled Fusao with its yellow radiance. For a moment he felt that he had died and was being transported into another world in a cloud of gold dust.

"I said come here, young boy, and write for me," Lord Nobunaga's voice cut across his thoughts and brought him back to earth.

With a start, Fusao bowed his way to the table, the cold sweat already forming on his brow as he felt the eyes of the entire group of people on him.

How was he going to write when his fingers were stiff and frozen with fear? But the samurai had ordered him to write, and he could not disobey that order even if the effort drew blood from his fingers. Yet, how could he write when Lord Okimoto's presence was stealing all the air from the room, leaving none for him to breathe?

The sweat was running down his back in little cold rivers of agony as he started to write. Fusao could only think of one thing to write.

"Today the Lord Nobunaga honored my undeserving family with his presence, and I felt as if I had died and gone to heaven..."

Fusao had hardly written half a page when the samurai, true to his reputation of unpredictability, grew restless and signaled that it was time to leave. Just as swiftly as they had arrived, the entire group swept out of the house, leaving its occupants in a kind of dazed bewilderment.

The only thing that lingered on in Fusao's mind was the glint of gold and steel as Lord Okimoto slid past him, leaving behind a wave of his heady masculine scent.

Chapter Ten

Mayumi scanned the train timetables for the next train to Minamimoto and was relieved that she had only 15 minutes to wait, one thing she could never stand was to waste time waiting for anything unless it was work or history related. Since it was a weekday and not peak hour, she hadn't bothered to pay more for a reserved seat, so it was better to be ahead of the queue for a good seat.

Armed with a can of green tea and a bag of rice crackers she had bought from a kiosk on the platform, she managed to find a corner seat in the last coach that was also usually the least crowded. The two-hour journey would give her plenty of time to go through her case notes and think about what she would say to the Fujitas.

As the sleek high-speed train glided out of the station, Mayumi took out the first few pages of the papers she had painstakingly deciphered for the last few days from her slim black business case and placed them on the tray table in front of her seat.

The haphazard scribbles of the first page reminded Mayumi of the person who had penned those words and she thought irrelevantly about how many days of hard and perilous walking it would have taken him to travel from one town to another hundreds of years ago. And yet here she was, making the journey in two hours on this fabulous product of human innovation!

Her mind wandered back to a long-forgotten history teacher explaining to a class of bored young students with better things on their minds than history and their roots about how women in Japan weren't permitted to travel alone even though they had the proper papers. Some took matters into their own hands and travelled dressed as men despite the dangers of being discovered and raped or abused along the way.

Did the writer of the papers have a wife or a sister perhaps?

"My goodness," she thought. "This unknown writer is really getting into me! I can't seem to stop thinking about him!"

She grimaced as she remembered her mother's exasperated warnings that if she messed around so much with dead people from the past, someday one of the spirits was going to get into her!

Mayumi shivered despite herself and was glad when her thoughts were interrupted by the cheery voice of the young girl wheeling a trolley down the aisle taking orders for drinks, snacks and packed lunches. She ordered a coffee and smiled as she remembered how her father always complained about paying so much for a cup of coffee on the train that wasn't even filled to the top! As Mayumi let the hot amber liquid course down her throat, no coffee had ever tasted more special, not even the thin watery "American coffee" served on trains in Japan!

Her vision blurred and she realized with a shock that she wasn't alone. A handsome young man with smoldering liquid eyes was riding alongside her on a magnificent black horse and she wondered vaguely why people in Japan still travelled on horseback. There was a thundering of hooves and a white horse appeared ridden by another young man of smaller build and Mayumi could see that he was of a humbler disposition. They were laughing gaily as the wind whipped their hair into a frenzy. as the younger man turned to face his companion, Mayumi was awed by the raw emotion and adoration that shone from his eyes. There seemed to be a kind of electric pool around them, and Mayumi felt herself drawn irresistibly into it.

"Minamimoto! Minamimoto Station!"

The loud announcement woke her up with a start and she realized with a shock that the train had stopped and if she didn't collect her things and get out fast, she was going to miss her station. Jeez, why had she fallen asleep? Wasn't the expensive coffee supposed to pump caffeine into her and keep her awake? What a rip off!

With the speed that only trained and habitual sleepers on Japanese commuter trains could muster, Mayumi grabbed her bags and dashed out of her coach just as the doors closed behind her and the train pulled out of the station for its onward journey within seconds.

Whew, that had been close!

For a moment Mayumi stood on the platform unable to focus on her surroundings because the images of the two young men were still vividly crowding her mind. Who were they and why did one man in particular keep entering her dreams? Was there anything they were trying to tell her? God, he was gorgeous, Mayumi thought and then almost laughed at

44

herself although it was really not all that funny. Her mother's words were buzzing in her head, about how she was so absorbed in her work that it wouldn't be very surprising that when Mayumi finally fell in love, it would be with a man of the past!

After the surging crowds and breakneck speed of movement in Tokyo stations, the serenity and slower pace of life in Minamimoto had a calming effect on Mayumi and she proceeded to the taxi stand, revitalized by the fresh mountain air and the excitement of meeting her clients on their home turf. The address she gave to the taxi driver was out of town and seemed difficult to find but after consulting a tiny map of even tinier roads and signs that only Japanese taxi drivers could decode, the affable taxi driver pointed triumphantly to a spot on the map and Mayumi knew he would get her there.

"It's on a small street way out of town," the taxi driver explained conversationally as he started up the engine and pulled off. "I think that's an area where an old samurai era house remains and the descendants of some notable samurai of this region still live there. You know, this town was the seat of a great samurai family who controlled all the rice fields and trading, and legend has it that the family was also notorious for other pursuits as well."

Mayumi smiled at the way the elderly taxi driver lowered his voice to almost a whisper as he touched on the other less than noble pursuits of the local samurai family, as if he expected them to rise from their centuries old, mildewed graves and lope off his head for defaming their good name!

* * * * *

A few miles away, Harumi Fujita was on her usual upright rocking chair watching a favorite gossip program on TV but today her mind wasn't really in it. They were expecting the historian from Tokyo anytime now and she was nervous about the meeting. She hadn't been able to sleep the last few nights just thinking about the bundle of old letters and poems and wondering, what did they say, who had written them and why?

The sound of a car screeching to a stop in front of the house interrupted Harumi's thoughts and she moved swiftly to the window to see the historian from Tokyo alighting from a taxi. Three o'clock, she was right on time. Harumi was pleased. She hated the younger generation who was always late and didn't care to uphold the traditional Japanese respect for punctuality. The old lady hurried to the front door and threw it open without waiting for her guest to ring the doorbell.

* * * * *

Caught off balance by this premature reception, Mayumi hesitated for just a moment before recovering herself to return the deep bow of her client. She noticed that with her steel grey hair piled high up in an elegant chignon and dressed today in a beautiful silver and pink kimono, Mrs. Fujita looked every inch a samurai's descendant. Suddenly Mayumi was very conscious of her faded jeans and simple white wrinkled shirt. Her sweater was unremarkable, and she wished she had dressed better for the meeting.

"Welcome to our home," the older woman said as she held the door open for Mayumi.

"Thank you, Fujita san, it's a real pleasure to visit your home, even the taxi driver spoke about it on the way here," Mayumi replied as she took off her shoes and slipped into a pair of slippers that Harumi placed in front of her.

"In fact," she added laughingly. "He was giving me a running commentary on the samurai family who presided over this region centuries ago!"

"Oh really?" Harumi san replied with a mixture of pride and a shuttered look of discomfort in her eyes. Mayumi could have kicked herself. Of course! The old taxi driver's comments on the samurai family had not all been complementary and there were probably a few rumors circulating in the local community that Harumi san would rather she didn't know.

It was the first time Mayumi had been to a samurai descendant's house and she looked around her with interest expecting the ornate entrance and grand reception rooms she had read about. She was disappointed because it was clear the entire house had been made over with modern wood paneling. Even the windows had very ordinary aluminum sashes and glass seen in most Japanese homes. The only evidence of its old samurai heritage was the rows of old wood block prints of kimono-clad warriors in various poses of swordplay that lined the walls. Harumi saw her looking at the prints and said, "Most of the house was burnt down during the war and we had to rebuild it with a small grant from the government. Miraculously, these prints survived the fire and looting during the war and represent some of the very few original things left of the old house. The castle, the main seat of my ancestors for centuries in the extreme north of this prefecture, is of course all gone except for a small tea house."

Mayumi nodded, somewhat relieved that there was, after all, a logical explanation for the almost indecent modernization of the house, stripping it almost entirely of its character and proud heritage.

Her client brought her to the sitting room decorated in the typical bare minimalist style of most Japanese houses, a low table in the middle of the room with four cushions placed around it and nothing more except for a few paintings of white cranes against a gold background hanging on the walls.

Harumi saw Mayumi looking at a very old painting hanging by itself in a corner of the room and said, "This is the only one that was saved from the priceless collection of paintings from the castle, the rest were either burnt or looted and God knows where they are now."

After pouring her guest a cup of green tea, Harumi went out of the room and returned minutes later with her husband and grandson in tow.

As soon as the usual polite greetings were exchanged and everyone had settled down on the cushions, Mayumi brought out her notes and laid them down on the table.

"I came in person for a preliminary discussion of the work I have done on the first few pages of the papers because I believe that sometimes it's a lot easier to talk like this in person especially for the first meeting than on the phone," she said. "As you know, the words and calligraphy are typical of that period and the translation and deciphering should be quite accurate because I used a good source for Edo period handwriting dissection."

In their first show of emotions, the family crowded round the papers trying to read the faded squiggles as Mayumi started to read and explain her findings, stopping only when the old lady at one point interrupted her.

"I don't understand, do you mean to say that this manuscript wasn't written by one of my ancestors? Are you saying that it was written by a peasant or someone of a lower class?"

"Yes, the characters are quite badly written and not at all the way a well-schooled samurai would write and of course, the contents are

47

indicative of the writer as well," Mayumi replied. "I know you have a million questions on your mind such as how a peasant of that era was able to write and how did such writings end up in the possession of your samurai ancestors, obviously treasured and lovingly preserved?"

When the old lady nodded, obviously too confused to say anything more, Mayumi continued," Yes, these are questions I ask myself too at this point. I don't have the answers yet but I'm sure our questions will be answered as I go deeper into these papers because, after all, that is what I am retained for, to unravel the mystery of these letters and what they mean to your family and ancestors. I prefer not to look for answers now by jumping from one part of the papers to another and feel that it's better to just follow the writings as they evolve, along its own timeline, don't you agree?"

Harumi nodded again, still unable to say anything else. Mayumi proceeded to go into the contents of the first three pages of the manuscript.

"Today the Lord Nobunaga came to our humble home with sheets of beautiful snow-white papers and ordered me to write for him…"

"Lord Nobunaga came again and this time he brought his son, young… magnificent, I am lost…"

By the time Mayumi finished with what she had translated so far, Harumi Fujita's eyes were shining with what looked like tears but when she thanked the historian, her voice was calm. The day's meeting left them with a lot of puzzling, disturbing questions that could only be answered much later and for the moment, they would just all have to wait for the tangled threads of history to unravel.

Mayumi promised to send all future translations periodically by post and at the rate of five pages a day, the whole assignment could be completed by the end of the month.

It was growing dark, and Harumi called out to her grandson to drive Mayumi to the Manamimoto station for her train back to Tokyo. Although not particularly keen on the company of the strange, diffident young man, Mayumi was grateful for the ride because she couldn't see any other means of transportation to the station and deeply shadowed by its arch of overhanging trees, the road did look spooky at night.

"Any living company tonight is surely better than none," she thought as she waited for Toyoki to drive her to the station.

Chapter Eleven

Fusao continued staring at the white sheets of papers before him while his father bowed the samurai and his entourage out of the house. When Naoki returned, he said in a flat, emotionless voice, but Fusao knew from the way a tiny muscle was working on his left jaw that he was anything but calm.

"Fusao, the Lord Nobunaga's son has invited you to the castle tomorrow for a visit and I've given the only answer that is expected of us and that is yes."

The sheets of papers Fusao had been holding slipped onto the floor. He, Fusao, rice farmer's son had just been invited to the samurai's home by his gorgeous son? Why, he didn't know of anyone in the village who had ever been to the formidable castle of their lord and master beyond the first guard post. Even the daily stream of tradesmen and suppliers were not allowed into the grounds and were required to leave their goods at that outer guard post!

The nearest Fusao had ever been to the castle was one summer when he had joined the villagers during the mid-summer festival to watch a magnificent fire display just outside the principal gate. It had been a good harvest that year and in a rare burst of generosity, the samurai had decided to put up a fire display for the whole village in the small courtyard in front of the first principal gate. They had all fallen back when two soldiers on horseback arrived to clear the way for the Lord Nobunaga's carriage as it left the castle. The bamboo curtain of the carriage lifted, and Fusao saw a young boy looking out at them with a kind of wonder in his face at the mass of humanity all bowing to them in one synchronized movement.

"That was the Lord Nobunaga's son, our next samurai!" a man standing next to Fusao whispered as the carriage disappeared into the distance leaving a cloud of dust behind.

That night, Fusao could not sleep. He lay awake, his thoughts alternating between excitement at his impending visit to the castle as an invited guest and apprehension at what he was expected to do for the samurai and his son. The ways of the nobility were strange and unpredictable, his mother had warned him, and peasants were just pawns to them to be used and discarded at will.

Would he be able to please his host, Lord Okimoto or would he fail and be sent away in disgrace or worse?

Fusao could see that his parents were worried and uncomfortable about this sudden interest the samurai and his son had with their son and they would rather be left alone to live their lives in obscurity and peace. Right now, they didn't know what the samurai wanted from their son and what would happen if Fusao couldn't give them what they wanted. It was dangerous, this unnatural crossing of class boundaries and would surely come to no good but the samurai's son had given an order, not an invitation and no one could say no.

To add to the feeling of doom and anxiety that had descended on their once peaceful home, the next day dawned cloudy with the threat of heavy rain looming in the grey, overcast sky. When Fusao woke up after a sleepless night, his father had already left the house.

"Father has gone to visit Uncle Joji to make some business arrangements," his mother said as she laid out his breakfast of rice, pickles and a steaming bowl of miso soup. But Fusao suspected that his father simply didn't want to be in the house when he left for the castle. For a moment he considered ignoring the samurai's order since it disturbed his father so much but Fusao knew it was impossible, no one who crossed the samurai and disobeyed a direct order could get away with it. As it was, he was already running late.

Fusao hurried through his breakfast and slipped into his best kimono within minutes. As he was leaving the house, his mother handed him an umbrella.

"Better take this, son, it looks like rain any moment now," she said but she would not look him in the eye.

For the first time in years, Fusao really looked at his mother that morning and noticed how the hard work of being a farmer's wife had etched deep lines into her face and hunched the shoulders that had once been straight, beautiful and strong. Today in particular, his mother looked pinched and deeply troubled. On an impulse, Fusao reached over and gave her a small hug. He felt little pangs of guilt that this trip, which was causing so much distress to his parents, gave him feelings of pleasurable anticipation from vague memories of the scent and sight of Lord Okimoto. Kuso, he was sick to have such thoughts of a feudal lord's son and heir!

Embarrassed at this unusual display of affection, Yuko pushed her son playfully away yet despite her gentle rejection of any kind of physical contact, Fusao could see that she was, nevertheless, happy for it. His mother stood at the door waving him off with a smile as he went down the road. Through her smile Fusao knew he had lifted some of her worries.

"Make sure you open up the umbrella when the rain comes," she called after him. "Otherwise, you'll catch a chill and your papers will get wet!"

"Don't worry, mother," he called back. "The papers are safe and well protected in a pouch inside my kimono."

The road to the castle was much better than all the other roads in the land and passed through the big, important houses of members of the samurai's immediate circle, courtiers, castle administrators and minor members of his family. Although it was still early and the storm looked set to burst any time, there were already quite a few people on the road, and they looked at him curiously.

The road led only to the castle and the people who used it, especially at this time of the morning, all knew each other. They were servants, tradesmen, messengers all in service to the samurai and his family in one way or another. Fusao was a new face on that road and because of that some of the travelers shot him curious looks. What made him think he would be able to get in anyway?.

The castle appeared after he had walked for 30 minutes and the sight of that imposing seat of unchallengeable power and wealth made Fusao's stomach turn. He felt nauseous with anxiety and the fear of uncertainty. What if he couldn't meet their expectations? Would he be punished or locked up in one of the dark rooms of the castle's dungeons that the villagers used to threaten their misbehaving children with? For a moment he panicked and considered turning back and making a run for it. But he didn't. Instead, he managed to control his fear and approached the castle's main entrance, thinking of the shame his family would face if Fusao had displeased the samurai and his son and ran.

The four guards who stood in front of the massive front gates were so intimidating that Fusao was glad he had been waved to the humbler side entrance, the one used by the servants as surely that must be the reason why he had been summoned to the castle, to become a servant to the samurai's son. Of course, if that were so, it was a little unusual that the samurai's son had personally attended to the selection of a servant, a menial task that was definitely beneath him and the job of his head servant.

Even the side gate was heavily guarded and as he approached it, two soldiers came out to block his way.

"What is your name and what is your business here?" one of them asked.

"My name is Fusao, and I was asked to come here by the son of our lord and master," he answered nervously, intimidated by the heavily armed soldiers whose swords were barely inches from his chest.

"You mean you are here to see the young samurai, Lord Okimoto? What is your purpose?" another soldier demanded.

Fusao hadn't anticipated this interrogation and taken aback, he said the first thing that came to his mind, "He asked me to come because he was entertained by my writing, I think. But… I haven't actually been told anything."

To his surprise, the soldier started to laugh and pointed a finger at him.

"Oh, so you are the writing farmer! We were told to wait for you!"

A few soldiers came over to look at him and joined in the merriment at poor Fusao's expense. He felt himself turning red at such unwarranted attention. Again his first instinct was to flee.

Eventually, another soldier, who was more authoritative and appeared to be higher in rank, came over and reprimanded the group and, like magic, the laughter died down and Fusao was swiftly brought to an inner chamber and asked to sit down with a bit more courtesy. What he thought would be a few minutes' wait dragged on and it was about a full hour before one of the soldiers returned and asked Fusao to follow him to the main building. He was looking at Fusao with a strange kind of new respect that made him even more uncomfortable than when he was the object of their ridicule. He could sense that there was something going on, an undercurrent and secret energy that no one was sharing with him, and this ambiguity frightened him.

Then as another two guards pushed open the heavy oak and steel doors and motioned him into the huge vestibule of the castle, Fusao forgot his fears, his apprehensions, everything but the fact that for the first time in his life and perhaps the last, he was inside the samurai's castle and it was like another world to him, one he had never expected to see.

His eyes took in the wonder of the outer guestroom he had been brought to and what seemed like miles and miles of fine and immaculately maintained tatami floor that felt like silk on his bare feet. What a far cry from the rough and prickly tatami mats at home that no amount of his mother's wiping could keep the stains away!

Beautiful scenes depicting snow-white cranes against a magnificent background of what he would later find out was real gold paint hung on the walls and as the tour of the castle progressed, Fusao realized that these gold screens of snow-white cranes were everywhere.

"The samurai must be very fond of cranes," he thought. "Cranes, symbols of peace and freedom! How ironic that a man trapped in such great power and wealth and never free from the watching eyes of courtiers, retainers and God alone knows how many servants, long for freedom and solitude! And yet he cannot survive without every pair of watching eyes to command and serve him."

A passage that went through a spectacular garden of carefully arranged rocks, water fountains and beautifully sculptured Matsu trees ended in a large airy room that had just a gleaming table in the middle and a pile of gold tasseled floor cushions. The only claim to opulence in that room was a heavy folding screen of exquisite lacquer inlaid with mother of pearl. Fusao had never seen anything so beautiful before and for a moment he stood mesmerized in front of the screen, tracing with his eyes every mother of pearl design on it.

In another corner stood a statue of a menacing samurai warrior in heavy armor. It looked so real that Fusao almost expected it to walk towards him and demand to know what a peasant like him was doing in the castle.

Fusao guessed he was in some kind of waiting room and the most important parts of the castle like the private quarters of the samurai and his family were deeper inside. The guards motioned him to sit down on one of the floor cushions and wait but no one told him what he was supposed to be waiting for and although he was bursting with anxiety, Fusao did not dare to question any of the formidable looking guards. The soft sounds of water told him that outside, it had started to rain.

He was left waiting for almost an hour and at one point when the guards left the room, he crossed over to the window and stared out at the rain falling gently into a little pond outside just to pass the time. Warm and dry in a room with silken tatami and the fresh smell of pine, Fusao felt strangely warm and protected from the driving rain and all the toils of his peasant world outside. In this cocoon of ease and comfort, the murky rice fields and his work wearied parents seemed very far away. Then he remembered his mother's words, that everything had a price tag and he wondered what price he would have to pay for this little piece of heaven.

The door opened abruptly, interrupting his thoughts. Lord Okimoto entered the room and just as abruptly, he waved away the two guards who had followed him in. With a deep respectful bow, they slipped out of the room, closing the sliding door softly behind them.

Fusao sprang up and lowered his body instinctively in the deep bow at a 45-degree angle that peasants had to execute in the presence of their feudal lords. His heart began to beat unsteadily as he realized, he was alone in the room with the awesome Lord Okimoto, the object of his sinfully impure thoughts since the day their eyes met at his rough, humble home.

"How dare you think of the samurai's son in this terrible way," he chided himself over and over again, but the thoughts would not go away, instead they came, each wave stronger than the last.

"I'm honored to be in your presence, my Lord" he whispered, overwhelmed by the knowledge that he was alone with this magnificent God like being, no guards, no servants, just the two of them together. Its disturbing air of intimacy sent a shudder down his spine, and he bowed even lower to remind himself of his place in society.

"Please get up, there's no need to bow to me. And when we are alone, please don't call me 'My Lord.' I have a name and it's Okimoto."

Fusao started to shake his head in protest, declaring that he could never call the son and heir of the Samurai by his name, it would be disrespectful and improper, and his father would whip him for that.

Lord Okimoto laughed. He reached over to stop Fusao's head in mid shake. "Well then, as the Lord Nobunaga's son and your master by protocol, I order you to stop bowing and stand up!"

Fusao obeyed and got up but he was confused and disorientated. Why was the samurai's son talking to him in such a familiar manner as if they were friends and equals in social standing? Was the world going mad or was this some kind of dream or joke someone was playing on him? Maybe the young man before him was not Lord Okimoto but someone from the village dressed up as the samurai's son to play some kind of sick joke on him? The young samurai's hand had even brushed playfully against him as he got up, the contact had been brief, but Fusao had drawn back instinctively for it was forbidden for any peasant to touch a samurai! Lord Okimoto seemed amused by the flustered Fusao and he started to laugh again.

When Fusao was on his feet, he realized how tall the young samurai was, almost a whole head taller than him and yet strangely Fusao did not feel threatened or intimidated. In fact, dear God, he felt almost comfortable and at ease with Lord Okimoto whom he should not even be allowed to look in the eye as an equal so great the social divide between them was.

Okimoto lowered himself onto a pile of floor cushions an aide had laid out earlier and patted another pile next to him.

"Come and sit beside me, Fusao, and relax, you're too tense. I promise not to bite you."

This light bantering coming from the samurai's son was so incongruous with the unsmiling stern image that the samurai always presented to their subjects, so much so that Fusao started to laugh and the ice between the two young men was broken. But the way Okimoto had caressed the word "bite" made Fusao's ears burn a little and he hurriedly sat down and busied himself with laying out the papers, brush and ink on the table in front of them. He presumed, of course, that was what he had been summoned to the castle for, to write.

Okimoto continued to look at him with a half-smile and Fusao felt his ears burning even more. Oh God, it was almost high treason but how that long languid body and lazy smile was igniting all kinds of forbidden emotions in him. If anyone knew of his daring licentious thoughts, he would be thrown into the dungeons for sure!

Fusao cleared his throat as the silence between them lengthened and smoldered and said, "My lord, do you want me to write for you today?"

"Remember, you are to call me Okimoto when we are alone," the young samurai reminded him. "It feels... nicer."

"Ye... yes... my lo... I mean lord Okimoto, I mean... Okimoto san," Fusao stuttered.

Okimoto started to laugh so loudly that the soldier obviously standing guard just outside the door opened it a crack to check if everything was all right, but the young samurai waved the overzealous guard impatiently away. He then shifted to a position in front of Fusao so that they faced each other.

"Yes, my loyal and beloved subject, I want you to write me something beautiful," he said.

"Do you want me to write about a flower?" Fusao ventured at random, he had no idea what a samurai would consider beautiful, so flowers seemed the best bet!

"No... something more alive."

"A beautiful bird in the sky then?"

"No... you can write about a person, a flesh and blood person with feelings and emotions."

"Shall I write about you my lord... Okimoto san?" asked Fusao.

"No... I want you to write about yourself. Look into this mirror, see the beautiful sensual man that I see and describe yourself!"

"No, I don't see any beauty in myself so I can't write about that," Fusao protested. "I am but a humble peasant boy and there's no beauty in that!"

"Yes, there is, and you will soon see it... take your time to discover yourself, who you are and what you really want."

Fusao took the mirror the young samurai held out to him and cradled it with wonder. He had never seen such a beautiful lacquer and gold mirror before. As he looked into it, he realized with great shock that Okimoto was right. The face that stared back at him was indeed beautiful, it shone with the luminous and unaffected innocence of trust, wonder and hope and he had never seen himself like this before. His long black hair shone like the beautiful black lacquer on the mirror and the face that stared back at him had full sensual lips, a nose that was fine and straight and a clear and smooth complexion. Fusao had to admit that his reflection was handsome and delicate.

A great desire to capture this moment forever in words overcame him and with Okimoto looking at him the whole time, Fusao started to write, seeking inspiration and feelings from his own image in the mirror.

Chapter Twelve

Toyoki was testing out his new mobile phone when he heard his grandmother calling him from downstairs. He had escaped to his room as soon as the meeting with the historian ended to avoid being drawn into any more discussion about his dead samurai ancestors. He'd had enough of them for one night! But now his grandmother was trying to get him downstairs again and it would be rude and ungracious for him to refuse.

With a deep sigh, he got up reluctantly from his study table. Lately his grandmother yelled at him a lot and there was hardly any privacy in the house. The traditional doors with no locks had never been changed so anyone could enter his bedroom and look through anything they wanted, and he suspected his grandmother sometimes went through his things. Perhaps he should think about getting his own bachelor's pad as soon as he found another job. Imagine bringing a lover home to this room with no locks and his grandmother probably never more than a meter away!

She was waiting for him now at the bottom of the staircase, fussing with the shoes at the genkan, every shoe in place, they all had to be arranged in a neat straight row.

Harumi straightened up when she saw Toyoki and said reproach-fully, "I've been calling you for the past 15 minutes! Can you do me a favor and drive Ms. Onodera to the station? It's getting dark and you know the buses are erratic after sunset."

"Just let me get the car keys and I'll get going."

The car was a late model higher range Toyota that his grandparents had bought for him when he started his first job. Toyoki's face softened as he backed the car out of the garage. The old people were wonderful to him, it was just that they could be stifling at times, especially his grandmother with her never ending quest of a wife for him. She just couldn't seem to understand that these days, even in Japan, young people of his age were looking for other goals in life than to get hitched up and produce the mandatory two children to prop up the nation's dismal birth rate! Besides, he had other visions and desires in life that he couldn't share with his grandmother, not yet anyway, because she wouldn't understand.

He waited while the historian, Mayumi, said goodbye to Harumi san and watched her idly as she walked to the car. Nice figure, good legs but too smart and uptight for his liking, definitely not his type. "sorry, Grandma, in case you are having any ideas, but it's never going to happen. Mayumi got into the car without a clue to her driver's thoughts and after a few failed attempts to make small talk, she lapsed into silence.

"What a strange young man," she thought. She had expected a man who had studied in the United States to be more open and talkative, but it seemed not so.

"What do you think about the papers so far?" Mayumi asked eventually, breaking the silence between the two of them.

"Well, they're fascinating of course," Toyoki replied, perking up in his seat, his face lighting up. Mayumi knew they had found a topic of common interest at last. "Although I think my O bachan's interest is more superficial, she just wants to be an important woman in the community and remind everyone she is descended from a great samurai family."

"Oh, then I must have disappointed her a lot when I gave her the bad news that the first few pages at least weren't actually written by anyone in her family."

"Well, it's too bad, isn't it? Facts are facts and you have to report your findings as they are, after all," Toyoki replied. "But as far as I'm concerned, it becomes even more of a mystery why a bundle of writings by someone obviously of a lower rank and outside the family should be so carefully preserved and treasured by our samurai ancestor. I think we need to know now more than ever who this mystery writer is and his place in the history of our family."

Mayumi looked at the pale faced passive young man beside her with new interest. At least he was supportive and passionate about his grandmother's quest to crack this mystery surrounding the memory of their samurai ancestors for centuries. For a committed historian and genealogist like her, any client's passionate desire to be involved was heartwarming She hated those clients who gave her a historical tracing about themselves or someone else as if it was a chore and thereafter showed no interest in her investigative reports except the final result nicely wrapped up in several computer print outs and delivered in an A 4 size brown envelope.

"Don't you agree?" Toyoki repeated insistently and Mayumi realized that, lost in her own thoughts, she hadn't been listening to her client.

"Yes, of course I agree, absolutely!" she replied praying that it was the right answer to whatever he had been asking her. He nodded and appeared satisfied. Mayumi was relieved that at least she had given him an acceptable answer!

They were mostly silent for the rest of the trip touching only on perfunctory details like when she would be able to come up with more information as she continued to translate the rest of the papers.

Chapter Thirteen

As soon as the sun rose, Fusao's father, Naoki, started the long walk home from Matsumoto where he had gone to spend a couple of days with his cousin, Joji. As always, the trip to Matsumoto was good because it was a big town and life there was less primitive. There was more trading and less farming and even the people looked different and were better dressed. they own folks who didn't live under the intimidating shadow of a feudal lord who owned them and their lands. In fact, Joji's family had left their village for Matsumoto soon after he was born because his mother, a woman from the town, just couldn't take the hard life of a farmer's wife anymore.

That had been a wise decision and today they lived in a house befitting successful rice traders and it was to Joji that Naoki sold the extra rice he hid from the samurai's account books every season. It was a great risk because if he was ever found out, he would suffer the samurai's wrath for cheating, but it was worth taking that risk because Naoki needed to put aside money for the grand wedding he planned for his only son, Fusao.

It was hard to be a peasant in bondage to a feudal lord, none of them owned the land they toiled in day after day, and they depended on their lord and master for everything. It was no wonder very few people in the village saw much reason to smile. A couple of times, the peasants rose up against their feudal lord demanding a bigger share of the crops but with no other weapons than sticks and kitchen knives they were easily put down by the samurai's soldiers and guards and the perpetrators were seized and never heard of again.

Yes, the Lord Nobunaga had been a terror in his hey days, so the villagers didn't really know what to make of the recent change in him. It made them uncomfortable to see him wind down to a benevolent almost fatherly figure and his occasional strolls down to the fields unnerved them. You never knew when you could unintentionally offend these powerful and unpredictable feudal lords so minimal contact was the best policy. Moreover, there were whispers about his son and heir because at 22, when most men of his rank were already married with children and mistresses on the side, he was still single and had never shown any interest in women. When the men got together over cups of sake, their favorite topic was to speculate about the love life of the young lord Okimoto and as the evening wore on, their imaginations usually got wilder.

Some even mentioned the unthinkable and it was this subject that sent a chill down Naoki's spine as he thought about his own son, Fusao and the young lord's interest in him. It had been alarming enough to send him to Matsumoto to discuss a pact made long ago with his cousin Joji.

Shortly after the birth of Aiko, the fourth unwelcome daughter of his cousin, both he and Joji had agreed that a marriage would be arranged between their children and with Aiko approaching her 13th birthday and Fusao already 15 years old, the time had come and Naoki's own uneasiness over the young lord Okimoto's unnatural interest in his son had made the matter seem more urgent.

Sometimes, Naoki felt that he was crazy and too presumptuous to imagine such things about Lord Okimoto's interest in his son but when Fusao was issued with an "invitation" to visit the castle, he saw with great clarity that his fears were very real.

His trip to Matsumoto had been a success because his cousin, anxious to marry off the last of his daughters as quickly as possible, had agreed to put the impending marriage of their children forward. Naoki sighed, the only difficulty he could see now was breaking the news to his son, he just couldn't understand it, any red-blooded young man would be eager to take a wife especially one as sweet as Aiko, except Fusao. But far from being interested in marriage to Aiko, Naoki could feel the sheer terror in his son every time the subject was broached. He couldn't, he shouldn't, he refused to think of the unthinkable about his own son. Fusao was a good and filial son; he would not go against his father's wishes for him to marry Aiko at the coming mid-summer festival.

Lost in his thoughts, Naoki didn't realize that he had reached home till he saw the clear distinct silhouette of Minamimoto's only castle in the horizon and was reminded once again of the young lord's undesirable interest in his son. He groaned inwardly. It had started with the wretched writing thing, of course!

How ironic it was that he had sent Fusao to Matsumoto at the age of 8 years to learn from his uncle more about life but instead the young boy had come back with a passion for writing and poetry, courtesy of another uncle, Toshiki, a retired official from the Shogun's court and the pride and joy of the family! Naoki had warned the boy not to get ideas above his station, but he knew from the tiny oil lamp his son lit when he thought his parents were asleep in the next room that Fusao had never given up his writing.

Sometimes, Naoki would call out irritably, "Put out that light, Fusao! I know what you're up to!" but at other times, he just didn't have the heart to deprive the boy of his only pleasure, so he pretended not to notice the yellow glow showing through the paper thin wall. There was no stopping his son and finally Naoki gave up as long as Fusao did not neglect his chores and his work in the rice fields.

As he got older, Fusao became quite well known for his writing skill. If anyone in the village wanted something written or read, they always asked him for help. In time, Naoki became quite proud of his son till one day the Lord Nobunaga became interested in Fusao and his writings and that pride turned to worry simply. It was never a good thing to be singled out by the samurai for special attention.

Their little house had some light and Naoki knew his wife would be boiling water in the kettle hanging over the fire which kept the whole house warm on a chilly night like this and a thin spiral of smoke coming from the back of the house told him that Yuko was probably in the kitchen preparing their dinner. It always warmed his heart to know that Yuko was there, cooking and making the house comfortable for them. There was something about having a woman around the house when a man returned home, and it really made the phrase "home and hearth" come alive. Naoki quickened his steps, eager now to reach home and share with his son the warmth of having a wife to come back to, for surely Fusao would have returned from the castle by now.

But the house seemed empty. After a few seconds his wife appeared but she looked very sad, none of her usual bustling self.

Alarmed, Naoki asked, "You look upset! Has anything happened?"

Yuko nodded and her eyes filled with tears, "A soldier came from the castle…".

"Yes, I know today is the day Fusao was summoned to the castle, I presume to entertain the samurai with his writing and poems," Naoki said. "But it should only be for a few hours, knowing the interest span of our samurai."

"No," Yuko shook her head emphatically. "The samurai's guard told me that Fusao will be spending the night in the castle."

Naoki's heart constricted with a mixture of fear and pain, but his voice was calm when he asked, "I see. Did he say when Fusao will return home?"

"No," Yuko replied with a shake of her head. "Oh Naoki, what are we going to do? I feel it too, right here, in my heart that this is the beginning of a terrible life for Fusao."

"I don't know yet whether there is anything we can do," Naoki replied and although he went through the motions of eating up all his dinner because Yuko hated to see any food go to waste, he tasted nothing. Yuko was right, what were they going to do to regain control of their son and his life from forces they didn't have the means to fight against?

That night Naoki slept fitfully, waking up at the slightest sound in case it was his son coming back from the castle but there was nothing, only the sound of the wind whistling through the tiny cracks on the walls. Where was Fusao sleeping and with whom? The answer to that conjured up such terrifying images that Naoki got up to down several cups of sake that eventually drove him into a drunken slumber.

When dawn broke and the birds started their morning ritual of breaking out in song, there was still no sign of Fusao. His parents dragged themselves up from their futons with heavy hearts and the shame of knowing that they had no control over their own son when they were up against the powerful samurai and his family.

There was nothing they could do but wait and get through the day till Fusao was allowed to return home.

Chapter Fourteen

Deep in the cloistered rooms of the castle, Fusao was so absorbed in his writing that he didn't realize when the sun went down, and the moon and stars of night took over till an attendant came in to light the lamps.

Earlier in the day, a servant had entered the room with trays of elegantly presented food served on fine china and lacquer bowls along with the finest green tea Fusao had ever tasted in his life. Both he and Lord Okimoto ate on the low table, sitting side by side, not speaking much, an unlikely couple from diverse backgrounds and yet strangely comfortable with each other.

And now as the day drew to a close, the yellow glow of the beautiful lamps cast an ambience of warmth and intimacy in the room and drew the occupants into its magic circle and, inspired by the magic of the moment, Fusao filled page after page with eager writings of himself and his thoughts while his powerful patron looked on, never taking his eyes off the young man and his passionate writing.

It was only much later after he had penned his last words for the day that Fusao realized that it was nightfall and his family would be waiting for him. He got up hurriedly and exclaimed in alarm, "Oh, I am so sorry I didn't know it is so late and I have outstayed my welcome. I must go, my lord… I mean Okimoto san, my family waits for me."

He felt a hand on his shoulder and the young samurai replied," I would be very happy if you stay the night here and keep me company. In this castle there are only old people and women, and it would be nice to have someone young in my company for a change!"

Fusao hesitated, wanting to stay but knowing his parents would be worried and that somehow it wasn't appropriate for him and Lord Okimoto to be spending the night together. As his father had already warned him, oil and water just couldn't and shouldn't mix.

Then he felt the pressure of the young samurai's hand on his shoulder increase and Fusao knew that it was not simply a request for him to stay at the castle but a pleasantly veiled order to do so.

"So, what do you say?" Lord Okimoto was saying. "Shall I ask the servants to bring in our dinner and then we can take four together."

Fusao was secretly glad that "No" was not an option open to him because deep inside he too wanted to spend the night at the castle with this man who was like a god to him.

When he didn't return, surely his parents would guess that he had been invited to stay the night at the castle and a considerate boy by nature, he wanted to ask that a message be sent to them so that they would not worry. But in this unequal relationship, the peasant could not order the samurai and his son to do anything so he kept silent, praying that his parents would understand.

But Lord Okimoto seemed to sense his young guest's anxiety and he said, "Don't worry, I'll send a messenger out to your parents to let them know you're spending the night here and will be perfectly safe under the protection of a samurai."

Fusao nodded gratefully, pleased that his powerful samurai friend had even considered his feelings. It was only much later that he saw the irony of Lord Okimoto's lofty assurance that Naoki would not have to worry about his son's safety because he was under the protection of a samurai because that "protection" was exactly what disturbed Fusao's father most.

In their humble cottage, the bath was just a wooden tub set up in an outhouse near the kitchen and they were considered lucky to have a bath at home. Most of the houses in the village did not have a bathroom and the villagers took their baths in the public bathhouse called the "sentor" strategically located just a short walk from the village square.

Every evening after dinner, lines of people snaked down the stretch of road that led to the sentor and Fusao loved to watch them banter and laugh. The hearty conversation, made the public bath ritual a time for neighbors to bond and exchange news and gossip with each other. In winter when it became dark before dinner time, some of the villagers carried little lamps to light the way and the yellow glow of their lamps made a very beautiful and heartwarming sight on cold wintry nights. It always gave Fusao a feeling of contentment and well-being to watch this line of yellow light balls bobbing steadily towards the public bathhouse.

Men and women were of course segregated in the public bath and boys went with their mothers until they were about five, then they had to follow their fathers as they grew older. Fusao remembered how he had cried when he was made to follow his father into the men's section but being small size, he managed to get away with it until he turned six. He much preferred the women's bath because there was always a lot of laughter and cheerful banter there. Most of all, he loved to watch his mother joining her group of friends to gossip and it was in the sentor that she put all her cares aside and really let hair down.

The women were totally uninhibited as they undressed and scrubbed themselves down before getting into the near boiling hot water of the large bath to soak themselves until the day's wear and tear were drained out of their tired bodies. Rain or snow, Fusao's mother would take him to the sentor because it was the only time she could socialize with her friends and neighbors. When he was six, she turned him over to his father and said, "You have to take him into the sentor now because he is too old to be with the women."

Fusao didn't really like the men's sentor because it was less cheerful and filled with the monotone grunts of bone weary men who talked only about their crops and, in bad seasons, how to pay their dues to their samurai landlords. The deep voices of the men and their bigger, bulkier bodies somehow intimidated Fusao and he longed for the soft musical voices and warmer curves of his mother and the other women.

Then one day his father came back from Matsumoto with the exciting news that some houses in the town actually had their own baths.

"I'm going to try and build one for us too so we don't need to waste time going to the sentor," he declared, much to his wife's horror.

They tried to dissuade him but Naoki was determined and every night after dinner, he would disappear to work on their "personal sentor," hammering together pieces of wood until one night, he triumphantly announced that it was finally finished and ready for its first trial use.

Despite her reservations, his wife eagerly boiled kettle after kettle of water to fill the square wooden tub with hot water but it was only after the 15th session was there sufficient hot water to put the scented bath powder inside and the whole family squeezed into the tub.

As he had seen the families in Matsumoto do, Naoki had also made a folding wooden cover to close up the bathtub after the last family member used it so that the water would stay hot inside and could be reused again the next day.

But after four backbreaking sessions of boiling and lugging 15 kettles of water just to fill the bathtub, a reluctant Naoki admitted that in Matsumoto, things were different. There, the hot water was pumped into the bathtub from nearby hot springs by bamboo pipes and no tired housewife had to labor like that just to put hot water into a bathtub. Emboldened by this admission from her husband, Fusao's mother promptly went on strike and refused to boil any more hot water!

So Naoki's lovingly crafted bathtub was pushed against the outhouse and soon forgotten and everyone went happily back to the public bath again.

Fusao was thinking of Naoki's bathtub now as he stood looking at the castle's private sentor in dumbstruck awe. With screens of bamboo trees and beautiful smooth pebbles scattered round glowing stone lanterns and a large bath made of shining slate grey stone, Lord Okimoto's bathroom was a far cry from the ugly functional village public bath Fusao was accustomed to.

"It's a beautiful furoba," he breathed.

"You like it?" Lord Okimoto asked, smiling at the charming and unaffected display of awe in his young companion. Sometimes he got so tired of the fake smiles and bowing servility of the people around him, all hoping for some favor or other from the samurai. Fusao's innocence was thoroughly refreshing and he felt the first stirrings of a powerful emotion for this young protege

Totally unaware of the feelings he had aroused in the young samurai, Fusao nodded emphatically and said, "Oh yes, even the smell inside here is so good."

They started to undress, as was the custom to wash before getting into the bath of hot scented water. Normally, Fusao did that in the public bath scrubbing down with scores of men of different shapes and sizes without inhibitions or a thought but somehow tonight he felt strangely uncomfortable and self-conscious, stripping in front of this gorgeous young nobleman whose eyes he could feel on his every move.

But later as they sat side by side soaking in the bath with the hot scented water draining away all the complications of unwarranted emotions, just two mortal beings, naked as the day they were born and stripped off all the barriers of rank and sex, Fusao felt so comfortable with his noble patron that his earlier inhibitions and embarrassing thoughts about Lord Okimoto seemed very far away.

His eyes closed as the exhaustion of a whole day of intensive writing started to take its toll on him and he had a hazy idea of someone lifting him from the furoba, drying his body and carrying him to another room where two soft futons smelling of pine trees had already been laid out.

Chapter Fifteen

It was late by the time Mayumi arrived home from Minamimoto and her cat was waiting resentfully for her, his disapproving eyes on the empty food bowl he had turned upside down in protest at what he perceived to be undeserved neglect by his usually attentive owner.

She had even forgotten to leave a light on for him, knowing his phobia for the dark and he snarled angrily at her.

Mayumi gathered her disgruntled cat up in her arms and said soothingly, "Sorry, Miki Chan, I didn't expect to return this late, don't be so mad!"

But after a good dosage of his favorite massage on the belly and chin, Miki promptly forgot about his disenchantment with his mistress and followed her cheerfully around while she fussed with his food bowl giving him an additional portion of the snacks she knew would win him over.

The huge Minnie Mouse clock on her study table belted out 11 chimes and Mayumi realized it was too late to call her mother as she always did after a long distance trip, it would have to wait till the following day.

"Mom probably waited up until her bedtime of 10:30 p.m., I should have remembered to call from the train, that's what mobile phones are for after all!" Mayumi thought ruefully.

She should probably take a shower and go to bed to prepare for another long day at the history museum the next day but the day's events were preying on her mind and she knew she would not sleep a wink till she had recorded everything onto her laptop.

After a quick shower, Mayumi laid the second set of old documents carefully on her worktable and trained her special magnifying glass over the old faded characters of the first page.

* * * * *

"Today Lord Okimoto has invited me to spend the day at the castle and I am torn between great excitement and fear," she read with some difficulty.

"What lies in store for me?"

"Is this the beginning of a wonderful friendship or a tragic end for me as my father thinks?"

"Oh God, tell me, can a feudal lord's son and a peasant be friends?"

* * * * *

Mayumi felt the change in the direction the recordings were taking, no longer random words and accounts of daily events but she was actually reading the "blog" of a young man agonizing over the beginning of a forbidden relationship across Japan's feudal class lines hundreds of years ago. The hand that wrote those words had long gone cold and turned to ashes, the heart that had soared to great heights of joy and bled with sorrow had stopped beating long ago, but the faded words of his emotions remained, determined to outlive the ravages of time.

* * * * *

"I know father is uneasy and unhappy that I am going to the castle. He is afraid that such a friendship can only come to no good for me. Mother told me he has gone to Matsumoto to see Uncle Joji but I know he left the house so early because he doesn't want to be here when I leave for the castle in the morning. Maybe he is right to be so apprehensive but I cannot stop myself even if I wanted to. Can he understand that? Can anyone?"

* * * * *

The phone on her desk rang and its shrill insistence cut across the centuries and brought Mayumi back to the present.

It was a call from Los Angeles, her friend, Michael who wanted to know why she hadn't called him for almost a week.

"Is everything ok with you?" she heard his voice floating into her ears from thousands of miles away and her first thought was how uncannily similar this phone call was to the written word of the peasant Fusao floating to her from across centuries away.

"Mayumi? Are you there?" Michael's anxious voice brought her back to the present and she said, "Oh Michael, I'm so glad to hear from you." And she was, the reassuring voice of someone dear to her from the present time and century reminded her that she was safe in 21st century Japan where powerful feudal lords and helpless peasants didn't exist!

"Poor Fusao, trapped in that world where, cursed with a tendency I am beginning to suspect, he never stood a chance!" Mayumi thought as she cleared her throat and answered Michael's "Hey, where are you? Mayumi chan!"

"Oh Michael, I'm sorry I had to save a document I was typing on my com," she lied. "It's so nice to hear from you!"

"I've missed you, Mayumi, no calls, no emails, nothing from you for almost a week!"

"I know, I know, Mike san and I'm really sorry again but I started working on a new case that really got to me, it was almost as if I stopped living and forgot about the whole world!"

"For as long as I know you, you've always been into every case you do!" Michael laughed. "It's my destiny to take a back seat to my historian girlfriend's cases!"

"That's not true!" Mayumi protested. "But seriously, this one's real weird, filled with samurai ghosts of the 18th century and an unresolved mystery! What do you know, Mike san, I think I've been hired to nail an elusive 18th century mystery! You should just see the documents I've been given to work with, real 18th century scripts and writings!"

Michael didn't laugh this time, he always took Mayumi's enthusiasm for her work seriously and that was one of the things she loved about him. Japanese men never considered a woman's career as anything more than a temporary prelude to marriage and when it related to an eccentric job like a historian, they found it "unfeminine", even intimidating, and she had received enough jibes for her career choice to make her mother lament that she would never be able to find a decent man and settle down.

Notwithstanding an impressive string of university degrees in history, genealogy and ancient writing, some even thought she worked exclusively with spirits and made her feel like a medium or a clairvoyant of some sort and certainly not many men wanted the challenge of pursuing a woman with a weird and "unladylike" career.

Mayumi was resigned to this so when she was accepted to UCLA in Los Angeles for a summer program of East Asian History, she readily accepted it for "a change of air."

That summer was the most liberating three months she had ever spent in her life, away from the watchful eyes of her family and the pressure of fighting to be a career woman in male dominated Japan. Los Angeles and UCLA was where Mayumi could be as eccentric and Avant Garde as she wanted and a woman could be anything she chose without being labelled "weird" or "unladylike" and there was no social pressure to be always on the lookout for a husband except by personal choice.

Men and relationships were the furthest things from her mind when Michael Williams came into her life one rainy afternoon as she sat in the Starbucks right across campus waiting for the rain to ease off before making a dash for the state of the art library that Mayumi loved.

"All the seats are taken. Mind if I share the table with you?" a tall dark haired senior asked. Before Mayumi answered, he had lowered his lanky form into the chair opposite splattering raindrops into her coffee as he did so.

Both of them started laughing and the senior said, "Now I'll have to buy you another cup of coffee. My name is Michael, by the way, graduate student from the Business Studies Department."

They dated all through the summer, finding out about each other's countries and cultures first hand. Michael was intrigued by the fact that she was a historian, first time a man did not withdraw just a little on hearing that and it pleased Mayumi immensely.

At the end of summer, Mayumi had to return to her life in Japan while Michael started a new job with a major newspaper company. They parted at Los Angeles airport with many tearful promises to constantly be in touch by emails, phone and whatever means they could so that they would not lose the magic of a budding transatlantic relationship.

But it had been tough, managing a long distance relationship with the demands of their respective careers. With each passing month, the emails became fewer and Michael, sensing the slipping away of his relationship with Mayumi like quick sand, took a month off from work and flew to Japan the previous summer.

Mayumi was deeply touched by his commitment to what she was

willing herself to accept as a mere summer dalliance for him. They spent a wonderful month travelling from Hokkaido to Hiroshima. She introduced him to the joys of Japanese onsens, or spas, and listened with great amusement as he raved about his first experience at a spa and the near boiling water which had almost scalded his whole body the first time he went in and the amazing kaiseki dinners that were served at every onsen which looked so beautiful it was almost impossible to destroy the perfection of every dish by eating them!

When Michael returned to Los Angeles, Mayumi felt very empty because she had got used to his big frame knocking into everything in her tiny apartment and the way he respected and supported her work as a historian and didn't consider her "odd" and less of a woman because of her passion for her work. Unlike the other Japanese men she had dated who "humored" her about her work as a temporary phase more than take her seriously, Michael actually shared her passion for history and her philosophy that "it is the past that shapes the present." On their last night, Michael told her he thought they were ready for a committed relationship.

But Mayumi knew that long distance relationships would eventually give more agony than happiness so she had plunged herself into her work and resolutely stopped sending emails to Michael.

For one agonizing week, she had paced her little apartment scribbling down her thoughts on countless scraps of paper, the pros and cons of a long distance relationship, could it work for a couple both committed to their work 10,000 miles apart? She could never ask Michael to leave his work at the LA news corporation that he loved so that he could come to Japan for an uncertain career future and neither could he ask her to leave the work she loved in a country she was comfortable in.

"Time is the best healer of all pain," her mother had once said and Mayumi had almost succeeded in thinking of Michael lesser each day till this insistent phone call and here he was crowding into her mind and soul again.

"Mayumi, are you there? Hey, this is an expensive transatlantic call!"

"Oh sorry Michael, yes I'm here and I'm so happy to hear from you."

And she was. to hell with her reservations about long distance relationships, she decided. She was so spooked by her 18th century "clients" she needed to hear a warm reassuring voice and Michael's was as good as any!

Chapter Sixteen

A soft morning light was filtering in. Fusao opened his eyes to a strange room and silk on his body. For a moment, he couldn't remember where he was. He wondered, why had his mother not called him before sunrise to dress and have breakfast before heading down to the fields? When had his hard lumpy futon become so soft, like a cloud of cotton?

He knew he should get up and find out but the soft silk on his body was so warm and comfortable his eyes started to close again. As he slipped into a deep sleep, he felt a movement and realized that he was not alone. Was he dreaming but did he feel someone touching his face with the gentlest of strokes, like the elusive flutter of a butterfly? He sighed, if he was dreaming let the dream go on forever.

"Fusao, my little farmer friend, wake up!"

This time it was not a dream and someone was shaking him vigorously, the way his father would do. Was he late for his day at the fields? God, his father would be angry!

He shot up but the face hovering over him was not the lined, weather beaten one of his father, but the young, unlined and handsome laughing face of Lord Okimoto trying to wake him up. And then Fusao remembered where he was and the events of the previous day and night and how he had ended up here in the castle and under the young samurai's futon came crowding into his head! Flushed with embarrassment and mortification that he had outslept his samurai host, Fusao struggled with the tangled silk sheets to get up, stuttering, "Oh my Lord, I am so sorry to have slept for so long, I can see the sun is already high in the sky!"

The young samurai laughed again and ran a hand lazily through Fusao's hair, "When will you learn to start calling me by my name? Maybe I have to order you to do that? Relax. Here we don't need to get up before sunrise."

There was a soft rustle and a servant appeared, bowing all the way.

"The morning meal is ready, my Lord," she whispered, averting her eyes and slipped discreetly away. Fusao watched her swishing kimono disappear and remembered how unnerved he had been the previous day by the silent, almost stealthy way the servants in the castle moved around, almost like an army of faceless, nameless shadows. They were so anonymous he wondered how their masters and mistresses told them apart if they bothered to do that at all!

The two young men ate their morning meal on a low highly polished lacquered table facing a beautiful indoor garden. The tranquility was broken only by the soothing sound of a small artificial bamboo water fountain and the occasional ripple of colorful carp swimming in the clear waters of a pond.

The rice at the castle was different from that eaten by peasants like Fusao and his family because although they worked the fields, the best crops of every harvest had to go to their feudal lords. It was soft and fluffy, nothing like the coarse grainy rice his mother had to soak for hours before cooking and it was more delicious than anything Fusao had ever tasted in his life.

"How ironic it is that rice farmers like us have never tasted the cream of our own crops," Fusao thought. "I can't wait to tell father about it!"

His joy and excitement over all his new experiences at the castle clouded a little as he remembered that he would have to face his father when he returned home later in the day. They had almost finished their meal when a servant bowed his way in and whispered something to Lord Okimoto.

It was obvious that he was not pleased with this interruption but he stood up and said, "My father summons me to his rooms and I must go."

"Yes, of course," Fusao replied. "And I must return to my home too My family must be wondering what happened to me last night!"

Lord Okimoto nodded. "All right but we will spend more time together again soon." He waved and a servant appeared as if by magic. "Show my young friend out by the front door today, not the back. He is my guest."

"Yes, of course, my lord," the servant bowed and Fusao followed him out of the room after saying his goodbyes to Lord Okimoto who seemed distracted, his mind obviously on the summons by his father.

Guest of his young master or not, the servant could see that Fusao was of his own class and kind and once out of sight of Lord Okimoto, his shoulders lifted perceptibly and there was even the merest hint of insolence in his eyes as he led his charge down a series of corridors, out of a large imposing door and down a minimalist but elegant rock garden and deposited him outside the castle gates with just a perfunctory bow and what looked suspiciously like a very soft snigger.

Like his own father, Fusao knew that the servant probably did not approve of this social interaction between a samurai and one of his lowest subjects. A peasant had no right to be jumping out of his little box to rub shoulders with someone from the highest echelons of society, never mind that it was at the latter's invitation and the servant made sure his peasant charge knew how he felt.

Fusao walked the half mile back to his home as slowly as he could, trying to delay the moment when he had to face his family and explain. He didn't know why he should feel guilty and jumpy because nothing sinister had happened, he had just spent a pleasant day and night providing the young samurai with the company of someone closer to his age, that was all.

"How different Lord Okimoto's relationship is with his parents," he thought. In all the time he had spent at the castle, Fusao had not once seen either Lord Okimoto's father or mother anywhere near them and it seemed he lived alone in a self-contained wing of the castle surrounded by servants, no sign of any family at all. In his own home, the word privacy didn't exist. Every family member had constant access to each other's lives and possessions and Fusao's only claim to some private moments was when he volunteered to go into the forest to gather wood for the crackling fire in the living room that kept the whole house warm. Sometimes he took longer than he should, stopping to sketch the animals which came out to watch him chopping off branches from the trees and dropping them into his wicker basket.

How different were the ways of the nobility when a son went to see his father only when he was summoned. Everyone knew the Lord Nobunaga had three children, two daughters and a son but Fusao hadn't seen any signs of Lord Okimoto's siblings at all. Fusao himself was an only child but he had seen the siblings of his friends and cousins never more than a few meters away from each other and certainly always at each other's throats!

The sun was high in the sky when he reached home. Fusao hoped that his father had left for the fields. But the straw hat hanging outside and the rush slippers on the wooden step told him that Naoki was still in the house, probably waiting for his son to return. Again, Fusao told himself he shouldn't feel guilty or be afraid. After all, he had been summoned to the castle and there was no way a peasant could disobey the orders of any member of the samurai family. Naoki was well aware of that so why did he feel as if he was returning from a clandestine outing his family didn't approve?

As soon as Yuko heard her son's footsteps going up to the front door, she rushed out from the back of the house, her face pinched with anxiety.

"You're back at last," she whispered. "Your father is very unhappy about the whole thing so please, Fusao, don't get into an argument with him even if he proposes something to you that you don't like."

Fusao looked at his mother's worried face and felt sorry for her. Like almost every Japanese woman, she lived in the shadow of her husband, his word was law in the house and he set the pace for everything in her life.

"Don't worry, mother," Fusao assured her. "Have you ever seen me talking back to father? Everything will be fine, you'll see, he just needs an explanation as to why I spent the night away from home, that's all!"

But Fusao wasn't quite so sure of that when he entered the house and saw the look on his father's face. Naoki said nothing, just waited with that stony expression that never failed to turn Fusao's blood to ice when he was a child. Although he was almost a grown man now, that look still unnerved him.

"So you're back," his father said sternly and plainly, he always did when he was angry.

"I'm sorry I stayed away from home last night without your permission but Lord Okimoto insisted and there was nothing I could do," Fusao replied. "You know how it is father, don't you, that no one in this village can disregard the orders of the samurai and his family."

Naoki's tense jaw muscles relaxed a little and he nodded, "Yes I know but still it is not proper and very disturbing for us that the samurai's son takes such a great interest in you."

There was a long silence as father and son sat facing each other. Then Naoki cleared his throat and said, "I hate to tell you this but I've heard stories about him and why at this age he still refuses to marry."

"What stories, father? What stories?"

Naoki shook his head and replied, "It doesn't matter, Fusao, because I've decided to put forward your marriage to Aiko. The wedding will take place next month. That should give us enough time to prepare and it's the only way to protect you."

"Yes, we will have the best wedding in the village. after all, Uncle Joji is an important man in Matsumoto," his wife agreed, glad that her husband had gone on to a happier subject.

They started a discussion about Fusao's forthcoming wedding as if he wasn't there and a necessary party to the event.

Fusao hardly heard them because his heart had turned ice cold. The ugly marriage serpent had raised its head again and this time it aimed to strike and make a kill and there would be no escape.

"No," he heard himself shout across the room. "I will not get married with such haste."

There was a stunned silence as his parents digested their son's outburst and daring defiance of his father's decree.

"You will do as I say, Fusao," Naoki responded harshly after a long moment. "You will not dishonor this family by refusing to marry Aiko and breaking a marriage contract I made with Uncle Joji years ago."

"Yes, a contract you made without asking me," Fusao replied.

"I am your father and I don't need to ask you. Do you think that just because the samurai and his son have taken a passing fancy to you that you can talk back so insolently to me? You honor this betrothal or you are no longer a son of this family!"

"Please, Naoki, don't say that, surely you don't need to act so hastily and we can discuss this more calmly," Yuko pleaded, tears streaming down her face at this sudden disintegration of order in her family.

"Stay out of this, wife," Naoki replied harshly, brushing her aside impatiently. "You don't understand anything. I have my reasons for doing this. We *must* save our son."

"Save me from *what?*" to his horror, Fusao heard himself demanding. He didn't know what was coming over him. He couldn't seem to stop himself from fighting his father whose word he had treated as law all his life. It was as if a strange force had entered and taken control of him, and there was no way he could stop this rebellion against his father.

Naoki was silent for a while then he replied and his voice was flat and weary, "I have my reasons for such haste, reasons you may not want to know or accept right now. You are in danger, my son, from a force we cannot resist. This is my only way of saving you."

A chill ran down Fusao's spine. An inner voice whispered to him, "Listen to your father, you know deep inside he's right, don't fight this and you will be safe and live to see old age."

But another deeper and more insistent voice urged him to follow his heart and grab the only chance he had of happiness no matter how crazy, how transient and socially unacceptable.

Almost in a trance, he replied and his voice sounded distant as if it had detached itself from his body and had a force of its own, "No, father, I will not marry Aiko, forgive me but I cannot do as you say."

He felt a stinging blow as his father struck him right across the face. The force of that blow stunned him momentarily. "Go then, get out of this house and never return till you are ready to honor this family!"

As if acting a part in a play, Fusao gathered up his slippers and ran out of the house, down the unkempt path to the road and the last thing he saw was his mother on her knees pleading with her husband, "Please, Naoki, I implore you, don't do this, he's only a boy, where will he go?"

The tears poured down his face as he ran and all he could think of was, his father had never hit him so hard before. He carried with him only the pouch holding a bunch of papers and his writing brush and ink which he had grabbed as he ran out of the house.

Chapter Seventeen

"I have been sitting under this tree in the forest for hours because Father has driven me out of the house and I don't know where to go," the anguished cry of the writer leapt out of the age stained paper before her. Mayumi felt her heart racing. His pain and fear was as raw and potent as the wind that was blowing in through the open window of her room.

"It is getting dark and soon, I must go to the castle and ask Lord Okimoto for help," Mayumi read on. "There's nowhere else to go, not even to Uncle Joji's place this time."

"And yet I am reluctant for my samurai to see me like this! Should I give in to Father and marry Aiko? I should but I can't! I am torn between my family and my heart and I don't know what to do!"

"Who can I turn to? Who can tell me what I should do?"

* * * * *

The writings had taken a different direction and was now more in the form of a personal diary than writings for the samurai and Mayumi was intrigued by it especially the page where several characters were blurred by what looked suspiciously like a drop of water or tear from eyes that had long since been silenced by death. She wanted to read on to find out more about the growing link between the writer and the young Lord Okimoto but the next page was blurry and difficult to make out and she decided to call it quits for the day.

But she could not stop thinking about the peasant boy and the young samurai and the suspicion about them that was growing in her mind. Perhaps they had tried to challenge a rigid and intolerant system a few hundred years ago to fulfil their own dreams and she wanted to know where this had led the ill fated pair.

"Damn, this is starting to get to me," she groaned. "I need to shake them off for a couple of hours or go nuts!"

80

On an impulse, Mayumi grabbed her jacket and headed to a nearby cinema complex. She would regret it later for sure because movies cost a hefty 1,800 yen in Tokyo but for now, what she needed was a good comedy drama to disconnect from the heaviness of her 400 year old case and she was prepared to pay any price.

Somehow the bright lights of the brand new shopping mall lifted her spirits and Mayumi spent the rest of the night shopping for some very much 21st century cosmetics. It felt good to be back in a world far away from feudal lords and castles with their dark secrets and morbid occupants, a world of bright lights and high technology that samurai, for all their wealth and power, would never know. somehow, that gave her a kind of wicked satisfaction.

Mayumi sighed as she realized that even here in the super modern shopping mall, she was still thinking of her peasant and samurai couple! That was the way she was, usually so absorbed in her cases that she actually lived and breathed the characters till she was done with them. Michael used to tease her and say that she was like a medium in a trance when she was in on a case and he could never have her full attention.

Her thoughts shifted to her own relationship and its problems. The distance was one thing but they also had other issues like cultural differences to sort out. Like most Westerners, he was open and demonstrative about his feelings and couldn't understand why Mayumi was shy about introducing him to her family and friends or, even when she did, why she treated him more as a friend and did not openly respond to his displays of affection. He was hurt that she would not let him kiss her in public or in the company of her friends and family and demanded to know if she was ashamed of him. She had a hard time explaining to him that her parents were painfully old fashioned and did not take kindly to any man pawing their daughter in front of them.

"People in Japan are just not used to outright displays of emotions and we're just not very physical," she tried to explain. "I mean, I love my parents to bits and am prepared to make all kinds of sacrifices for them and vice versa but I guess you won't think of that by the way we don't seem to hug or display our feelings openly. In fact you might even think of our relationship as cold and distant but it's not like that at all."

Michael had understood eventually but it had taken some time to make him see how things were in Japan.

Chapter Eighteen

After he left his home, Fusao ran to the little clearing in the woods nearby where he had often rested when he went on his wood gathering expeditions. The morning sun had dipped behind the clouds and it was cool and dim in the clearing and for the first time, Fusao ignored the little birds who came out to sing for him. They seemed peeved by his rejection and after a while, the little creatures flew off, plunging the whole clearing into silence.

"Even the birds have left me in my time of sorrow and despair!" Fusao thought listlessly gathering together a small bundle of twigs.

He was deeply troubled as random thoughts raced through his mind. Where would he go from here and what was he going to do? He should go back to the house, apologize to his father and agree to marry Aiko chan, yes, that was his duty. But his whole body and soul cried out against it and he could not understand why. Other young men his age didn't seem to mind getting married so why was he so different from them? He felt the same sexual urges and the same physical awakening as them and yet somehow, he had always known that he was different. Fusao discovered that when he was 14 years old and his friends had paid a prostitute to dance for them. As the group watched, glassy eyed and gaped mouthed, tell-tale bulges straining against their thin yukatas, Fusao had felt nothing, no physical attraction, no stirring of emotions, nothing in his own body. But when the oldest boy in the group tore off his yukata and gyrated with the scantily clad prostitute in a suggestive dance, it was his magnificent body that set Fusao on fire.

As the pair disappeared into a room to continue their dalliance followed closely by the group of leering boys, Fusao fled and ran all the way home, horrified at what had happened and disgusted with himself. What had his father said just a few days ago? A monastery in the next village had become embroiled in a shameful scandal because a devotee had stumbled upon a couple of monks in a compromising sexual position and Naoki had called them men who fornicated with each other like animals and ought to be locked away.

"What kind of man shows interest in another man?" whispered his wife, shocked. "It's unnatural and can only come to no good. I'm sure if this gets to the samurai and the Shogun, the perpetrators will be severely punished. "

She shuddered and turned to Fusao, "Did you hear that? Such men should be condemned for committing sins like that."

And eyes shining with full confidence that such things would never happen in her own home, Yuko added, "Thank goodness no one in our family will ever do such things!"

That night, Fusao refused to go to the public bath where he had to bathe with naked men of all ages, shapes and sizes, choosing instead to scrub the guilt off his body in his father's home made bath. The water was almost freezing and it stung his body bringing out all the goosebumps but Fusao felt an almost insane relief. It was only by punishing his treacherous body this way that he could wash away all the dirt of what he was beginning to discover about himself.

"I am disgusting! I am a sinner! I am an animal!" he kept repeating to himself as he sat in the bathtub shivering violently in the ice cold water until his body started to turn blue. He was still there when his parents returned from the public bath to pull him out and wrap warm blankets round his frozen body.

"What got into you?" his mother screamed. "Have you gone insane?"

Fusao caught a very bad chill and for three days he battled with high fever and breathing difficulties while his mother forced hot soup down his throat. On the third day, his fever subsided and he woke up drenched in sweat but luckily out of danger.

His mother cried with relief and said, "You're all right now, my son! I don't know why you did such a silly thing but please promise never to do it again."

Fusao hung his head and replied through cracked lips, "I'm sorry to cause both of you so much worry, I must have fallen asleep in the bathtub but I promise this will never happen again."

He kept quiet about why he had done it, managing a weak smile as he wondered what his mother would say if only she knew. Kuso, he should just have died instead of being trapped in this great joke of a male body, forever alone and different in a society that would never condone his feelings. He kept his secret so carefully guarded that no one ever found out about it but the shroud of deceit and secrecy he had to carry everywhere weighed heavily on Fusao and robbed him of the carefreeness of youth. To the rest of the village, he was just another somber young man subdued by the hard life of a peasant. Only he himself knew about the rot that had invaded him, slowly chipping away at his body, mind and soul, like the rotten core of an apple.

Now alone in the woods and not knowing what else to do, Fusao took out the sheet of papers he had stuffed into a pouch round his yukata when he left the house and began to write. He was glad his uncle had taught him to write because when everyone else rejected him, he still had these few pieces of paper left to turn to. He didn't know whether anyone would ever read his writings or when but for now it was all he had. A large tear slipped out of his left eye and fell on the paper making a big blurry black blob on one of the words he had just written. Fusao rubbed the offending tear angrily away. A man was a hunter, a warrior, and a man shouldn't cry!

A sudden flash of light cut through the gathering darkness and Fusao realized that night would be falling soon and the sky had grown dark and heavy with rain. Where would he take shelter? He raked his mind for a place to go as he emerged from the woods and wandered aimlessly down the dirt road. Perhaps he could go home and pretend to tow the line just to take shelter for the night? But, no, that wouldn't be right and went against the tiny grain of self-respect he still had for himself.

The temple, of course, that was where all the destitute people like him went, never mind that speculations would be all over the village why the aloof Naoki's son was sleeping at the temple. Then a cloud of dust temporarily blinded him as a carriage roared by, only to stop beside him. Fusao saw Lord Okimoto's face peering out of the bamboo curtain.

"What are you doing out here in this kind of weather?" the young samurai called out and Fusao took the hand that he had extended.

"Oh my Lord Okimoto," he almost wept. "I have been driven out of my home by my father and I have nowhere else to go."

The young samurai gave an order and an aide hurried over from the front of the carriage to open the bamboo door and help Fusao inside. He had never been in a carriage before and despite his current plight, Fusao gaped at the polished seats that lined the walls of the tiny cabin and the bamboo screens that shielded them from prying eyes outside. It felt exclusive and gave one a sense of power and a strange detachment from the common folks walking the streets outside.

Fusao took the seat opposite his young benefactor and held on so tightly that the knuckles on his hands showed white as the slight rocking motion told him that they had started to move.

"Come, tell me what has happened to you," the young samurai said as he put his hand casually on Fusao's in a way that made Fusao's skin crawl with goosebumps. Fusao shivered involuntarily. He prayed that Lord Okimoto would not notice this forbidden and illicit lust and push him out of the carriage in disgust. How dare a peasant lust after his feudal lord and master in such a way, Fusao couldn't imagine the consequences if his feelings were exposed!

He became acutely conscious of his work hardened hands and tried to draw them away but Lord Okimoto held on to them with just enough pressure to let him know who was in control.

Encouraged by the young nobleman's interest in his plight, Fusao poured out his heart to him, recounting his father's plans for an arranged marriage with his cousin and his refusal to comply which had resulted in his being driven from home.

When Fusao had finished his story, Lord Okimoto, who had been listening intently, asked, "And why are you so against marrying this cousin? Do you perhaps have any special reason?"

Fusao hesitated before replying in a rush," Well, Lord Okimoto, I don't have, shall we say, interest in women!"

"Then do you have interest in, shall we say, men?"

Fusao felt the rush of blood to his face and neck but he nodded then hung his head in deep shame at what he had actually admitted. Oh Kuso, what had he done? Admitted to being a doseiai to, of all people, a samurai, he would be thrown out of the carriage for sure. Fusao closed his eyes, prepared for the worst.

Then he felt someone's arm on his shoulders and he was drawn into the deep embrace of his young feudal master. It was at that moment Fusao realized with great shock and a burst of deep happiness that he had found his soulmate at last in a most unlikely place and person, a samurai belonging to the highest level of a society which was out of bounds to peasants like him.

"Take me to live with you," he whispered. "I will work for you as a servant and serve you in any way that pleases you." A slight smile played across the lips of the young samurai.

Chapter Nineteen

Lord Okimoto took Fusao back to the castle and installed him as his personal aide, officially entrusting him with services of a personal nature like organizing his clothes and meals so that they could have maximum contact without arousing the suspicions of anyone. At night, he slept in a small room annexed to the young samurai's chambers so that he could always be in attendance. But still, they had to be careful because on Lord Nobunaga's orders, there were always at least two guards stationed to watch over the safety of the younger samurai, even at night.

And suddenly, without much time to prepare or even think about it, Fusao found himself thrust into a world that was like nothing he had ever seen before. Each member of the Nobunaga family had his or her own stable of servants and clothes were chosen with great care each morning, depending on the activities or functions of the day. In his home, meals had been Spartan and predictable, rice, bean paste soup, pickles, grilled fish almost every day and it was only during the new year that they could have meat on the table.

But here at the castle, the cooks had to think of new and elegantly presented dishes every day and serve them in the porcelain and lacquer bowls. Even the servants' clothes and meals were far better than that at home and sometimes Fusao found himself thinking wistfully of how his mother would gape in wonder at such a lifestyle and how he could never show it to her.

For the first two weeks nothing happened, he learnt the ropes of serving at the castle from the other servants and hardly saw Lord Okimoto who was travelling to the north with his father to inspect some land. Amidst all the excitement of being in a new environment with scores of servants, Fusao realized that he was lonely. The other servants couldn't quite place his position at the castle, a servant by designation and yet holding some special position with Lord Okimoto; so they left him alone. A few, he suspected, were even resentful of the way he was thrust into their midst in an immediately preferred position.

There was, however, a young servant charged with the cleaning of Lord Okimoto's quarters by the name of Michio who struck up a friendship with Fusao. Michio frequently hung around the kitchens because of a pretty young maid there that he was enamored with so he heard the gossip around the castle and knew all about the politicking and scandals that went on among the servants.

"Okuno san, the chief housekeeper is an informer, he reports everything to our masters so you have to be careful of that one," Michio said. "And sooner or later, you will see Setsuko around, she's our mistress, Lady Momoe's chief maid and they say that in the night, she steals off to the rooms of the young male servants and sleeps with them!"

"Once, a servant saw a lady in white with long flowing hair walking away from the male servants' quarters and he nearly had a fit thinking he had seen a ghost but it was only Setsuko coming out of the bed of her lover for the night! If the Lady Momoe knows how her favorite maid spends her nights, she would be livid! But Okuno forbids anyone from telling on her because he too is one of her nocturnal playmates!"

"Maybe you might receive a visit from her soon! I might have a go at her myself but I'm trying to win Yuki chan over so I must behave!"

"What about Lord Okimoto's mother?" Fusao asked. "No one ever really sees her."

"You mean the Lady Michiko? Oh, she's not Lord Okimoto's mother, but the old samurai's official wife who couldn't have any children so he took the Lady Momoe as a second wife and she is Lord Okimoto's real mother. The Lady Michiko is said to be a little queer in the head, she hardly talks to anyone and keeps mostly to her chambers. The servants see her sometimes in the gardens just sitting and staring at the sky but we hear her playing the Koto in the music room almost every morning without fail. She always plays those sad, wailing tunes that really makes our hair stand on end! The Lord Nobunaga ignored her after it was established she couldn't have children and that probably sent her over the edge!"

"The Lady Momoe is a different kettle of fish! She looks all soft and pliant and beautiful on the outside but she's really as shrewd and hard as nails. In fact, she's the force behind Lord Nobunaga and controls everything that goes on in this castle and as the master grows older and more dependent on her, she becomes even more powerful."

"She's a lot younger than him, you know, and the only person who can control her is her son Lord Okimoto. That's why he has managed to get away from the stable of beautiful young women she parades regularly before him to nudge him into marriage and producing an heir for the family. But until now, that's one area Lady Momoe hasn't been able to control and it's making her nuts!"

There was a lump in Fusao's throat as he asked casually, "And so far has Lord Okimoto shown any interest in marriage?"

Michio shook his head, "None at all but you know, sooner or later, he will have to do his duty and produce an heir. His mother is only tolerating him because she believes he's still young and can wait a couple more years. In the end, Lady Momoe always wins!"

He drew closer to Fusao and lowered his voice to a whisper, "There's talk among the servants especially those who are directly under him that Lord Okimoto has, you know, strange tendencies and desires. They say he fancies men and sometimes sleeps with boys! But don't you ever dare repeat that because if it gets to Lady Momoe's ears, there'll be hell to pay!"

A strange unfamiliar feeling gripped Fusao's chest so tight he thought he was going to choke. In a matter of months, he would recognize that powerful emotion as an extreme and acute attack of jealousy which would eventually be his downfall, but for now it was a new and harmless emotion for him.

"And is Lord Okimoto with any young man right now?" he whispered and a burst of relief shot through him like a lightning bolt when Michio shook his head again and replied, "No, we haven't seen him with any young man for some time. It is rumored, though, that he has a new interest but no one knows who yet."

"Michio!" the ominous voice of Okuno thundered down the narrow passageway. "Stop your gossiping and get over here immediately! There's so much to be done. The masters are returning home today!"

Without another word, Michio straightened his yukata and hurried away in the direction of the chief housekeeper's voice, leaving Fusao breathless and heady with all the information he had just been fed.

His heart beat faster as he thought of what Michio had just said, the servants whispering about a new interest, he had to be even more careful now because if Lady Momoe should ever have an inkling of what was happening under her very nose, his life, not only at the castle but in general, would be over!

Chapter Twenty

Mayumi read the words over and over again, just to be sure her translation was correct. She had spent the whole night and right into the early hours poring over the old scripts. The badly written characters were already jumping haphazardly before her eyes. Michael was arriving in three weeks' time and she wanted to finish the whole translation and crack the case before then. Besides, her clients were coming to see her later in the afternoon and she wanted to have something substantial for them but even she hadn't expected to stumble upon such a twist of events and facts in their family history. Would they believe her? Certainly the starchy Harumi san would insist that such proclivities didn't exist in conservative 18th century Japan!

But there they were again, the words she had deciphered for the third time. "Tomorrow Lord Okimoto is returning to the castle and I can't wait to see him!"

Mayumi had tried not to think too much of these words. After all, friends were always excited to see each other and in this case, Fusao clearly hero worshipped the young samurai for having come to his rescue. In any event, even men had crushes on each other without any other more sinister objectives, she remembered her own crush on a glamorous and popular senior at the university and that didn't make her a lesbian!

Moreover, even though they were separated by a few centuries, human emotions were basically the same so she would read a few more entries before passing judgement on her subject. Perhaps it was better to postpone seeing her clients until she was sure about their ancestor, after all, this was no minor slur they would be discussing but a propensity that was barely tolerated in 21st century Japan!

Mayumi picked up the phone and called Toyoki praying that they had not already left the house to come see her. She was in luck that morning. After just a couple of rings, the old lady Harumi answered the phone.

"No," she said. "We weren't going to leave for Tokyo until after lunch so it's all right. Shall we go down to see you, say, on Monday instead?"

Mayumi checked her calendar and replied, "Monday is fine. I'm sorry about cancelling last minute but I really need to check more into some facts to confirm a very crucial finding so even if you come today, I won't have anything concrete for you."

"It's really all right, Mayumi san," the old lady assured her." We don't want to rush you, after all this has waited for centuries to be discovered so what do a few days delay matter, right?"

Mayumi laughed, "Yes, of course, but don't worry, I'm sure it will not be another century before we get to the bottom of this case!"

She had hardly put down the phone for a few minutes when it rang again. It was Sayuri, her friend from her first job at the Yokohama junior high school where she had taught history to gangly teenagers.

They were both history teachers and had become very close. After Mayumi left the school, they continued to stay in touch and met at least once a month for a small catch up.

"Yumi san, it's the last week of the month so we're supposed to meet! It's your turn to call, remember? But what the hell, you are a busy business lady these days so I decided to call you instead! I'm staying in Tokyo tonight after a teachers' conference. How are you for dinner?"

Mayumi had felt a little lonely and out of sorts the whole morning so she was delighted to hear Sayuri's voice and the prospect of having a night out with her was uplifting.

"Oh, Sayuri, how nice to hear from you! An appointment with a client for late afternoon was cancelled so I'm free tonight. Shall we meet at the same place, in front of JR Shinjuku Station?"

Mayumi could hear the little clucking sound her friend always made when she was thrilled about something. Dear sweet Sayuri, she always showed up at the right time, like the day she broke up with the only boyfriend she had dated with long term plans and had cried herself silly and Sayuri had just shown up like that with a huge teddy bear and some flowers.

"Yes of course, around six? Make sure you don't eat anything until then because we are going to an izakaya and eat ourselves silly!"

It was Friday night and the trains were packed with after office workers heading down to Shinjuku's glittering bars and nightlife for dinner and drinks. When the train arrived at Shinjuku station, Mayumi was ejected with the huge wave of Friday night revelers and swept almost to the entrance without even having to make any effort to move! Although Mayumi was born and bred in Tokyo, she could never cease to marvel at this tide of humanity that swept everyone along like a massive herd of sheep. Tonight she let it sweep her right out of the train, up a flight of stairs right to the front of the central exit where Sayuri was already waiting, her familiar flamboyant bag making her very visible even in the crowds milling around.

Mayumi smiled, the bag stood out like a sore thumb but it was Sayuri, her somewhat bizarre lifestyle and personality making her a challenge that most Japanese men didn't dare take up. But Sayuri was okay with being single and indulging in her passion for travelling without a care in the world. She was happy to live the simple life of an increasing number of single working ladies in big cities like Tokyo, living with their parents and working hard to support their passion for travelling to exotic places and branded goods. Mayumi found her friend's uncluttered lifestyle and philosophical views relaxing and it complimented her own life of a self-absorbing career which often drained her emotionally and a long distance relationship which she didn't know what to do with.

Sayuri spotted her friend and waved effusively, her long pony tail bobbing up and down as she ran towards Mayumi. Tonight, she was dressed in a brightly colored dress of the latest baby doll fashion with accessories and spiral earrings to compliment. Mayumi was sure Sayuri had gone back her cousin's apartment in Tokyo, where she stayed when she came to visit, to change out of the correct suits she had to wear when she was at school or on official business.

"I just love Shinjuku on Friday and Saturday nights, don't you?" Sayuri said gaily as they weaved in and out of the crowds on the sidewalks, their faces glowing from the glittering neon lights on almost every building. As Michael said on his first visit before he got used to Tokyo, the neon lights and the night district of Shinjuku were simply awesome and breathtaking. They were like live pulses beating away the blues of overworked Japanese salaried workers while tourists like him gaped at the sheer audacity of the sleaze in the back alleys.

After some good natured haggling, they decided to go to their usual izakaya, Tsubohachi, the crazy, smoke filled Japanese "tapas" bar crammed with young people where the selection of dishes was delicious and the prices unbelievably low. As usual, the Friday night crowds ensured that they had to wait in line for almost 45 minutes to get a table but they didn't mind. Michael had once commented on how amazing the infinite patience of Tokyoites to wait in line was. Armed with iPods and books, they could queue patiently for hours, a kind of quizzical contrast between the fast pace of life in Tokyo and the patience to stand still and wait for hours.

The two friends updated each other on a month's news of themselves over huge mugs of draft beer and the small dishes of food that soon covered the square wooden table they shared with another couple.

Mayumi told her friend about her latest case and her suspicions that the gay relationship between her samurai and peasant subjects was the key to the whole unsolved 18th century mystery surrounding Harumi san's proverbial family skeleton in the cupboard.

"Wait a minute!" she interrupted excitedly." I was researching some historical samurai figures and I remember coming across a notorious young feudal lord who was rumored to be gay and was nicknamed "The Magnolia." He took it for his personal seal. As I recall he was brutally attacked in his castle in the north in 1765 and no one was ever held accountable for that. Sounds suspiciously like your guy!"

"Was he from the Nobunaga clan?" Mayumi asked, unable to believe the uncanny coincidence as if the young gay samurai was begging to be discovered. She shivered involuntarily, maybe he was crying from across hundreds of years of death for his story to be told and accepted?

Sayuri nodded, "Yes I believe so because at the time, I liked the sound of the name."

But as they started eating, Mayumi changed the subject because tonight she wanted to have fun and away from an 18th century samurai ghost.

Chapter Twenty-One

For the last week, the castle had been particularly quiet because the masters were away in the North and even the formidable Lady Momoe had gone to take the onsen (hot spring) waters in Tohoku. Only the diffident and self-effacing Lady Michiko was left to "man the fort" and she was so light weight and oblivious to everything and everyone around her that the servants had a field day.

Even Okuno san relaxed his usually tight grip on them but the male servants missed Setsuko's "night rounds" because Lady Momoe had taken her along to the hot spring. For Fusao it was a time to learn as much as he could about life at the castle without the pressure of Lord Okimoto's electrifying presence.

But although he had grown to like the easy and indulgent life at the castle and sharing the lives of the rich and privileged, Fusao could not forget his parents and how he had failed them as a son. He was still haunted by his father's angry face and the helplessness with which his mother had watched them fight the day he left his home. Would they ever be able to bridge the widening gap between them and could his parents ever understand and accept him for the way he was?

His mother probably could but his father's stubborn pride would never allow him to accept a son who had disgraced the family in such a shameful and dishonorable way.

"Is it over?" he asked himself. "Fifteen years of close family ties severed just like that?"

Fusao felt a sudden desolation, a boy on the brink of manhood and trapped in a body and emotions he could not control or put right. Had the devil himself cast an evil eye on his mother when she was pregnant and turned him into this freak of nature? The hot tears stung his eyes as he remembered that even his own father had called him a pervert and he brushed them away hastily as he heard footsteps running towards him.

It was Michio, flushed from a successful and romantic tryst with his increasingly cooperative ladylove from the kitchens. Fusao looked at him wistfully. How nice to be like Michio! Born with all the right functions that were approved and supported by society, he would never have to live a life of shame under cover or know the pain of such a life.

Unaware of the dark thoughts that were going through his new friend's head, Michio announced, "The masters and Lady Momoe are coming back tomorrow and so ends our days of sake and laughter! Okuno san is busy beating people up to put everything in order because Lady Momoe can make things very difficult if she finds anything out of place!"

Michio went on rambling about Lady Momoe's long list of defects but Fusao hardly heard. He was feeling again that breathless rush of air into his head making him feel light headed and almost weak. His heart refused to stop pounding out its excitement because the gorgeous Lord Okimoto was coming home, was this powerful, heady and unstoppable emotion love? For the past one week he had tried to stifle it with cold logical reasoning and reality checks, but it kept bouncing back in huge all-consuming waves to drown him. He was like putty in the hands of this awesome emotion for a man who had been placed within his reach, by a miracle or by a curse.

As soon as he could escape from Michio, Fusao went out to the castle gardens to think. The whole place shone with a tranquility and beauty that was perfect, from the carefully shaped hedges to the Matsu trees arched at just the right angles and the water of the small pond was so clear that every single carp swimming in it showed up in a beautiful riot of red, yellow and smoky grey. It was hard to connect this tranquil, unhurried setting with the complex force of emotions, pain and warped lives of the people inside the castle.

He thought of Lady Michiko lost in her own world of oblivion and the Lady Momoe and her conniving ways, Lord Okimoto and his secret life, of the old samurai who, at the twilight of his life was manipulated by all of them. Even the servants had their own complex sub plots of scheming, manipulations, depravities and undercurrents.

Moved by the power of his new experiences and the beauty of his surroundings, Fusao took out the little sheaf of papers he always kept hidden in a secret pocket in his kimono and began to write.

"Tomorrow Lord Okimoto is coming back to the castle and I can't wait to see him."

"I am on fire for him! Will it happen? Will it be tomorrow night, or will it be never?"

Chapter Twenty-Two

"I'm on fire for him!"

With those words Mayumi felt certain at last that she had been right all along, it was a shocking but undeniable discovery and she really didn't know how her solid background and conservative clients would take it. That was the trouble with such clients sometimes, they asked her to dig into their roots but when she uncovered ugly facts that didn't quite suit them, they refused to accept the truth and some even accused her of fabricating lies.

It wouldn't be easy to present such "improper" facts to the impeccable and socially correct Harumi san who was obviously very proud of her samurai lineage

She tried to visualize how Harumi san would react to the news that one of her noble ancestors had been an infamous renegade samurai with definite homosexual tendencies.

"Probably with denial," Mayumi decided finally. "And the insistence that homosexuality is a deviation of modern society that didn't exist in Edo Japan!"

She had gone over her interpretations at least five times and read up Sayuri's research on a certain notorious homosexual young samurai of the time before arriving at her conclusion. After all, one did not accuse someone's highly respected ancestor of being a homosexual without being absolutely sure, especially someone like Harumi san who believed that there was going to be a proud and honorable, if not happy, ending to her ancestor search.

The small antique clock in her office struck the hour and Mayumi knew her clients would arrive soon because Japanese people were seldom late for an appointment, especially people of Harumi san's generation. As if to prove her right, the doorbell rang at two o'clock on the dot and Mayumi got up to open the door for them.

Today, it was only Harumi san and her grandson because her husband had caught a bad cold and couldn't make the trip. Mayumi could see that they were nervous, even the usually indifferent and aloof Toyoki and her cat, Miki, who was in a rare frisky mood, proved to be a welcome distraction, lightening up the atmosphere with a display of entertaining feline tricks.

"He's a very playful cat," Harumi laughed, rescuing the dangling ends of her shawl from Miki's flailing claws and everyone relaxed.

Mayumi brought out the shift of papers she had been deciphering, feeling the anxious eyes of their owner on her and consulted her notes to play for a little time. The tension in the air was so brittle it felt like a thin layer of ice that could crack anytime and Mayumi was wondering how to start when Harumi said quietly, "You said you have some news for us that might be disturbing so you can imagine how anxious we are."

Mayumi took in a deep breath. "All right, let me explain what I've noticed so far. As you know, these papers actually started as random writing, some of them uncoordinated and quite badly written, but gradually I noticed that the writing improved considerably and started to change direction, became more of a diary about the writer's daily experiences and feelings, description of events, places and people."

"I established that the writer was a peasant who lived in a village called Minamimoto, the place you are still staying, son of rice farmers. I did some historical checks on this place and found out that in that era it was a very important rice producing region. Peasants like the writer were subjected to feudal lords the most powerful of which were members of the Nobunaga clan, your ancestors."

"How, you might ask, did a peasant boy's writings find their way into the home of the most powerful feudal lord in the region and kept by them for generations as if they were important documents?"

"The connection came through Lord Okimoto, the son of the grand samurai, Lord Nobunaga who ruled over that region in the 1700s. "

"Wait a minute," Toyoki interrupted. "But I thought in those days, the samurai and their families never ever interacted with peasants. It was almost a taboo."

"Yes, you are right of course," Mayumi replied. "Except that as he grew older, Lord Nobunaga became very eccentric and one of his eccentricities was that he liked to wander down to the village and watch his peasants at work in the rice fields. Then he heard about a young teenage boy called Fusao who was quite a prolific writer in the village and paid several visits to his home to watch him write."

"It was, to all intents and purposes, very unconventional and unprecedented behavior for an important samurai like Lord Nobunaga to interact with common people and peasants, even to the extent of visiting their homes. But he was the master, he owned everything and everyone and he could do anything he wanted with his subjects. In the teenage Fusao's case, it was just a passing fancy with the samurai to take an interest in his writing, but it brought on a chain of traumatic events that created the history we are looking at now."

"On these erratic "courtesy calls" on his subjects, he sometimes brought his son, Lord Okimoto and that was how the two young men's paths first crossed."

"Fusao's parents were nervous about the samurai's interest in their son because to the peasants, it was best not to be noticed by their masters who could be cruel and harsh and confiscate their lands on a whim or if they were displeased in some way. But more trouble was to come when Fusao's father noticed, to his horror, that the young Lord Okimoto was showing more interest in his son than he was comfortable with. You see, the samurai's son was whispered among the villagers to be 'different' because he was more interested in men than in women."

Mayumi paused as she saw the looks of disbelief on Harumi's face but Toyoki was listening with an expression of what she swore was a curious mix of fascination and triumph.

"No, don't stop, go on, we want to hear it all," Harumi whispered.

"Well, if Lord Okimoto wanted Fusao, there was nothing his parents could do so his father, Naoki decided that the only way to save his son was to get him married to a cousin who had been promised to him in marriage."

At this point, Harumi put up her hand to stop Mayumi and cried, "What do you mean by all these insinuations on my ancestor? You can't be saying he was a… a… homosexual? No, you must be wrong, it was a perversity that didn't exist in those days!" she said and her voice was sharp. "You must be mistaken. My ancestors were not some riff raff in the streets but highly respected samurai and honored in the entire Tohoku region."

"I wish I could say you are right but these few pieces of paper point unmistakably in that direction, I'm sorry, Harumi san, I know it's something you don't want to hear but I must lay the facts to you as I find them," Mayumi replied. "You want me to go as near to the truth as possible, don't you?"

Harumi stood up suddenly and stretched out her hands for the papers.

"I don't like the way things are going so I've decided not to proceed with this case," she said firmly. "Just return the papers to us and I will settle your bill and we'll forget about the whole thing."

Mayumi's heart sank, she was prepared to finish the case even on her own time but she hadn't expected Harumi san to demand the papers back and except for a few pages, she didn't have a photocopy of the whole diary for herself.

She was wondering whether there was any way she could stall the return of the papers when Toyoki, who had been listening intently to the exchange, laid a hand on the old lady's arm and said, "No, O bachan, I don't think we should stop just because we are hearing facts that are not pleasant for us. we have to find out the truth about this family skeleton so that we can lay the ghost of our ancestor to rest. I found most of those papers, O bachan, and I insist we should not stop until we find out the truth."

There were very few things Harumi could ever deny her only grandson and this was no exception so she slowly sat down and inclined her head to Mayumi.

"I suppose my grandson has a point but you know my level of toleration for explicit sexual details so just spare me any graphic accounts should they appear in any of the entries of the papers," she said stiffly and Mayumi felt almost sorry for the old lady.

How perplexing it must be for her to be thrown suddenly into the 18th century homosexual world of an ancestor who had been her pride and joy and somehow gay sex in whatever era and Harumi san just didn't go too well together!

A few minutes later, her clients got up to go. Toyoki asked his grandmother to give him a few minutes with Mayumi.

"There are more things in those entries you didn't mention to us, I am sure about that," he said looking pointedly at the sheets of papers still in her hands.

"Yes, some words of passion I felt would hurt your grandmother's sensibilities," Mayumi replied. "Look at these words "I am on fire for him," for example, your grandma would freak out if I had shown her these parts!"

"So Lord Nobunaga's son was a gay!" Toyoki said thoughtfully. "Well, that is just perfect! Everything falls into place now."

"What do you mean?" Mayumi asked casually and thought she saw the shutter come down on Toyoki's eyes as he replied, "Oh, nothing, just some things that went through my mind, that's all, nothing important."

Chapter Twenty-Three

The masters' return to the castle did not cause much of a stir except that the pleasantly laid back and relaxed atmosphere of the last few days had to go back into storage until the next time Lord Nobunaga and his family decided to make another trip.

It was clear that the trip to the hot spring had not relaxed Lady Momoe and she was in a foul mood. Fusao and the rest of the servants could hear her screaming at Sayuri and the rest of her personal attendants and at least two of them got dismissed that day. But they always ran to Lady Michiko who would take them in so they never had to leave the castle and when Lady Momoe calmed down, she would order them to come back to her and they got shuttled to and from the two ladies of the castle with the ease of a ball.

That night, Lord Okimoto said that his muscles were tired after the long trip and requested Fusao to give him a massage in his room with some special oils he kept in little colorful jars in a shining black lacquer cupboard.

"This one," he said pointing to a small brown jar. "It makes one feel sensual…"

He slipped off his silk kimono with the ease of someone used to nudity. For Fusao too, male nudity was nothing new, he had bathed naked in public baths his entire life and seen men of all ages in all shapes and sizes. However, the beauty of this man took his breath away. From the rippling muscles on his broad shoulders to the slim taut waist and long lithe legs, Lord Okimoto was every doseiai man's dream. Keeping his eyes averted, Fusao prayed that his emotions and desires would not be too obvious as he started massaging away the tired knots on Lord Okimoto's neck and shoulders.

"Lower, go lower down, Fusao, don't be afraid," Lord Okimoto said and Fusao's cheeks flamed as he realized that the gorgeous samurai was teaching him the art of seduction. It was painfully clear that Fusao had never been with any man and Lord Okimoto was both intrigued and touched by his shyness and unspoiled innocence. He himself was no stranger to taking sensual pleasures from any young man he wanted but somehow, this young boy, a nameless peasant from the village and one of his lowest subjects, moved him and made him feel strangely protective and in no hurry to rush him.

In fact, he surprised himself by this unusual desire to exercise restraint and give as much pleasure to Fusao as he himself was receiving. Lord Okimoto had led a charmed and privileged life, the only son and heir of a long line of great samurai and since the day he was born, nothing was spared to get him anything and anyone he wanted. He was not used to waiting for his pleasures and yet with this doe eyed young gazelle of a boy, the samurai could restrain the tension in his loins and wait for the right moment to unleash the floodgate of exquisite pleasure on that firm boyish figure. Lord Okimoto realized that he had fallen in love with the peasant boy and it was this love that brought on more tenderness than the raw physical passion of lust that he had always felt for his sexual partners whom he used relentlessly and then discarded without a thought.

When he was barely four years old, a betrothal had been arranged with the two year old daughter of another great samurai family from the south and when his chosen bride reached the age of 13, a missal had arrived every six months requesting that plans for their marriage be commenced, a duty he had so far been able to ward off. But now that the Lady Sachiko had reached the ripe old age of 17, it was becoming increasingly difficult to hold back and he expected and dreaded the ultimatum that was bound to arrive someday soon…

Okimoto couldn't remember at which exact point of his life that he realized he was doseiai and would never be attracted to a woman. One day he had bathed naked with a distant cousin from a less influential branch of the family and felt something come alive in him. It was wrong, forbidden and he had a fiancée waiting to marry him and a duty to produce an heir for the family, so he lowered himself into the scorching water of the bath, determined to cleanse himself of these unholy thoughts and desires.

But that night, his cousin had climbed into his futon and proceeded to seduce him with such skill and passion that Okimoto realized that it was no use holding back. For some reason he had been born doseiai, he would always be one and there was not a thing he could do about it. He had become hooked onto the intense pleasure that only a man could give him and every night, his cousin would creep into his futon and convince him that it was his destiny to be doseiai and there was no need to fight it. By the time his cousin left the castle to return to his own family seat in Hokkaido, Okimoto was a confirmed gay and there was no turning back.

In the months to come, Okimoto realized that it was difficult being doseiai. He had to be careful not to expose his secret to his family and a society which could never accept something so unnatural as a relationship between two men, no matter how high up the social ladder he was in. When he saw a boy he fancied, he could not openly pursue him as he could a woman and be labelled with nothing worse than a normal young man with a healthy appetite for sowing his wild oats.

So far he had never been caught red handed and although he suspected his mother was beginning to suspect something amiss, he knew she would not do anything until she had figured out a way to deal with him.

Lord Okimoto had never been emotionally involved with any of his lovers and he made it a point not to have the same boy more than twice. He was thus worried about his unusual weakness for this boy Fusao and although he was sure about the boy's sexual orientations, Lord Okimoto had made up his mind not to have sex with him until he was sure he could detach himself emotionally. Still, the self-imposed restraint was killing him.

The first time he had laid eyes on the young peasant boy was when he accompanied his father to their home to watch him write. Okimoto had never been inside the home of a peasant and found the hard mud floors and flimsy wooden walls that hardly kept the wind and cold out, at best distasteful. Then the young boy his father had come to see appeared and he forgot about his rough surroundings. Fusao was beautiful with a shock of jet black hair setting off his pale, almost translucent skin which shone with a kind of open wonder that was captivating. Okimoto felt what he swore was his heart move when the boy's huge eyes fixed on him and he turned away, annoyed with the tricks this mere peasant boy was playing on him. Was it possible to find someone to love in these surroundings? Could love be found in one momentary locking of their eyes? Why would fate be so cruel to him? He was the Lord Samurai's son and one day he would own all these people, how could he possibly fall in love with someone he owned?

They met a couple more times after that and then his father lost interest in what he called "the literate peasant" and to his relief Okimoto was able to put Fusao out of his mind for a while. Until one stormy night, when Fate threw them together again. He was returning from a sword fighting match when a dark shadowy figure appeared beside his speeding carriage, waving frantically. At that moment there was a flash of lightning and Okimoto saw that it was Fusao. He screamed for the carriage drivers to stop, took a soaking and shivering Fusao inside and brought him back to the castle.

As he felt Fusao's tender hands stroking his back all the way down as he had requested, Lord Okimoto closed his eyes at the sheer pleasure that sensual touch invoked in him and fought the temptation to have his way with Fusao right at that moment, on the tatami floor of the room. With a great effort, he restrained himself. He wasn't sure how far he could go with the boy and the young samurai didn't want to frighten him away. For the first time in his life, the revered Lord Okimoto, heir to the most powerful samurai seat in the region, allowed a nameless peasant boy to play with his feelings and make him exercise restraint and for the first time too, someone else's needs were becoming more important to him than his own.

No, Fusao wasn't ready yet so tonight they would sleep together and hold each other but that was all. He had to slowly stoke the fires in his young protégé until he was ready and then their union would be spectacular and lasting.

They took a bath together in one of the castle's many scented baths. For tonight, Lord Okimoto chose one of the outdoor baths which faced a natural rock garden on the eastern side of the castle. The small bath of clear scented topaz water was surrounded by large rocks with a stone frog at one end that spouted water from its mouth to create the lovely sound of running water.

They were silent, breathing in the cool crisp air under a carpet of stars in the darkening sky while the hot scented water covered their bodies in a wonderful blanket of warmth and well-being. Fusao had never felt so comfortable and content in his life.

Although Lord Okimoto hadn't made any moves and gone all the way yet, there was a kind of quiet intimacy between them as if they were meant to be together and this feeling of spiritual bonding was more powerful and beyond any physical union and it was enough for them that night.

Rei Kimura

"It's as if our souls have searched and found each other in this union of great love. I don't know where we are going or how we will end but tonight, right now, it's magic."

Chapter Twenty-Four

Autumn had given way to the first chill of winter and the whole castle was in mourning because the old samurai, Lord Nobunaga lay dying in his room. No one knew quite how it had started. One day he caught a chill from riding in the rain, which wasn't really a cause for concern as he normally recovered from such ailments fairly quickly. But this time, something had gone wrong, the chill developed into pneumonia and no amount of herbal remedies from all the best physicians in the prefecture could bring him out of it.

Lady Momoe sat quietly weeping in the corner and his son Lord Okimoto faced the daunting task of ending his carefree days and taking over as head of the Nobunaga clan, and, as his mother put it tearfully, without even a wife at his side.

The servants went about their work with heavy hearts wondering what would happen to them if their old master passed away. Lord Nobunaga had been around for so long that most of them didn't know any other master or any other life without him.

"Lord Nobunaga is dying and my beloved will become the next samurai head of the family and be forced to marry… what are we going to do?" Fusao thought.

Fusao had escaped to the rock garden to write when Lord Okimoto left his rooms to visit his father and assess the situation. It was a lovely day and the warm sunlight, birds singing gaily among the trees and the dazzling colors of the carp swimming in the pond all seemed to be mocking the sorrow and darkness that lay within the castle.

* * * * *

Michio was sweeping the leaves from the front yard angrily. He was mad with the old samurai for dying suddenly on them and the uncertainties that could throw his fledgling romance with Yuki, the kitchen maid out of the window. Besides, Michio respected Lord Nobunaga who treated his servants well and knew most of their names unlike the aloof Lord Okimoto who hardly knew they existed. He shivered, besides, Lord Okimoto was "queer" and there were some really murky things going on in his life. The thought of him being their lord and master wasn't appealing at all.

He saw Fusao sitting in the rock garden and debated whether he should air his concerns but decided against it because his friend was writing furiously. Michio's brow creased as he remembered some disturbing gossip he had heard a few days ago. What was it Okuna san had said about Fusao? That he slept with Lord Okimoto in the same room? Did that mean that he was becoming one of the young samurai's "boys?"

"Oh No," Michio said to himself. "Not Fusao, he's too nice for this kind of mess!" But just in case, he decided against going up to Fusao to air his grievances and anxieties about Lord Nobunaga's son and heir. Things were changing with the shifting of power every hour and it was not the right time to take risks with anyone.

* * * * *

Up in the castle, Lord Okimoto let himself quietly into his father's room and was immediately struck by the stench of sickness and death that no amount of perfumed scent the servants had put everywhere could kill.

He averted his eyes, unable to see his father's usually robust body wasted to a shriveled carcass of himself. From the rasping way he was breathing, Lord Okimoto knew his father would not live to see the end of the week.

"Come here, son," but when Lord Nobunaga spoke, his voice was surprisingly clear. "I have something important to ask you."

The young man approached his father's deathbed and knelt down beside him covering the frail clammy hands with his.

"It's all right, father. I'm here," he said, his heart constricting as he felt the old man's hand tightening on his in a surprisingly strong grip.

It was then that the old samurai opened his eyes and looked straight at his son in a clear, unflinching stare.

"Okimoto, my son," he began. "I know about you, I've known for some time about your secret ways and the boys you bring into your bed.

In the beginning it hurt me a lot and I asked myself, Why, why, why my only son and heir? I tried to change you by bringing all those women to you hoping that it was just a passing phase but no, none of it worked and I realized that your… condition really was serious and irreversible."

He paused for a moment, gasping for breath before continuing, "I know it's not your fault and perhaps God made a mistake and put a woman's mind into your body, but I think I accepted you as you are years ago. But remember, you are the heir to the very powerful and prestigious Nobunaga line and whether you like it or not, a duty sits on your shoulders, to marry and have children."

"What I am asking you is to promise your dying father that you will fulfil this duty and marry Sachi, your fiancé, and produce an heir to continue our family line. I am asking you from my deathbed, Okimoto so please say you will not deny me…"

The tears stung the young samurai's eyes as he whispered to his father, "You knew all this time, father and yet you did not push me away with disgust? Father I don't deserve your love and I promise you that I will do my duty by this family and marry my betrothed."

The old samurai nodded his head and said, "Thank you, my son. This is all I want to hear, that you have promised to continue our noble Nobunaga line… I can now die in peace."

That night, the old samurai lapsed into unconsciousness and never spoke again. Two days later, he was gone.

* * * * *

Lord Nobunaga's funeral was as grand and spectacular as his life had been and he was laid out in a magnificent silver kimono in the stateroom of the castle for four days and visited by the shogun and powerful samurai from near and far. Fusao, watching with the other servants from an inner room, was mesmerized by the sight of this steady stream of dignitaries.

The night before the Lord Nobunaga was laid to rest in the family mausoleum near the castle, Fusao found Lord Okimoto sitting alone in his room, banging his fist against a bag filled with beans he kept for punching when he needed to let off steam. They hadn't been able to spend any time together since the old samurai fell sick so Fusao was delighted to find himself alone with Lord Okimoto at last.

The young samurai stopped punching when he saw Fusao. As if it was the most natural thing to do, Fusao moved towards Lord Okimoto and wrapped his arms around him.

"My heart is heavy with the prospect of what I must do, a promise my father made me give on his deathbed, that I marry Lady Sachi, and produce an heir to perpetuate the Nobunaga line," Lord Okimoto said. "Oh Fusao, tell me what I'm going to do!"

His words shot its lethal poison of agonizing pain through Fusao's heart and he could feel the young samurai's desperation as if it were his own. There was nothing both of them could say, they could only feel and bleed.

Fusao knew what he had to do. He had to give himself to Lord Okimoto and through the fusion of their souls and bodies would come a love so intense, so eternal, nothing could tear them apart, not the ravages of time, not even promises made on a deathbed. They would defy all the cruel laws of nature and society that made their love forbidden and illicit and even if they were defeated in the end, at least they would have their time, here and now.

Chapter Twenty-Five

The day of the funeral dawned bright and clear as if the heavens wanted to give Lord Nobunaga a good send off. It seemed that with her husband well and truly gone, Lady Momoe had steeled herself and assumed control of everything. She had never really depended on her son and now more than ever she had to admit that he was weak, self-indulgent and did not have the makings of a great samurai like his father although the same blood flowed in their veins.

Lady Momoe realized that it was up to her to keep the Nobunaga clan together and afloat and push Okimoto into a marriage as soon as possible and hope that he would produce at least one son with the gumption and strength of the old samurai to take over. Until then, it was all up to her. But she would have to tread carefully and work behind the front of her son because feudal Japan was still not ready yet to tolerate matriarchs and if it ever went out that Okimoto was weak and disinterested in assuming his position as head of the Nobunaga clan, there would be a scramble among all the minor cousins to take control. This she would not allow.

When she thought of her son, Lady Momoe's lips curled, it would not be easy to force him to marry the girl he was betrothed to because she had her own suspicions about his sexual leanings, an unmentionable thought that disgusted her. What had gone wrong that she, daughter of one of the most prestigious families of the North and from an impeccable bloodline had produced a son like that? She just wanted to blot it from her mind and never discuss it with him. But now things had changed, the can of worms could be opened when she confronted him with his impending marriage. But Lady Momoe knew in the end Okimoto would fulfil his duty because she had heard him making that promise to his father on his deathbed and that was one undertaking no son could ever break.

Even she had not married for love but through an intricate system of matchmaking to join two important families and feudal seats and avert a big potential scandal. Her face clouded as she thought of the handsome young man who had been her brothers' tutor and with whom she had fallen so madly in love that they had considered at one point running away together. But her own mother had caught them in a compromising position one day and the young man and his whole family were sent away never to be heard again. A marriage was then quickly arranged for Lady Momoe herself with an older but prominent samurai from the central part of Japan who needed a young second wife to replace a first who could not bear children.

Lady Momoe's pleas fell on deaf ears and in the end, to protect herself from any more pain and suffering, she developed this hard impenetrable shell and that was how she found the strength to go through with the marriage and try year after year to produce heirs for her husband. In the end, after two miscarriages and two daughters, Lord Okimoto had arrived and his mother cried with joy at the birth of the long awaited heir.

But there was one memory she would carry to her grave and no one could take that away from her, the three glorious months in her life when she had known love, passion and a physical intimacy that could never be arranged by a matchmaker.

It was so incongruous and improper that for a moment she wanted to laugh hysterically, but, while walking in her husband's funeral procession behind her son holding their ancestral tablet, Lady Momoe was thinking of Takuya, her lover of a distant life, and the night they had got carried away and ended up making love on the tatami floor of her brother's room. It had been a great risk because the sliding doors had no locks and anyone could just walk in but they were so young and so in love and so desperate with the impossibility of their relationship that they had thrown all caution to the wind.

Afterwards, as they held each other, frightened about what they had done, her mother had walked in and thrown Takuya out of their castle in a rage that went on for days until she had found a suitable match for her disgraced daughter in Lord Nobunaga. Never mind the age gap or that he was already married and Lady Momoe would be his second wife, at least she would be safely married. After all, she had lost her virginity and had nothing more to lose.

Virginity in a bride was a must have in marriages and Lady Momoe ought to have been nervous on her wedding night but somehow, the pain of losing her lover had numbed all her feelings and she went to her marriage bed, prepared for the worst and apathetic and unwilling to please her husband. If she was thrown out of the marriage, so be it. It wasn't one she had wanted anyway.

The minute her new husband made love to her he knew she was not a virgin and she waited for him to denounce her for her lack of virtue. But to her surprise, he said nothing and afterwards he held her tightly in his arms until she fell asleep. For the next few days she waited for him to confront her but he said nothing and was the usual attentive new husband and gradually, Lady Momoe realized that he was not going to question her about her past at all but take her for what she was. It was then she realized what a good man Lord Nobunaga was and although she knew she would never love him with the heart wrenching passion that she had loved Takuya, she would always respect him and care for him. A month later when she discovered she was with child. She wasn't even sure whose child it was but deep down inside her, she hoped it was Takuya's, a link that would always connect them together and a link that might someday lead her to him. Lord Nobunaga was delighted and didn't suspect a thing.

But Fate stepped in and when she was into her third month, she woke up one night bleeding profusely and the baby was gone, she had suffered a miscarriage and she cried bitterly because she had lost her link with Takuya forever. The next day the midwife came to clean her up. Mistaking Lady Momoe's lifeless body and white face for grief over her lost baby, the midwife whispered soothingly to her, "It's all right, a lot of women lose their first child, you will soon have another."

She said nothing. From now on, she would be the unfeeling, emotionless and faultlessly dutiful wife of Lord Nobunaga, and nothing more.

But as the years went by she found her husband depending more on her. she developed quickly a strength and business acumen she didn't know she had. In the years to follow, few doubted that she, Lady Momoe, was their de facto feudal lord and ruler! She had travelled very far away from the shy beautiful young girl who had dared to dream of impossible love and happiness with a tutor with neither substantial wealth nor social position in feudal Japan.

In recent months after she discovered her son's sexual leanings and questioned herself about where she had gone wrong in bringing him up, Lady Momoe had thought more of her wild past and concluded that, perhaps, Lord Okimoto received his inclinations from this wild streak of his mother before it was suppressed and finally snuffed out.

Her own past had taught Lady Momoe the pain of unrequited and forbidden love. Afterall, she was his mother and wished him happiness and not the pain that had destroyed her life. so if it had been a girl he wanted no matter from what social status she would have allowed it but, a boy? No, no mother could allow or approve such unnatural dalliances! There was no other way. after the funeral, she would have to broach the subject of his marriage with her son. Tears streamed down her cheeks as she thought about her own lost youth and how she must condemn her son to the same fate her own mother had years ago. As Lord Nobunaga was lowered into his final resting place, everyone presumed that Lady Momoe was crying for her husband.

In front of her, hardly a few meters away, her son stood, head bowed and he too was thinking of the promise he had made to his father on his deathbed and the obligation to honor that promise weighed so heavily on his heart that he had to close his eyes tightly to prevent the tears from spilling out.

"We Samurai are warriors and we never ever show our tears and weaknesses to the world," Lord Okimoto would often draw strength from his father's favorite words in the days ahead as he faced the frightening prospect of being head of the Nobunaga family and feudal lord of the whole prefecture.

Having kept the stiff upper lip that was expected of him in public for days, the new grand samurai let go of all his pent up emotions in the privacy of his own quarters. As tears flowed freely down his face he whispered," A few months out of a lifetime, that is all we are asking."

Chapter Twenty-Six

As soon as the last guest had left the castle and the servants began to clear up the formal reception hall, Lord Okimoto escaped to the peace and quiet of his rooms. He had been conscious the whole night of his mother's eyes on him, and he knew what was on her mind.

"Can't she even wait until after the mourning period?" he thought bitterly. Sometimes he couldn't fathom his mother, there was something in the way she looked at him that made Okimoto wonder whether she knew the truth about him. He even fancied she pitied him which was strange given her strict regard for discipline, family honor and being socially correct.

Okimoto laughed, the death of his father and the long drawn out funeral must have made him soft in the head that, for one moment, he could entertain even the slightest hope that the Lady Momoe would condone his way of life. Oh no, his mother was a stickler for social correctness, class distinctions, impeccable lineages and nothing was ever going to change that.

Tonight there were none of the usual servants and attendants in his rooms, they were all busy down at the reception hall and in the kitchens. Okimoto was glad. He opened up the sliding doors and stepped out onto the balcony outside. It was a clear night and the sky was filled with a million stars. The beauty of the carpet of lights high above him was breathtaking but Okimoto saw none of it. In the distance, he could hear the mournful sounds of a Koto from Lady Michiko, his step mother.

Okimoto could feel himself sinking into depression. With his father's death, he was forced to admit that he was not ready to take over as the Grand Samurai, head of the family and feudal lord to all the people in the region and question whether he would ever be ready. He knew that his mother, Lady Momoe would be the real grand samurai. For the first time, he was looking at himself as a big joke, not worthy to be the son of a great samurai. Okimoto could not even make love to a woman to produce an heir, something every normal man, and even the most humble of peasants, could do What was he good for except to live a life forever under cover? In the weeks to come, he would be forced into a marriage to honor a promise he made to his father and he didn't even know how he would go through it and spend his wedding night.

The young samurai walked over to a wall in the corner of the room that was mounted with his collection of swords and drew out one from its Sabre. The sword shone, bright, dazzling and hard in his hands. All he had to do was plunge it into his stomach and all his pain and agony would be gone. He pointed the sharp end of the weapon to his body but as he felt the sword grazing his skin, Lord Okimoto panicked, flung it away from him and ran from the room.

'I am a coward! I am a coward!" he chanted the words as he ran, as if in a trance. "I don't have the strength to even kill myself!"

* * * * *

He ended up in an abandoned teahouse at the far end of the castle grounds, where the young ladies of the castle, including his sisters, were once given lessons in tea ceremonies. Now it stood abandoned..

Okimoto leaned against the rough straw of the fence that surrounded the teahouse, breathing heavily as he watched the shadows of the Matsu trees moving gently in the breeze. He was lost in this teahouse where he started to cry, great heaving sobs that he could let out because there was no one there to witness his shame.

He was so steeped in his own misery and pain that he did not feel the gentle touch on his shoulders and the arms embraced him, holding him tight. Was it one of the fabled castle ghosts making his nightly rounds ministering to him with such tenderness?

But it was not a ghost. It was Fusao who had seen Lord Okimoto rushing wildly out of the castle and had followed him, alarmed by his state of mind. Without a word, they pushed open the tiny door of the teahouse and started to kiss, long deep kisses.

The tatami floor of the long unused teahouse was dusty and their bodies crushed the dry leaves that had blown in through the open windows making crackling sounds that seemed to mock their illicit passion. They didn't care. To them, their love, their passion, and their need for one another was as natural, pure, and real as any love between a man and a woman.

* * * * *

Later, long after their passion was spent, the two young men lay on that dusty, dirty floor, clinging tightly to one other and talking.

"You know, of course, that soon I must marry a distant cousin I was betrothed to from childhood and now that my father is dead, my mother will not allow me to avoid my duties any longer." Okimoto softly grazed the smooth skin of Fusao's cheeks. "Anyway, what is more important, I made a promise to my father as he lay dying that I would marry and although no words are adequate to express my grief, I will not shirk this duty."

He gave a bitter laugh and continued, "It's strange, isn't it, I am the samurai, the most important man in this prefecture and I can have anything I want except for the one thing and one person I really want. In the end, although it may sound strange, I'm defeated by my own position and power."

For a moment Fusao could not answer. The lump in his throat was too great, he was moved by Okimoto's profession of love for him and hurt by how impossible their relationship was. In the end, their families, society and even the spirit of Lord Nobunaga would come down on them with such great force that their love, no matter how great, would buckle and crumble into ashes under such a great weight of denunciation. Perhaps it would be far better for them to outwardly conform and go undercover with their secret love.

Aloud, Fusao said, "You know, it's funny how we are caught in exactly the same situation. My father wanted me to marry a distant cousin too that was promised to me almost at birth but being what I am, I just couldn't do it. That night you found me, he had driven me out of his house for disobeying him."

"Yes, it seems almost like destiny the way our lives are travelling along the same paths," Okimoto replied. "I dream of the day when society will accept people like us who do not love as other people do, of a time when we can walk openly in the streets and even live together without being spat at. But I know it will not happen in our lifetime and I am in despair about what we are going to do."

Fusao stopped stroking his lover's thigh and looked away in pain. Yes, he knew the world was not ready to accept the kind of love they shared. He knew he would be killed just being caught here making love with his master.

If their situation was not so grave, both of them would have laughed at the irony of a situation where a young feudal lord was asking a peasant, one of his lowest subjects what to do instead of issuing orders that had to be followed, no questions permitted.

But centuries of feudal codes could not be undone so easily, not even with an intimate relationship across strict class lines. Fusao voiced his opinion hesitantly, "I have an idea and it may be the only way we can save our relationship."

"Then speak up and don't keep me in such agony," Okimoto replied, and there was the slight hint of a feudal lord's impatience in his voice. Old habits die hard and when Okimoto realized his tone of voice, he softened it with a gentle caress which sent a wave down Fusao's spine.

"Strange how a man with such a gorgeous physique and arrogant disposition can be so gentle and loving." he thought but didn't dare to say aloud. Fusao finally spoke again, "I'm thinking, let's make a pact! We both know you must marry to keep your promise to your father and to satisfy your family but it doesn't mean we cannot carry on with our relationship behind the safe cover of that marriage."

Okimoto was silent for a while, then he reached over and kissed Fusao on the lips, a long and lingering kiss that spoke of the depth of his feelings.

Then he looked deep into Fusao's eyes and said steadily, "But you realize of course that if I marry, and you know I must, it would mean I have to try for an heir with my bride. In my case, that is a very crucial duty that I have to secure the continuity of the Nobunaga line. I have never been with a woman and God knows how I am going to do it but I have to try. Do you understand what I'm saying?"

Fusao swallowed. It would not be easy to understand but he had to try. So he nodded and said, "Yes, of course I understand that and although I admit it will be very hard to see you consummate your marriage with a woman, I have to accept it. I will accept anything to remain near you."

The moon had risen high in the sky and little slivers of light were filtering into the teahouse through the cracks in the walls and the howling of a pack of wolves. It was getting late and the two needed to get back to the castle. Reluctantly, the two men stood and started the long walk back, holding hands until they were within sight of the castle. The whole place was awash with lights as was the custom to leave all the lights on for seven nights in case the spirit of the dead wanted to come back for a visit.

Both Fusao and Okimoto parted just before the main door with a hurried kiss and entered the castle separately. Fusao was hurrying down the dark narrow passage leading to his room, his body still glowing from the warm embraces of his young samurai lover when he felt a heavy hand on his shoulder.

"There you are!" the voice of Okuno identified the owner of the hand. "Where did you disappear to? Please remember that just because Lord Nobunaga is dead, it doesn't mean that there are no more rules and regulations in this castle! We do have a new master and the watchful eyes of Lady Momoe are still on us. So if a servant wants to leave the castle, he has to ask me for permission. But because we are still in mourning for Lord Nobunaga, I'll let you off this time but make sure this doesn't happen again!"

Fusao had forgotten about rules and regulations when he saw Lord Okimoto fleeing the castle. Fusao's only thought was to follow him and make sure that he would not harm himself but he could not possibly explain this to Okuno so he hung his head and apologized, "I am so sorry, Okuno san, I don't know what came over me but I think it was the shock of seeing our master dead. I promise I'll never do it again."

"All right then," Okuno replied, mollified by Fusao's attitude. "Get to your room and have some sleep, it's very late. Tomorrow we have a busy day sorting out old Lord Nobunaga's rooms and installing Lord Okimoto in his new quarters as our new lord and master."

* * * * *

Fusao reached his room without meeting anyone else and much later when he was sure no one was around he crept over to Okimoto's room and peeped inside. The young samurai was sprawled on his futon breathing quietly in an exhausted sleep. In Okimoto's sleep he had kicked the blanket off. Fusao moved quietly in to pull a thick soft blanket over Okimoto to keep out the cold night air. He looked so peaceful and happy that it was impossible to remember the tormented spirit that was trapped within, just like Fusao himself.

Back in his own room, unable to sleep, Fusao took out two pieces of paper from his treasure trove of stationary and began to write, straining his eyes in the poor light of the room.

"Lord Nobunaga is dead and we have started a new era. Tonight, we made love in the old teahouse and I had a glimpse of paradise! But now I am alone in my room and I am hurt because Okimoto sama must marry soon. Although I have promised to accept the inevitable, it is so hard!"

"Will I ever get used to seeing my beloved with a woman who is recognized as his wife and partner while I must live in the shadows forever? Will this heart ever stop feeling the pain of living a life under cover?"

"I don't have the answers, by all the stars in the heavens, not tonight!"

Fusao continued writing until his eyes could not take it anymore. Then he carefully stored the pieces of emotional writing into a rough wooden folder and placed it inside the little chest of drawers that held all his possessions.

"My writings will survive me perhaps to all eternity and one day, someone will find it and tell my story and my pain to the world," was Fusao's last thought as he drifted into sleep at last.

Chapter-Twenty-Seven

The next few days saw the castle buzzing with news of another impending event, the new grand samurai's marriage that was to take place immediately after the 49 days mourning period for his father was upon them. It was a welcome respite from the months of sorrow and dreary mourning that had accompanied the old samurai's illness and eventual demise.

"After all these months of sadness over Lord Nobunaga's illness and his death and funeral, it's about time we had some happy event, don't you think so?" Michio said as he accosted Fusao in the kitchens where both of them were preparing to take orders from Okuna san for the day. "And a married grand samurai will somehow look and feel more stable and assertive, especially one as young as Lord Okimoto."

Fusao said nothing because his friend's innocent comments had pierced his heart with so much agony and distress he had felt as if a poisoned arrow had gone through him.

Concerned by Fusao's silence, Michio peered up at his friend and asked worriedly, "Are you all right, Fusao? You look very pale, maybe all the excitement and extra work of the last few days have been too much for you?"

Fusao was afraid he might give himself away and with a supreme effort, managed a smile as he replied, "No, I'm fine, really. Must be something I ate this morning that doesn't quite agree with me. Don't worry, it'll pass and I'll be right as rain! My mother always said I have this finicky tummy which plays up at the slightest aggravation!"

"Oh, that's all right then, you just looked so down that for a moment I was worried something serious was troubling you," Michio replied and the moment of awkwardness passed.

But even though Fusao was relieved that he had not given himself away this time, it did nothing to lift his spirits because he was beginning to see how it was always going to be for him, living and working at the castle to be close to his young samurai lover and yet having to see and hear about his new life as a married man and watch him with a woman. Men like them had a bond, an understanding that they shouldn't, couldn't be with a woman. Despite Fusao's promise to accept the situation, he felt betrayed by Okimoto's forthcoming marriage, notwithstanding the circumstances and his lack of choice in the matter.

Fusao sighed wearily. the human heart had a way of refusing to obey the commands of the mind and the brain. He knew with certainty that his pledge to suffer in silence would be very tough to uphold and at times, almost unbearable. The road ahead stretched in an endless tunnel of turbulent waves swirling from deep despair to the exquisite joys of a love and passion that kept him trapped inside. How long could he stay in that tunnel before he ran out of air and passed out?

Michio peered up at him again and said, "I swear something is bothering you, Fusao. You really look like death itself! Maybe I should go and tell Okuno to give you some time off."

"No, Michio, no!" Fusao cried, horrified. "Please don't do that, I'm already in his black books for going out of the castle without permission last night. I'll get sent back home if you do that."

Michio slanted a look at him and said a little hesitantly, "No, you won't be sent away, they say you are sort of Lord Okimoto's favorite servant."

"Well, maybe that's because I am a good servant, Michio! Have you ever thought about that?" Fusao laughed trying to make a joke out of such a touchy issue. "But when he is well and truly married, I'm sure his wife will throw me out. They also say that a new wife never wants her man to keep all the old habits and favorite people of his unmarried days!"

Fortunately, the love of Michio's life, Yuki, the kitchen maid, appeared and he immediately forgot about Fusao and his problems. While his friend was distracted with Yuki, Fusao beat a hasty retreat but for the rest of the day, although he performed his tasks with his usual meticulous attention to details, his heart was heavy. He hadn't seen Lord Okimoto since the previous night and it was killing him. He kept wondering where his lover was, whether he still remembered their intimacy and the unbridled passion of their bodies glistening with sweat at the teahouse with the moonlight filtering in. And when Lord Okimoto shifted away to his new and bigger quarters befitting the head of the castle, with more servants and guards, how would they get to see each other?

By noon, Fusao found himself hanging around the young samurai's rooms hoping to catch a glimpse of him. Instead, he found Okuno san striding towards him, a paper in his hands.

"Everyone, go down to the kitchen," Okuno shouted. Automatically, Fusao retraced his steps to the kitchens on the heels of a group of castle maids and helpers who had started to follow Okuno san.

When almost all but the outdoor staff were gathered round him, the head servant said, "Our new samurai, Lord Okimoto, has given me a list of the servants he selected to serve him in his new quarters."

Okuno san consulted the piece of paper in his hands and rattled out the names. "Kiku… Sawada, Michio, Uno…"

Fusao waited with his heart in his throat. would he be included? Or had Lord Okimoto tired of him after only two nights and planned to discard him?

After rattling off a few more names, Okuno called his name out "Fusao… Yuki…" and Fusao's spirits soared to such great heights he thought he wound faint from its rapid ascent from the depths of depression. He would continue to work for Lord Okimoto and be near him again. At that, moment nothing else mattered.

In the afternoon Lord Okimoto "summoned" Fusao to his new rooms ostensibly to help arrange things. For the first time Fusao saw the new grand samurai's quarters which spanned almost the whole western wing of the castle. With none of the Spartan functional look of his old quarters, this new wing boasted of several large rooms with beautiful paintings of cranes and pine trees gracing the walls. It was then Fusao realized with a heavy heart that this wing was designed to accommodate the family Lord Okimoto was expected to have after his marriage.

But he didn't want to spoil this rare moment alone with the young samurai so he said wistfully, "I missed you today. Is it going to be difficult for us to spend any time together?"

Lord Okimoto nodded somberly as he took Fusao's hand and pulled him down to sit beside him. "There's so much of my father's duties I have to learn. I tried convincing my mother to continue to rule since she enjoys being de facto samurai more than I do. But she's insisting I fulfill a bare minimum to, you know, keep up appearances with the people."

"It'll be hard to meet in the castle because there will always be people around me. I'm thinking, Fusao, we can make the teahouse our meeting place, after all, no one ever goes there so we'll be very private. The problem is getting rid of these bodyguards my mother insists I need now that I am head of this family and the whole prefecture."

It was his turn to look wistfully at Fusao as he said, "It was so much better before my father died when my parents were there to take care of everything and I was just their son, living in a small, secluded corner of the castle and free to do anything I wanted. We had so many good moments lying together at night and bathing together. I love you, my little peasant boy and nothing that will happen in the next few weeks will change that."

"Sometimes, I feel like leaving all this, a life I don't really want. We could run away together, you know, be farmers in my own land and we don't need to hide from people. But who am I kidding? Where would we go that we could be accepted? People like us, Fusao, will never be accepted, here among my class and even out there among the farmers. Where would we go where we could be respected and lead open lives and be proud of who we are?"

Before Fusao could reply, there was a rustling of silk and the door slid slowly open. It was Lady Momoe. It was as if she had been listening outside and simply chose an opportune moment to interrupt their conversation before they got carried away. It reminded them how easily they could be discovered and exposed in the castle.

"There's something we need to discuss," she said to Okimoto, ignoring Fusao who had sprung automatically to his feet. A servant in feudal Japan did not sit next to his master and carry on a conversation as if they were equals..

Lord Okimoto inclined his head slightly. Fusao took the cue and slipped silently out of the room. Their stolen moment was over and they were once again, master and servant in the eyes of the world.

No love, no matter how strong, could withstand the powerful dynamics of a rigid system. Fusao wondered sadly how many more of these stolen moments they would have before they were defeated.

Chapter Twenty-Eight

"Today for the first time in days, I found myself alone with Okimoto sama at last. But it didn't last long, Lady Momoe appeared and our moment was taken away from us."

"A touch, a stolen kiss, it has to be enough for me today…"

* * * * *

Mayumi stared at the badly written words. She was deeply moved by the emotions of the young peasant boy and the samurai and their impossible love for each other. Unlike the previous pages, this particular one was written in a sloppily as if the writer had written it under very poor light or in some kind of distress.

Earlier, Toyoki had called her and both of them agreed that they should try to put faces to the writer of the papers and his samurai lover.

"I just feel that we should know what they look like after being so closely connected to them through the peasant's writings," Toyoki said. "Do you think it's possible to find any information about these people? After all, the Nobunaga clan was very powerful among Japan's feudal lords of that period so there has to be some records of them."

"A few weeks ago, I was with a friend and she mentioned coming across a notorious gay samurai who fits the description of our Lord Okimoto Nobunaga in one of her research pieces, same era and same mysterious end at a young age," Mayumi said. "I'll call her and ask for her source and go investigate. I can't promise but maybe there could be some sketches. Just remember, photography didn't exist then so all portraits had to be drawn. Maybe there could be an image of the samurai but most certainly not of Fusao."

"Yes, that's true," Toyoki agreed. "Pity because it's more Fusao, the writer of this diary, so to speak, that I am interested in but I guess we'll have to settle for my infamous samurai ancestor."

"Do you know, my grandmother is still nervous about this whole thing and what else you will unearth to tear down our impeccable bloodline?" Toyoki added, laughing. "But she knows she can't stop me from seeing this thing through so she has decided to go along with us."

It was Mayumi's turn to laugh, "In that case, I'd better not dig up too much dirt if I want to get paid! But seriously, I think I should track down my friend's source and see whether we come up with any relevant information or if we're lucky, even a picture or two."

They agreed on a date to meet for a discussion the following week. As she put down the phone, Mayumi thought of how much Toyoki reminded her of Lord Okimoto, in particular, the similarly intense way he looked at people that Fusao described in his diary. But of course Toyoki was the samurai's descendant and had his blood flowing in his veins after all, so inheriting some of those looks and habits was expected.

She glanced at the clock in the wall, still enough time to call Sayuri about her research source because she was a notorious night owl and never went to bed until 2 or 3 a.m. but getting her out of bed in the morning was like scaling Mt Fuji in summer. It was fortunate Sayuri taught the afternoon sessions in college! Mayumi smiled as she thought about the famous hotel "ladies' spa packages" they frequently attended together and trying to get Sayuri out of bed in time for first, the cruel and unreasonable breakfast time of 7:30 a.m. at most Japanese ryokans and then before the cruel 10 a.m. check out time! There were times when Mayumi just gave up, threw Sayuri back on the futon and went for breakfast by herself. Yes, at 11:00 p.m., chances were that her friend would still be up all right!

The fact that Sayuri answered the phone almost immediately told Mayumi that her friend was sitting in front of her computer probably chatting with one of her "stand by" boyfriends because the telephone was right beside her desk top. Mayumi smiled again as she thought of Sayuri and her flamboyant, thoroughly 21st century lifestyle, she hardly fitted the bill of a college history teacher but ironically, she was considered one of the best in her field!

"So who is it tonight, Tanuki, Robert or…?" Mayumi teased.

"Matsumoto, he's new and he's absolutely gorgeous," Sayuri replied, unabashed and continued matter of factly," But I don't think he will stay with me for long, he's too free spirited."

Then Sayuri changed the subject to the matter at hand, knowing that her friend was never bothered much about male playmates or affairs of the heart, "Now what is it you are really interested in?"

"Ok, to cut all the preliminaries short, do you remember what I told you about my latest case, the gay samurai and his peasant boy lover?"

"Oh, yes, of course. Hard to forget something like that, isn't it?"

"Well, you were telling me that night you did some research and came across a historical piece similar to my case profile? My clients have asked me to try and put faces to their renegade ancestor and his lover and to be honest, I myself am more than a little curious about what the two Edo period non conformists looked like!"

"What I want to know is, when you were doing the research and I know you go deeply into everything you do, did you happen to come across any pictures of Lord Okimoto Nobunaga?"

"No, I don't think so. If there were I would have surely remembered with such an interesting story," Sayuri replied. "But then I only researched one source and there must be others that you could look into. Wait, I saved the source on my computer and there could be other links, let me pull up the document."

Mayumi heard the typing of keys as Sayuri recalled her document before saying triumphantly, "Look, here are three or four links that you could check out and maybe one of them may have images of your samurai!"

She rattled off the links which Mayumi entered into her electronic organizer and they ended the conversation with Sayuri's good natured teasing, "Good luck, Mayumi! I swear you are half in love with this fascinating samurai but remember, he was a gay so…"

Mayumi hung up, chuckling by herself at her friend's playful nature.

Mayumi spent the rest of the night and into the early hours of the morning checking out on her computer the links her friend had given her. One of them entitled "Scandals of Edo period samurai in Japan" especially caught her eye.

It spoke about the Nobunaga clan and the matriarch Lady Momoe Nobunaga who effectively ruled the whole region after her husband's death because her son, the real samurai, Okimoto Nobunaga, was soft and rumored to be a homosexual who died young, at the age of 28 years old in a sword fighting incident.

Further down was a note "Picture gallery of Edo period samurai" and Mayumi hit the button excitedly. Was she going to get a look at the infamous Okimoto Nobunaga at last?

She drummed her fingers impatiently as the whole panel of images downloaded slowly, black and white sketches of kimono clad samurai staring proudly back at her. When they had all come out on her computer screen, she slowly scanned the whole panel going through their names, one by one, making sure she didn't miss out any. She was halfway down the list when she saw one who looked different from the rest, he was obviously very young and didn't have the arrogant and craggy, rugged look of the typical warrior type samurai. Her heart began to beat unsteadily as she knew even before she read his name that she had found Lord Okimoto Nobunaga!

Excitedly, Mayumi zoomed into the picture and almost fell off her chair, the enlarged face staring back at her was the splitting image of Toyoki, the grandson of her clients. It was as if a blurry Toyoki was staring at her, dressed in the fancy costume of a samurai. In fact Toyoki looked like Okimoto Nobunaga reincarnated!

Mayumi reached out to switch on her printer and watched as the enlarged picture of Okimoto Nobunaga came slowly out of the machine and she could put a face to at least one of her subjects at last!

Chapter Twenty-Nine

As soon as the official 49 days of mourning for Lord Nobunaga was over, Lady Momoe wasted no time to fix a wedding date a discreet two weeks later for her son and the Lady Sachiko. It would be a grand wedding uniting two powerful samurai families from different parts of Japan. The exchange of gifts between the two families had started the very day the official mourning for Lord Nobunaga ended and until the actual marriage rituals were completed, Lady Momoe lived in fear that her unpredictable son would renegade on his promise to go through with the wedding.

The whole castle was bustling again but this time with preparations for the most important wedding of the century. Every day, commissioned tradesmen poured in to show samples of food, kimonos and hundreds of other wedding necessities to Lady Momoe. Then came the jewelers with their magnificent collection of gold and precious stones to craft the finest wedding jewelry and lacquer ware befitting the daughter of a powerful northern samurai.

The main player in the forthcoming nuptials, Lord Okimoto, however, showed no interest at all and in exasperation, his mother demanded more involvement from him.

"You should show more interest in your own wedding," she said. "I am the only one making all the decisions here and people are asking whether the bridegroom has any opinion. Remember, you are the samurai now and the least you can do is behave like one."

Her son merely shrugged and replied, "You should be satisfied, mother, you got what you wanted, a wedding made in heaven in the eyes of everyone. But for me, it's merely a duty, my heart and soul are not in it as you know very well. So no, I don't have any opinion about anything."

"Don't take that tone with me. You may be the head of this family now, Okimoto but remember, I am still your mother and I deserve some respect from you. Besides, we had an agreement. You get married and produce an heir or two and then you can do whatever you want with your life, discreetly and within reason," Lady Momoe replied, annoyed by her son's uncharacteristic display of contempt for her and an event that was crucial for the survival of the whole Nobunaga dynasty. Couldn't he even understand that?

She sighed, depressed by her son's lack of interest in his position as the most important man in the prefecture. Why couldn't he be more responsible and conduct himself with the dignity befitting his status instead of creeping around with servant boys and indulging himself in unnatural and disgusting pleasures? Her lips curled, he thought she didn't know all about the things he did with that shameless servant boy but of course she did, her spies had made sure of that! If he were not her son and a Nobunaga samurai, she would drive the two of them out of the castle to work in the rice fields until their backs broke and their feet were bruised and blistered.

The tears stung her eyes and for the first time since her husband's death, the tough Lady Momoe whom everyone called the iron lady, felt thoroughly alone, holding up a centuries old dynasty with her bare hands. Couldn't Okimoto understand that no matter how strong she was, she was still a woman and there was only so much she could do?

"Help me! Just help me!" the samurai's mother cried.

She herself had suffered and understood the pain of unrequited and unfulfilled love from her own distant past and perhaps, she would have sanctioned it if her son had fallen in love with a lower ranking woman or even a servant girl! But a man? How could she, or any mother, even among the peasants, sanction such an unnatural union of shame?

The tray of jewels she had been holding slipped from her hands and she watched, fascinated as the colorful stones rolled away from her in all directions. At that point, Lady Momoe realized that if she was not careful, she could crack up. With great effort, she pulled herself together and ordered the nearest servant to pick up the jewels and arrange them back onto the tray. The steely resolve returned and Lady Momoe turned on her heels and walked determinedly to the small reception where another group of kimono craftsmen were waiting for her.

"Whatever happens, even if I have to drag Okimoto to the temple for his wedding, the show must go on," she thought grimly.

That evening, she saw Okimoto striding across the vast castle gardens, heading to the northern part of the compound and within minutes another figure followed in the same direction. Lady Momoe's lips tightened. She had her spies and she knew where they were heading.

As a mother, her heart broke. Her first instinct was to drag him back to her bosom and purge all the evil desires out of him. But as a woman, no matter how powerful, Okimoto was head of the whole Nobunaga dynasty and effectively her lord and master and she could not control him or shame him in public. To dishonor him was to dishonor herself and the whole dynasty he headed. All she could do was pray that after he was married, he would discover the warmth and fulfillment of a normal relationship with a woman as nature intended man to have.

Ever since Lady Momoe first suspected and then confirmed Lord Okimoto's sexual inclinations, she had searched herself and the family trees on both sides for an answer why and how this could have happened. Was there any bad genes or anything she had done, or was it the male tutors she had imposed on him that had brought this curse on her only son? But everything came up negative, the genetic compositions of both the families were blue blooded and impeccable, the tutors were married and completely respectable and she herself had never done anything to turn him in the direction of men.

* * * * *

Unaware of the agony he was causing his mother, Lord Okimoto made his way to the teahouse where he had arranged a tryst with Fusao. It had been a depressing and harrowing week with reminders of his impending arranged marriage pouring into the castle every day in the way of gifts and congratulatory messages from courtiers, other feudal lords and family from far and near. Even the Shogun sent an emissary with a gift of magnificent lacquer ware in gleaming black embossed with pure gold sprigs of plum blossoms and a message penned in his own hand.

Then one evening, a pair of magnificent Arabian bred horses arrived from a feudal family of the Ryukyu islands, shiny ebony torsos and long elegant legs, they caused quite a stir in the castle as they were intended to. Even Okimoto had to admit that such a fabulous gift was fit for the emperor himself and later in the night, he brought Fusao to the stables to admire them.

To Fusao who had never seen a thoroughbred horse at such close quarters, much less ride one, the pair looked haughty and arrogant with wicked gleams in their luminous eyes but since Okimoto was obviously enthralled by them, he held his tongue. He too had been miserable all week as he wandered around the reception hall of the castle that was the epicenter of the wedding preparations for Lord Okimoto. Worse still, because he was the only servant who could write, Okuno san had assigned him the task of recording the presents and congratulatory messages as they poured into the castle.

The two long tables that had been put up to lay out the magnificent wedding gifts soon grew to four, all groaning under the weight of more gifts that arrived steadily each day and kept Fusao busy recording them. The director of operations, Lady Momoe sat at one of the tables to receive tradesmen vying to present their products and services for the wedding. It made Fusao uncomfortable to be so near her for such a long stretch of time and several times, he caught her staring intensely at him.

"Oh kuso, I think she knows about Lord Okimoto and me!" he thought and then chided himself for his paranoia. That wasn't possible, they were always so careful and had never been caught in any compromising position.

As soon as he could, Fusao went out into the rock garden to think. But even in the usually tranquil and healing garden, there was no escaping the wedding. The gardens minimalist calm had been transformed into a garish fairyland of colorful lanterns that he himself had helped put up. Michio found him there and started to complain about the kitchens overflowing with food and the best sake from the prefecture breweries. Down in the villages, although there was much excitement about the wedding of the century, people were also grumbling that there was no good sake left anymore because all had been commissioned for the castle.

That morning an extraordinary thing had happened. Fusao was in the courtyard helping Michio and two other servants from the kitchens trundle a huge barrel filled with sake to the liquor storage outhouse when he saw a familiar figure wheeling a cart towards the tradesmen's door. It was his father. for a moment, Fusao hesitated wondering whether he should run over to greet Naoki. Fusao had left home for more than a few months and lately, he had started missing the quiet strength of his father and the gentle caring of his mother and the simplicity of life in their little cottage with its straw and mud thatched roof.

Life at the castle was a rollercoaster of ecstatic joy and pleasure when he and Lord Okimoto were together but it could also plunge into an abyss of dark black despair when he went back to his other life and Fusao was left behind by his Samurai lover. The emotional pendulum of his life at the castle could swing from one end to the other suddenly and without warning and that was taking its toll on him. When he didn't see Lord Okimoto for days, Fusao would toy with the idea of leaving the castle and returning to his home to ask for a compromise but then the samurai would summon him again and his resolve would melt away like ice in the sun as his heart soared yet again to scorching heights of joy.

On an impulse and risking a painful rejection, he left the barrel of sake with the other servants and ran up to his father, shouting, "Father, father, wait, may I speak with you?"

The older man turned and stared at him as if he couldn't believe what he was hearing and for a moment Fusao's heart sank, his father was not going to acknowledge him and there was no chance of reconciliation.

Then Naoki's weather beaten face creased into a smile and he dropped the cart he was pushing to reach out for his son.

"Fusao!" he said. "I must bring this new rice to the castle but I have a few minutes to talk. Your mother and I have been worried because there was no news from you so when I heard that the new samurai needed new rice for his wedding feast I volunteered my crop straight away to enter the castle and try to look for you!"

"Thank you, father, thank you," Fusao replied and there were tears in his eyes as he held onto his father's hand. "Tell mother not to worry, I'm fine and working here as a servant of all services."

He could have bitten off his tongue when he saw his father's face darken at the words "servant of all services" and added quickly, "I mean I help the chief housekeeper, Okuno san in everything, look at those lovely lanterns in the gardens. I helped fix them yesterday and you should just see them at night!"

Naoki's face lightened and he looked around appreciatively, "I can see it'll be a very grand wedding, even better than when Lord Nobunaga took Lady Momoe as his second wife, I was hardly out of my teens then but that was a wedding made in heaven for us villagers!"

Fusao could tell that his father was in high spirits because Lord Okimoto was getting married and their "special" friendship would have to end but he didn't enlighten Naoki on the fact that it was far from over.

131

Better let him think that and be at peace, for Fusao had caused enough pain for his family after all.

There was a shout from one of the guards for him to get a move on and Naoki picked up the cart hastily and said, "I have to go, Fusao, but please come back and see us soon, you can even return home when you want! Your mother waits for you every day!"

Although he didn't mention it, Fusao knew that his father was trying to tell him that soon Lord Okimoto would be safely married so the pressure for him to marry Aiko chan in the immediate future would be eased and they could afford to wait awhile to marry.

Someone tapped him on the shoulder and he turned round to see the personal valet of Lord Okimoto pressing a note into his hands before slipping off as quietly as he had come. With trembling fingers, Fusao opened up the sealed note and a dark red stained his normally pale face as his heart soared to dizzying heights, Lord Okimoto wanted to see him tonight at the teahouse! He was glad his father had left and was not there to witness the exchange. Naoki must never know that the wedding would not end his liaison with the samurai.

For a moment, Fusao stood frozen to the spot not seeing anything else but the note in his hands. Then he hurried to his room to hide it in his drawer and, deciding that he would not be missed by the hawk-eyed Okuno san if he lingered for just a few minutes, he took out two pieces of paper from his wooden file and began to write.

"Today I almost made up my mind to leave the castle and return to my father's house. But Lord Okimoto has just sent me a note asking me to meet him at the tea house tonight and once again, I am lost!"

"Dear Inari Okami, tell me what to do, my love for Okimoto sama is like a powerful potion, a sickness that has caught hold of me and I cannot escape. I am caught like a fly in a net, will I die the same way, trapped in a net?"

"Will I ? Will I?"

Chapter Thirty

For the rest of the day, Fusao could not concentrate on his work, nightfall had never seemed further away and even his friend, Michio, became impatient with him.

"The way you are daydreaming, Fusao, I could swear you are in love!" he scolded and Fusao smiled wryly. Little did Michio know how right he was or perhaps he did? Sometimes the slanted way his friend looked at him made Fusao wonder whether he knew more than he was letting on. But somehow with Michio, he didn't mind so much because Michio was kind and never judgmental. Even if Michio knew what was going on, Fusao didn't have to be afraid or feel small for being what he was.

After an eternity, nightfall came at last and Fusao took a quick bath in the castle's public bath for the servants, changed into a fresh kimono and waited till Okuno san had disappeared into the kitchen to supervise the following day's breakfast menu before letting himself out of the castle.

Tonight there was no moon and a thick layer of clouds stubbornly blocked out the stars from the sky. Once Fusao had left the part of the castle grounds that was lit up with the lanterns, it was almost pitch black. In his excitement at seeing Lord Okimoto again, Fusao had forgotten to bring a small lantern to light the way but fortunately, he had walked this route enough times to find his way in the dark. Still, the eerie silence gave him the creeps and he quickened his steps to reach the tea house and feel the comfort of his lover's arms around him.

In the servants' quarters, stories flowed freely about numerous ghosts wandering the grounds of the centuries old castle, one of the most famous being that of an amorous lady ghost who appeared on dark moonless nights looking for a young man to feed her libido. It was said that she had been the young concubine of an old samurai who couldn't satisfy her and it wasn't long before she succumbed to the temptation of several of her husband's young minor feudal lords. When the samurai discovered his wife's infidelity, he was furious because she had cuckolded him and stained his family honor. He had her killed and dumped her body into one of the many lakes that dotted the castle grounds.

Nobody ever found her body but it was said that some nights she appeared looking for a young man to satisfy her. A number of male servants had reported sighting the "love ghost" and several years ago, two young men had disappeared after being last seen in the castle grounds. One night, they had simply vanished without a trace after another servant reported sighting the amorous ghost and, rumor had it, that she had taken them to the other world to be her permanent "attendants."

It was not a story for the faint hearted out on a murky night like this and Fusao shivered as he cursed himself for having forgotten to bring a small lantern with him as it was said the "love ghost" kept away from even the smallest of lights. Something whizzed by him in a flurry of feathers and light breeze. Fusao screamed but it was only a bird trying to find its way home in the dark. He quickened his steps and ran all the way until he saw the welcome flicker of lights from the teahouse through the clumps of trees that surrounded it.

In the panic of possibly encountering the "love ghost", Fusao had forgotten his own love interest, Lord Okimoto, very much alive and desirable and as it came back to him, he ran lightly up the moss-strewn path leading to the teahouse, his straw slippers hardly making a sound.

Okimoto san had arranged the teahouse a little, there were fresh mats on the floor and the low table and floor cushions looked well dusted and cleaned. On the table sat a bottle of sake, two sake cups and a shining black lacquer box of food.

Fusao was touched that Okimoto, a samurai with hundreds of servants at his beck and call, had taken the trouble to clean the teahouse and carried food and drink all the way from the castle for the little servant boy he loved. Strange, he thought, how love could turn a person's life upside down and reversed their roles and even social status. Somehow, there was dignity and meaning for a great man like Okimoto to be performing menial tasks for his lover, tasks that were done only by the lowest ranking servants in the castle.

"Hello, Okimoto sama. I'm sorry to be late," Fusao said, trying his best to sound casual despite his heart racing. "I ran almost all the way, it's so scary out there, without even a light to guide me and the 'love ghost" wandering around'."

134

Okimoto laughed and said, "Let me be your love ghost tonight. It won't be so bad, will it?"

Then he sobered and patted the seat beside him, "Come, my little one, let's have something to eat first."

The sake was the finest and the food was his favorite, sushi made from the freshest seafood but Fusao paid no mind to what he was eating. Seeing Lord Okimoto again had raked up sad and poignant feelings about the following week when he would be officially married and things between them would have to change.

That night there was more tenderness in their love making than passion, both men thinking of the dreaded events of the next week but, not wanting to spoil the few precious moments they had, neither of them spoke of their thoughts and sadness.

They made love slowly and gently; taking the time to enjoy the body of one another with a sweetness they rarely had the time to express before. Their lovemaking was usually passionate with a certain urgency to it. But tonight they took their time to explore and enjoy each other to the fullest. The lovers spent hours caressing, kissing and touching until they both collapsed, drenched and spent.

Later, satiated and exhausted from the weight of their emotions, both of them fell asleep until the first slivers of light began to lighten the sky. Fusao opened his eyes to see a bird perched on the windowsill watching them. Still hazy from sleep, Fusao could not remember where he was. Then he heard the quiet breathing of Okimoto beside him and felt the strong protective arm flung across his chest and he realized that they had spent the night at the teahouse.

For a moment he panicked because Okuno san would find him missing and dismiss him from the castle and he would never see Lord Okimoto again. Then he almost laughed. What kind of irony was it that he had been spending the night with Lord Okimoto himself, the feudal lord and master of them all.

Fusao continued to lie there, not wanting to move and wake Okimoto because it felt so nice to be wrapped in those strong, protective arms. Slowly he drifted back into a deep sleep again. But something strange was happening, the castle was gone and in its place were smaller houses lining a broad street filled with metal boxes which had wheels smaller than their carriages and they seemed to be moving on their own without any horses or men to pull or carry them.

A young man came out of a large house at the end of the road, got into one of the metal boxes and rode off. Fusao realized with a shock that it was Okimoto san but he was different, his hair was cut short and his clothes were different too. He wore none of the heavy dark kimonos but light plain clothes with clean fuss free lines, his face smooth and carefree, showing nothing of the strain of duty, responsibilities and tortured emotions.

"Fusao, wake up, we must be getting back!" someone was shaking him and he opened his eyes again, this time to look into the face of Lord Okimoto. He was back to his anxious face and dark heavy kimono.

"I had a dream and I saw you in a different place with different clothes and life and you looked very peaceful and happy!" he blurted out.

"Peaceful and happy? Me?" Okimoto laughed bitterly. "That must be a different world indeed!"

He stretched out his hand and pulled Fusao to his feet, "Come, my love, let's take a short walk outside before we return to the castle and you can tell me more of your dream."

Morning had just broken and the sky was awash with yellow light breaking through the clouds as small clusters of sparrows huddled around, chattering like groups of women gossiping in the village. Dewdrops glittered on the leaves of the trees shielding the teahouse from casual sight and on the soft grass under their feet. It was a glorious morning filled with promises of a wonderful day but for Fusao and the young samurai, it only brought more sorrow of the realities of themselves, their lives and where they were going.

But here in this remote corner of the castle grounds, in this abandoned teahouse where no one ever went, this was their little world. They could hold hands, kiss under the canopy of trees with the birds serenading them because this was their moment in time. They were so engrossed in each other that neither of them noticed a movement in the bushes which sent a little flock of sparrows fluttering away or a slight figure in green kimono blending with the foliage around and slipping quietly away.

Chapter Thirty-One

Mayumi declared a day off for herself, even though it was a Wednesday, to compensate for all the late nights she had spent over her latest case. She had woken up that morning feeling burnt out and unable to concentrate and whenever that happened, she knew it was time to take a break. That was the good thing about working on her own, she could take any day off whenever she wanted to!

Although the weather was beautiful, Mayumi didn't feel energized enough to tackle the awesome crowds of Tokyo so she decided to just stay home and relax with a good book and perhaps pay some attention to her poor cat whom she had neglected woefully the last couple of weeks.

It was wonderful just to empty her mind and do nothing more intellectual than potter around her apartment. She even managed to repot some of her plants while Miki fussed all over her.

"I can really get used to this kind of life," she thought. Then the doorbell rang and she groaned. "Oh No! Who on earth could that be?"

Mayumi considered not answering the persistent doorbell but after a couple more sharp rings, she gave up. A diehard addiction to doorbells, she was always afraid that she might miss something important. Reluctantly, she got up from the tiny balcony and crossed over to the front door.

"It'd better be important," Mayumi growled as she peered into the peephole. For a moment she was stunned. Looking back at her from the other side of the door was Toyoki, the last person she expected to see at her doorstep. What was he doing here? Didn't she always make it clear to her clients that her home was her sanctuary and she didn't like them knocking on her front door?

Mayumi hesitated. She could just pretend no one was in and wait for him to leave because she really shouldn't encourage her clients to appear on her doorstep whenever they wanted. But on the other hand, it could be important because Toyoki was not the kind of person to go to a woman's home without a very good reason and it was a Wednesday and she was expected to be at work anyway.

Instinctively, she removed the head-band from her forehead and fluffed out her hair before opening the door.

Before she could say anything, Toyoki blurted out apologetically, "I'm really sorry to intrude on your privacy and I can assure you this is not normally what I do but I have found something I really need to show you. I went to your office and found it locked so I reckoned you had taken the day off, then I tried calling your cell phone but it was off too so I really had no other way to get you except to come here!"

"Well, I don't usually encourage my clients to follow me home, so to speak," Mayumi replied but on seeing his dejected face, she softened her reproach with a laugh. "But I guess you must have a very good reason for doing that so come in and tell me about it."

"Thank you, I really appreciate that," Toyoki said as he sat down on a brightly colored chair noting the eclectic clutter and hanging plants in Mayumi's apartment that made him feel comfortable and relaxed. Then he remembered what he had come for and held out a small brown envelope to Mayumi.

"I found these deep in one of my grandmother's many "family history" chests, I guess she left this out when she passed the rest of the writings to you," he said.

Mayumi took the envelope, all her peevishness at being disturbed on her day off gone. As she went through the five pieces of yellowed paper and realized with great excitement that they were sketches of some of the places mentioned by the peasant boy in his writings.

"Look, Toyoki," she said. "This is a sketch of the castle, another of what was obviously Fusao's house in the village and this very interesting sketch is, I believe, the abandoned teahouse he mentions as the place he and Lord Okimoto had their secret trysts!"

"So our peasant was an artist as well as a writer! And looking at these very well done sketches, I would say a good one too!"

"Well, we don't know for sure yet who made these sketches. They could have been done by his samurai lover too! But I guess it doesn't matter to us who did the sketches, just that they give us an insight on what the places looked like."

Toyoki let out a low whistle as he held up a final sketch of two men in a tight embrace with their kimonos falling away from their bodies. One man was taller and better built and the other slender with a beautiful face, obviously an erotic sketch of Lord Okimoto and Fusao.

"This is a fantastic find, isn't it?' he said. "They make all the things and people we have read about in Fusao's writings come alive."

"Yes, it is indeed," Mayumi replied. "You know, Toyoki, I think we should make a trip to the site where the castle was and maybe talk to the people around. They might know something of the local history that could shed some light into what happened to your ancestor. Do you know where the castle was sited?"

"Yes, I did a little research and it seems that Minamimoto was a village during the Edo period about 50 km from the present town of the same name. The castle was sited a little north of that village," Toyoki replied. "My grandmother even kept a map of the old village of Minamimoto and I think I brought a copy along. Here, have a look. As you can see, it's not that far from Tokyo, about 150 km heading up north."

Mayumi took the map and spread it on her work table to study, then an idea struck her and she said on an impulse, "I'm thinking, why don't we drive up there now? As you just said, it's not that far. we'll be able to find it and get back here before midnight. Are you game?"

Toyoki was taken aback by this suggestion, he was not one to do anything on impulse without careful thought and planning and he wasn't even ready to make any trip, especially one of this nature.

"You mean, like right now? This is kind of sudden, isn't it? Are you sure it's a good idea to do it today?" he asked.

"Well, why not? If you have your car, we can drive up there or if not, take a train and find our way to the site," Mayumi replied. "Look, if we don't go today, it'll be hard to find another day that both of us are available. Come on, just give me a minute to change into jeans and we can be on our way."

Her enthusiasm was infectious and Toyoki was ashamed of his initial reluctance to make the trip. Yes, she was right, there would never be a right time to go on this very important mission. He had just been plain lazy thinking only of getting back to his house and chilling out for the rest of the day especially as he was due to start a new job the following week.

The thought of being there at the castle where everything had begun

139

and ended for the star crossed gay couple was beginning to appeal to him and he said, "You're right, let's go!

Mayumi was ready in less than ten minutes as she had promised, and Toyoki was amazed that she spent more time apologizing to the long suffering Miki than on getting ready. Most of the women he knew including his mother and even grandmother spent hours in front of the mirror and drove him nuts.

She grabbed two bottles of mineral water on their way out and passed him one.

"Here, take this! It'll be quite a long drive and maybe there won't even be time to stop for a drink," she said. "Do you have a road map in the car?"

Toyoki nodded, "Yes, my grandmother, bless her soul even stapled a road map of the area around the site of the castle, obviously she intended to go there someday. You know, of course, it's in the same prefecture as we live but right in the extreme north, a fair distance from our house."

Both of them kept a companionable silence as they drove through the usual thick traffic of Tokyo and headed north. As soon as they left the city center, the traffic began to thin out to a pleasant flow as they queued up to pay Japan's exorbitant toll charges to use the beautiful highways that cut traveling time by half.

"My boyfriend, Michael, always complains about the toll charges in Japan, that they're unbelievably high," Mayumi said as Toyoki took the toll card and they sped down the expressway.

"Oh, you have a boyfriend? And from his name, I gather he's a foreigner?"

"Yes, an American I met while studying in Los Angeles but we are on kind of rocky ground right now. It's hard, you know, long distance relationships and all that cultural difference stuff doesn't help either and of course, my parents aren't very happy about it. They want me to settle down with a good solidly Japanese man and contribute to the homogeneity of Japanese society!"

"And my mum has said she prefers a live one and not the dead historical figures I am so fond of and as a parting shot to me last Valentine's Day, she said the only Japanese men I seem to be interested in are the dead ones! If only she knows that my life currently centers around a couple of centuries old dead gay men, Lord Okimoto and Fusao, she would have a fit!"

Toyoki's face creased into one of his rare smiles and he said, "I like your sense of humor, it's hard to find a woman who can laugh at herself these days, especially in Japan. I was also educated in the U.S., in Michigan. I got used to the life there so when I first came back, it was kind of hard to fit in back here, I was too outspoken and not respectful enough of superiors. I led a pretty wild life in the States, you know, smoking pot and all that stuff but I had to really clean up my act before I came back or else O bachan would freak out! I've changed jobs twice already and I've decided that Japanese corporations just can't appreciate my working style so I start work with an American company next week."

They lapsed into silence and before long, Mayumi dozed off and did not stir until she felt Toyoki tap her on the shoulder to tell her that they had arrived. Machido was the small town that had grown around the castle site since Minamoto moved to its present location and was quite typical of small towns all over Japan, narrow streets lined with traditional noodle and sanbei shops. Almost all the shops had retained their old wooden structures and, propped up by precariously worn looking beams, appeared to be on the verge of collapsing at any time but were actually strong enough to withstand the earthquakes that frequently tested their resilience. Nestled among the clusters of houses and little side streets were tiny plots of rice fields. Mayumi could imagine how it had been hundreds of years ago when Fusao's family and the other villagers farmed the lands, producing rice for their feudal lords.

The whole town was quiet and peaceful even on a weekday with a kind of old world charm, as if time had stood still and never quite made it to the 21st century. Mayumi felt that if she closed her eyes, she could almost hear the sounds of horses on the street and the samurai's carriage going by as hundreds of peasants working in the rice fields watched with a curious glee. And there was Fusao working alongside his father in their rush sandals and writing furiously on his precious scraps of paper when the day's work was done. All the things he had written about had happened in this very place, events both happy and tragic revolving around the lives of people who walked or rode in these narrow streets. it was hard not to feel their presence.

Both Toyoki and Mayumi were overwhelmed by the atmosphere of mystique in the town as they drove in silence as far up the road leading to the castle as they could until they found a small parking area with a sign pointing to the castle site. If they had expected the castle to be as it had appeared in the sketch, rising tall and proud from its lofty hilltop perch as it looked down on the peasants slaving in the fields below, they would have been disappointed. Where there had been a castle, was now a flat piece of land with a big sign explaining that this had been the site of the powerful Nobunaga family's castle that was burnt down during the war. But several arrows pointed to four or five remaining structures, part of a wall, a corner of what had been a moat surrounding the castle and three piles of stones that marked the place where the main entrance to the castle had been.

Mayumi ran her fingers over the crumbling stones ignoring the sign not to touch anything and thought about Lord Okimoto and the rest of his family and their influential visitors who would have walked in and out of this entrance, but not Fusao for his position had been that of a favored servant at best and he would have been assigned the servants and tradesmen's door at the back or the side entrance for minor officials.

Apart from these few relics, nothing else was left of the castle except memories recounted in the diary of a servant and lover of its samurai master. Perhaps at night, their ghosts came alive to resurrect its former glory and seat of power. By day, however, there was nothing much left of the castle. Still, for both Mayumi and Toyoki with their intimate knowledge of its history and life, it was enough just to be there.

A magnificent aged darkened, solitary Matsu tree stood almost in the middle of what they could imagine was the courtyard of the castle. Toyoki wandered casually over to read the information on a wooden board in front of the tree.

"Mayumi, come here," he called out excitedly." Look, it says here that this tree was planted by Lord Okimoto Nobunaga himself on his wedding day! That makes it almost 400 years old!"

"Just imagine what kind of stories this tree can tell us if only it can speak!" Mayumi said, running her fingers over the old gnarled branches of the tree that its caretakers had lovingly propped up with wooden poles.

"Like an old, old man leaning on a walking stick!" Toyoki said softly. "And yet so determined to go on."

Mesmerized by its magic, they stood there for a long time looking at Lord Okimoto's tree, serenely gazing out at the world just as it had done for centuries, untouched by the passage of time and people.

Then Toyoki said briskly, to break the spell of the tree, "We should really go and look for the teahouse now. According to this map it was in the far north west corner of the castle grounds."

"Look!" Mayumi called over from where she had gone to study some signs. "Here's a sign which points to 'The Wataru Teahouse!' It has to be Okimoto and Fusao's meeting place and it's sited in the right location, northwest! Come on, let's go!"

They went up a small path leading northwest. As they went further up, the foliage became wilder. The deep, shadowy atmosphere reminded Mayumi of Fusao describing his long walk on dark moonless nights through whispering trees and foliage from the castle to the tea house to meet his lover, Lord Okimoto.

* * * * *

It took a good 40 minutes of walking to arrive eventually at a point where the thick foliage gave way to neatly trimmed hedges and a lovely serene garden filled with sculpted shrubs and a little pond with colorful carp swimming around. A small stone bridge connected one edge of the lake to the other. The whole scene reminded Mayumi of the fairy tales her mother had read her as a child of little girls wandering into the woods and stumbling onto magic lands filled with flowers and happy scampering forest creatures who could talk.

Beyond this picturesque garden was a Japanese teahouse in the traditional style. For a moment, both Mayumi and Toyoki stared at it, taken aback. They had expected a dejected run down shack, not the perfect reconstruction of a teahouse that did not at all resemble the one in the sketches. What was even more unexpected was that the teahouse seemed to be open for business. Behind the teahouse was a small parking lot that opened out to a busy road visible behind the screen of hedges.

"Are you sure this is the same teahouse?" Mayumi asked and Toyoki nodded.

"Most definitely! It's on the exact spot marked on the map so it has to be the same teahouse. The current owners must have rebuilt it in the present style."

The sliding door of the teahouse opened gently and discreetly. A young lady in a beautiful blue kimono stepped out, bowed gracefully and called out, "Irasshaimase welcome!"

"What now?" Toyoki asked.

Mayumi nudged him forward and replied," Let's go in and have a cup of tea, that way we can look around the place and ask a few questions."

The minute she stepped into the teahouse, Mayumi knew that they had come to the right place. Perhaps it was the way the proprietors had tried to recapture the atmosphere of what they imagined the teahouse had been like inside but it definitely felt like Fusao and Lord Okimoto's teahouse.

Unlike most teahouses in Japan, this one had low tables and the guests sat on crimson floor cushions. It was exactly the way Fusao had described it in his diary. Even the warming stove in the center of the room was the same..

"OH MY GOD!" she whispered to Toyoki. "Just look at this, even the way the warming stove faced the window and Fusao and Okimoto used to lie there watching the birds on the window ledge singing to them, it's almost exactly the same as the way he described it! Forget about the new structure, the fresh tatami and the shining polished tables for a moment and it's very easy to go back 400 years and imagine the two of them here! It's heart-breaking to be here and remember how they lived, loved and suffered!"

The beautiful girl in kimono who had greeted them at the door came over and took their orders, the house's finest green tea and accompanying sweet bean paste condiments. She disappeared and returned to grind the fragrant tea-leaves and prepare the tea right in front of them in a time honored ritual.

Mayumi waited until she had finished her beautiful ritual of traditional Japanese tea preparation and laid everything in front of them before asking, "Do you know who owns this tea house?"

"Oh, my father, Noboru Miyamoto is the owner."

"If your father has a moment, I would really like to speak to him," Mayumi replied. Her heart had started to beat quickly. Could this owner somehow be connected to Fusao? A descendant, perhaps, no, maybe not because Fusao was gay who didn't or couldn't have children.

The girl disappeared behind the red noren hanging across the door and called for her father. A few minutes later, a man came through the noren and bowed to them. He was stout and did not have any trace of his daughter's grace and beauty and Mayumi concluded that the looks must have come from her mother then. She had to confess, she was a little disappointed. She had expected a man with the elegant good looks of Lord Okimoto.

"I am Noboru Miyamoto. My daughter says you wish to speak to me?" he said and waited politely.

Mayumi returned the bow and replied, "Yes, and thank you for taking time off to talk to us. You see, we are doing a project about this area and would like to ask you whether this is the teahouse that historically belonged to the castle?"

"Yes, the whole area was once part of the castle grounds and this teahouse has been in my family for a long time and as rumor has it, was acquired by someone who was in service to the reigning samurai at the time."

"When my grandfather first decided to reopen this place as a teahouse, it was in a really bad condition and took a lot of restoring to reach what you see now," Miyamoto waved his hand airily around the room. "No one in the family wanted to do anything with this teahouse until my grandfather because it is said to be haunted. Some people say they've seen a young man standing by the window staring at the sky and sometimes another man joins him but he is usually alone."

He shrugged and continued, "I guess every old place has its own ghost stories so we've learnt to live with ours but to be honest, I have never seen anything. My family has lived here for generations and some of my ancestors were in service to several generations of the Grand Samurai Nobunaga."

"They were an interesting lot, the Nobunagas with their full share of 'royal' scandals the most notorious of which was the mystery surrounding a young samurai called Okimoto Nobunaga who died very young in some reckless sword fighting match, went a bit out of his mind, I think. He was reputed to be doseiai… gay and had a preference for young boys!"

"Was this teahouse ever used by the samurai and his family or guests?" Mayumi asked.

"No, as far as my information goes, it was abandoned in the mid 1600s after one of the samurai's consorts complained that she had seen a lady ghost wandering around who threatened to destroy the lives of anyone who came and disturbed her peace. After that they built another teahouse closer to the castle and this one was abandoned."

"Who knows whether any of these ghost stories are true or not," Miyamoto san shrugged his ample shoulders. "But no one wanted to take any chances so they kept away from it for hundreds of years."

"Can I have a look around?"

"Yes, of course," Noburo Miyamoto said. "We're almost closing anyway and there won't be any more guests around at this time."

He bowed again and disappeared behind the noren, followed by his daughter.

Before the noren had swished back on them, Mayumi was already on her feet snapping pictures of the teahouse with a tiny digital camera she always carried with her.

It was just one large airy room with neatly laid out low tables in straight lines and a stack of crimson floor cushions in the corner for the guests to sit on. But as Mayumi went over to the window with its shoji, or rice paper screens, and looked out, she gave a loud gasp.

"Toyoki, come over here and look at this!" she screamed and when Toyoki came and joined her, she pointed to a Matsu tree right outside, its branches growing upwards to curve and come together again like a heart.

"Toyoki, this Matsu tree!" she whispered. "Fusao mentioned it in his diary and the heart formed by the unusual joining of two of its branches as a symbol of their love! I can't believe that 400years later, we are looking out and seeing the same thing. Okimoto and Fusao were here and they made love repeatedly in that spot there right beside the open stove, it's all mentioned in his diary!"

She stood there at the window feeling the power of the two star crossed lovers wash over her knowing for certain now that the stories of frequent sightings of the two young men's ghosts had been true. They were Okimoto and Fusao revisiting the place where they had often consummated their forbidden love for each other. Their spiritual power grew and became stronger and suddenly Mayumi felt an oppressive need to get out of the teahouse.

"Let's go, I think we've seen enough for today and it's a long drive back to Tokyo," she said and without another word, they placed the money for their tea and sweets on one of the tables and began the long walk back to Toyoki's car at the castle site car park without a word. Mayumi could feel that Toyoki too had been overwhelmed by the strong spiritual presence of Fusao and Okimoto at the teahouse and wanted to leave.

The sky had lost most of its light and whatever was left was shut out by the trees. Mayumi and Toyoki walked in near darkness with only the birds and forest creatures for company. it was eerie and they quickened their steps, almost running back to their car.

Mayumi was relieved when they finally reached the open space of the castle site and saw signs of life in the few remaining visitors and a national heritage staff waiting to close up the place.

"Whew, it's spooky in there!" she said and realized that her hands were wet and clammy.

"Yes, it's not exactly a teahouse you would want to go to relax with all that talk of ghosts, but a lot of people must like it," Toyoki replied. "Next time, we should drive along the main road and enter from the other side presuming, of course, that we need to come here again."

"But I'm glad we came today," Mayumi said. "It makes Fusao's writings and emotions come alive and I am beginning to understand him much better."

* * * * *

The traffic back to Tokyo was heavy and it was almost midnight by the time they pulled up at Mayumi's apartment. She knew Toyoki still had a two hour drive. She reached into her bag and passed him an envelope.

"I have a surprise for you, Toyoki," she said. "Here, have a look at this!"

Toyoki took the envelope and drew out the single sheet of computer print out. As Toyoki glanced down at the sheet, his eyes widened as he studied the black and white picture of himself in samurai clothes.

"Who on earth is this? Is this who I think it is?"

Mayumi nodded triumphantly, "Yes, it's Lord Okimoto, I found this sketch of him in a picture gallery of samurai in Japan. Isn't it incredible. He's the spitting image of you or I should say you are the spitting image of him!"

Chapter Thirty-Two

"Today is my Lord Okimoto's wedding. Everyone is excited about the event and ceremonies, everyone, except me," Fusao wrote with so much force on the piece of paper in front of him that it tore but he continued writing, trying to empty his tortured mind of its helpless emotions. But it didn't work, the pain kept coming back to attack him in waves, giving him no respite.

"I have been pacing this room the whole night, like a wild beast in a cage and my hands long to rip this bleeding heart out so that it can hurt no more."

"Someone, give me a knife so that I may commit hara kiri on myself for I cannot bear to see my lover given to another in marriage!"

Earlier, he had watched Okimoto plant the customary Matsu tree in the eastern garden as a symbol of the new life his marriage would bring him. Fusao had to remind himself over and over again that it was a symbolic marriage which Lord Okimoto had to go through against his will to keep the honor of his family.

Fusao told himself that the marriage had nothing to do with their love that was stored safely in that corner of their hearts where no one could find and destroy it. No, he couldn't die yet. He had to stay alive to guard that love. Slowly, he removed the sharp hocho he had stolen from the kitchens in the morning to commit hara kiri and threw it out of the window, watching the sun glinting on its steely blade as it spiraled away to land on a hedge a few meters away.

Later, unable to stay away, Fusao joined the crowds outside the castle to watch the carriage carrying Lord Okimoto and the Lady Momoe to the temple where his marriage would be solemnized, with all the traditional rituals and ancient ceremonies of samurai marriages. The carriage window was left slightly open and Fusao had a glimpse of the bridegroom's face, expressionless and inscrutable. Like a white Noh mask, it did not show any emotions at all for his impending marriage or response to the bowing crowds. Somehow that grim unhappy face eased Fusao's suffering a little.

The servants of the castle had been allowed out to watch and cheer the wedding carriage with strict instructions to return to the castle as soon as it had gone past. But Fusao stayed in the street watching until the convoy of carriages disappeared in billowing clouds of dust. Still he did not follow orders and return to the castle. Instead, his feet seemed to have a will of their own. To his horror, Fusao found himself running after the wedding carriage, never stopping until he reached the temple where his lover's marriage was to be solemnized.

It was a public temple where even peasants were allowed to go and pray but Fusao didn't want to be seen by anyone so he hid behind a large spreading tree close enough to watch the ceremony but still out of view. He felt strangely detached as if he was watching a play being acted out on a stage but he knew that this nonchalance was only a temporary respite, and soon reality would sink in with such ferocity that his pain would know no bounds. But for the moment, the couple in the heavily embroidered white kimonos were just strangers as they stood before the head monk of the temple receiving blessings for their marriage and prayers for fertility.

When the wedding party disappeared into an inner chamber of the temple to continue with the rituals inside and Fusao couldn't see them anymore, he came out of his hiding place and started the long walk back to the castle. Head down and shoulders hunched, Fusao had reached the lowest point of his life since he became intimate with Lord Okimoto. Fusao was unsure whether he could carry on living with this heavy stone inside him.

Witnessing the couple marry in the temple with so much approval and acceptance by society had made him realize with great finality that what he and Lord Okimoto had would always be considered unnatural and improper, a warped and disgusting distortion of the human mind and body, viewed with loathing and vilified. Society would make them feel unclean and turn the beauty of their love into dark, sordid lust.

Fusao had always thought everyone was so wrong. After all, they had not chosen to be this way, nature had made them like that for a reason and the love and emotional commitment they felt for each other was just as real and as beautiful as that between a man and a woman. But today, on the saddest day of his life, he began to question himself, whether perhaps he had been wrong and maybe society was right. People like him and Lord Okimoto were selfish, self-indulgent and disgusting. Maybe if they made a bigger effort to overcome their selfish needs, they could force themselves to change and conform.

When he returned to the castle, he crept into his quarters to make an entry in his diary before reporting to Okuno san for a punishing day of work and toil.

"In maybe 30 or 40 years' time, I will be dead and I won't care about anything, my body and my mind will be cold and silent, freed from all feelings, emotions and pain. But right now, I am alive, flesh and blood, mind and soul, and I don't know how I will get through the next few weeks."

But it was that night which tortured Fusao most because it was Lord Okimoto's wedding night and he would be alone with his bride, the beautiful and irresistible Lady Sachiko. Would he consummate his marriage? The very thought of that made Fusao nauseous and insane beyond reason. He wanted to rush over to the east wing of the castle where the couple would be spending their wedding night and beg Lord Okimoto not to betray their love but he also knew if he did that, he faced certain arrest for being a nuisance and threatening the safety of the samurai and his new bride.

With great effort, Fusao managed to control himself so that he could stay on at the castle and remain in close proximity to Lord Okimoto just in case they could still meet at the teahouse and have their stolen moments. He had to accept his new role now as the "lover in waiting" and convince himself that in the end his patience would pay off.

"My love knows no shame or honor for I am prepared to accept any crumbs Okimoto sama offers me," he wrote in his diary that night. Then he hid himself in a little used storehouse and started drinking steadily, cup after cup of sake he had stolen from the kitchen until he collapsed in a drunken heap on its grimy floor.

The next morning Michio heard the sound of snoring from the storehouse and went inside to find his friend sprawled on the floor, stone drunk. With all his might, because Michio was of slim build, he dragged Fusao back to their quarters, cleaned him up and used a scalding towel to revive him before Okuno san made his rounds of the servants and discovered Fusao incoherent and drunk.

150

Fusao never knew what Michio thought of his little episode because his friend never asked for any explanation when he managed to recover sufficiently to go through the rest of the day without being noticed by the hawk eyed Okuno. That was the sweetest thing about Michio, although he had his own opinions about Fusao's distress, he never asked his friend any questions. Michio was just there to help haul him back to reality whenever Fusao went too close to the edge.

And in the days that followed, it was Michio who covered up Fusao's mistakes and helped him get through the nights without getting stone drunk.

* * * * *

On the other side of the castle, Okimoto Nobunaga stirred from a fitful sleep to see the morning sunlight filtering through the thin rice paper window screens into the room. For a moment, he couldn't remember where he was and why there was another futon next to him. Were they in the teahouse and did Fusao spend the night with him again? Okimoto turned over, hoping to see Fusao snug under the sheets next to him. He was horrified to see instead the face of Lady Sachiko, gentle and sweetly asleep. Okimoto felt the blood rushing into his face, staining it a bright red.

Yesterday he had married Lady Sachiko and last night had been his wedding night. For the first time in his life he had spent the night alone with a woman and it had been a disaster. His new wife was the most beautiful woman he had ever seen, even more beautiful than his mother had been in her hey days and most of all, she was gentle and everything a man could wish for and desire. He hated himself for not being able to love her or feel anything for her beyond acceptance that she was his wife and he had certain duties towards her.

As they entered their chambers he didn't know who was more nervous, he or she. With a small polite bow, because they were, after all, just strangers, he told her to prepare for bed first as he escaped to the long balcony outside their bedroom. There was a full moon that night and he could see the rocks and shrubs in the garden bathed in the silvery moon light and just a few meters away was the Matsu tree he had planted that morning as a symbol of life and fertility.

"Oh Moon Goddess," he thought. "I am expected to make love to this woman and impregnate her as soon as possible. How can I when I can't bear the thought of touching a woman?"

The answer came to him. "Just try, Okimoto, remember your promise to your father, close your eyes and pretend it's Fusao you are touching."

He took a deep breath and turned back into the room where his wife was already lying on the futon next to his, the covers drawn up to her chin. Without thinking, he undressed, stripping off his yukata layer by layer until he remembered he was not alone. He did not want to be naked before a woman. Reaching out, he snuffed out the light that illuminated the room in soft romantic tones and was grateful for the darkness that followed.

What was it one of his tutors had once told him? That darkness hid everything, emotions, defects, ugliness, fears, loathing and that was what Okimoto was doing now, hiding behind the cloak of pitch-black darkness because that was the only way he could betray his soul and his lover, Fusao, and make love to a woman.

Quickly, before he had time to think, Okimoto reached out to his wife and felt her stiffening up at the unexpected touch of a man as he tried to feel something, anything as he slowly parted her yukata and ran his hands over her body. Her skin was soft to his touch and his hands moved over the unfamiliar curves of a woman, soft breasts and rounded hips that did not excite him. He wanted the hard lean muscles of a man and a flat, masculine chest to bury his face in. Okimoto tried to stimulate himself by stirring up memories of the hot passionate nights with Fusao at the teahouse but every time he felt himself stir, the soft flesh of his wife got in the way and all the passion ebbed away.

Kissing Fusao always made him insane with desire. He tried to arouse himself by kissing Sachiko but a woman's lips were different and they didn't do anything for him. Okimoto realized the more he tried, the more he was going to fail and show himself up even more to Sachiko. So with a gentle kiss on her forehead as he would a child, Okimoto said, "I'm sorry, I guess I'm just too tired tonight with the stress of all the wedding preparations the last few weeks."

Sachiko touched his hand timidly and said, "It's all right, we should just try and sleep tonight."

"Thank you, Sachiko, tomorrow will be better, I promise you," Okimoto whispered, glad that she had been so nice about what he hoped was a temporary impotence and although it made him feel terrible about himself, he was relieved to get away from her onto his own futon.

But long after his wife had fallen asleep, the young samurai lay awake wondering what they were going to do if this inability to consummate their marriage continued. Sachiko was a lovely person and she didn't deserve a man like him, a man who could only be aroused by the muscles and hard angular body of a man. He moved as far away from his sleeping wife as he could and allowed himself the luxury of a few tears because his life was such a mess.

Then Okimoto brushed the tears fiercely away from his eyes and willed himself to stop crying. It would not do for a samurai bearing the famous strong Nobunaga genes to be seen the next morning after what everyone hoped was a night of passion with eyes swollen from crying instead. Amaterasu, he silently prayed to the Shinto Goddess for guidance. Everyone looked up to Okimoto as the strongest and most powerful man in the prefecture and he was expected to behave like one! Only Lady Momoe, his mother, knew all his inner secrets and fears and how weak he really was.

When he woke up next morning, Sachiko had already dressed and left the room and Okimoto was glad that he was alone and didn't have to face her after his failure on their wedding night. For a moment, he lay on the futon reluctant to get up and face the world and the happy knowing smiles of his mother and the servants.

Oh, how he longed for Fusao and his lean hard and lithe body pressed against his and as he felt himself becoming aroused just by that thought, Okimoto realized with great relief that he was not impotent, he just couldn't be aroused by a woman.

Chapter Thirty-Three

Fusao hadn't seen his samurai lover for almost three weeks and he couldn't concentrate on anything he was doing. Had Lord Okimoto settled into his new role as husband and no longer needed him, Fusao? Were they happy and would Lady Sachiko soon become pregnant with the child that the Nobunaga family needed so badly? His mind raced with a hundred questions day and night. This time, not even pouring his thoughts out on paper could help to exorcise the pain and jealousy that possessed and overwhelmed him with its terrifying ferocity.

Michio was put in charge of some of the rooms in the east wing of the castle near Lord Okimoto's chambers and Fusao had been returned to the west wing by Okuno san very possibly on the advice of Lady Momoe herself. At the end of an excruciating third week, when he could stand it no longer, Fusao approached his friend and asked him as a favor to let him do the east wing rooms for just a few days.

Michio looked at him and said sharply, "Do you really think that's a good idea, Fusao?"

"It's nothing sinister or anything, Michio," Fusao replied, hoping he didn't sound too defensive. "I just want a change of duties. It's boring here in the main kitchens, always doing the same things every day."

"Please don't beat around the bush, you know very well what I mean," Michio said, looking at him steadily. Fusao froze, realizing that his friend knew, and had known, all along about him and Lord Okimoto.

"Yes, maybe it's not wise but right now, my heart rules my head. Please, Michio, I promise I won't do anything silly, I just want to be there to see him for a few days, that's all," Fusao pleaded. "You know what love is like and how you are prepared to take any risk for Yuki chan. Sometimes, the head cannot control what the heart feels."

He waited while Michio thought about it. "I don't know whether I'm doing the right thing but all right," Michio said. "Just for a few days and make sure you keep your promise and nothing happens! Remember if we draw attention to this exchange, both of us will be fired for sure."

"I promise, Michio, I promise," Fusao replied and his eyes glistened with the tears he had been holding back for weeks.

It was fortunate that Michio was assigned to care for the Lady Michiko's quarters in the east wing because only she would not notice the exchange and question it but it was close enough to Lord Okimoto's own rooms to satisfy Fusao's purpose. That evening after their duties were done, Michio took Fusao to the east wing to show him where things were and although they did not bump into Lord Okimoto, it was enough for Fusao to know that he was there, just meters away. And although he would not be doing his samurai lover's quarters, it was near enough to hope for the occasional contact with Lord Okimoto and see how things were between him and his new bride.

It was killing him not knowing how things stood between Lord Okimoto and himself because if there was no hope for them, Fusao had made up his mind to leave the castle and return to his parents' home. The pain of living like this, in a limbo, was becoming more intolerable each day, waiting for the summons that did not come. He tried to tell himself that Lord Okimoto needed time to settle down into his new life before making any attempts to resume their relationship or even establish some kind of contact. But as the days turned to weeks, Fusao became desperate. He needed a sign, any sign about how things stood between them.

The next morning, he started work at the east wing very early taking care not to cross the paths of Lady Momoe and Okuno san, the two people who could thwart his plans to see Lord Okimoto. Michio had pointed out the newlyweds' chambers and Fusao found himself moving in that direction, stopping only when he saw a soldier who also served as the samurai's bodyguard standing at the first of a few sliding doors leading to the inner chambers. Fusao remembered his promise to Michio not to cause a stir and a servant loitering around the samurai's chambers so early in the morning would surely attract the attention of his bodyguard.

As if to prove that point, the soldier stirred at the sound of footsteps and Fusao beat a hasty retreat to Lady Michiko's quarters at the far end of the east wing. He would return to look for Lord Okimoto later at a more decent hour when there were more people around and he wouldn't be noticed.

Down in the east wing kitchens, work had already started on the breakfast menu for the samurai and his family, no small task because each member had different preferences and the menu had to be changed every day giving the cooks real challenges to think up new dishes or present the same dish in a different form.

Sato, the chief cook, was a perfectionist and each dish had to be a perfect coordination of color, taste and presentation. The other assistant cooks lived in fear of his famous temper and intolerance of any culinary mishaps and rumor had it that in his home in the village, Sato san was thoroughly hen pecked by his domineering wife and came to the kitchens of the castle each day to unleash his frustrations on the staff under him. On good days, he was just a grumpy old man but on bad days, he could be a real tyrant! One plus point was that Sato san had a very bad memory for faces and names and it was unlikely that he would notice that Fusao had taken the place of Michio as long as he kept a low profile.

As Fusao's main duties were taking care of Lady Michiko's rooms and in the kitchens, Michio had told him all about Sato san and this morning. He noticed with relief that the portly cook was having a "good day" because he was just fussing around quietly, without any of the barking of a bad day.

Despite his preoccupation with Lord Okimoto, Fusao watched his new temporary work place with interest, especially the servants who were better dressed, more personable looking and well mannered, probably because they served the samurai and his family directly. If there was such a thing as ranking among the servants, he would say they were the "higher ranking" servants. He suddenly felt gauche and unpolished among them and wondered what they would say if they knew that he was sleeping with their revered lord and master and knew him more intimately than even his most personal servant!

Working in the kitchen was much better than the mindless task of cleaning and Fusao discovered that he loved the art of creating beautiful food presentations. For the first time, he even thought about what he would do if he ever left the castle, maybe start a restaurant and spend his whole life creating good food!

The first day passed without incident and although he found reasons to hang around Lord Okimoto's chambers, neither he nor Lady Sachiko appeared. Fusao felt his bile rising. Could they be so enamored with each other that they remained cloistered in their rooms?

But the bits and pieces of gossip he caught in the kitchens cheered

156

him up considerably, especially the whispered exchanges of the servants about the couple's wedding night.

"You know, Seiko, Lady Sachiko's personal maid cleared her futon next morning and no sign of the virginal stain! As Lady Sachiko is definitely a lady of great virtue, we have to presume that the marriage was not consummated!"

"And next morning, Lady Sachiko was up at the crack of dawn! Which new bride, I ask you, would want to get up so early on the morning of her wedding night?"

Fusao's heart was soaring. Maybe, just maybe, he had been wrong and Lord Okimoto did not love or desire his wife! They had not consummated their marriage yet and he hoped they never would. He felt selfish and wicked for wishing such a thing but Lord Okimoto was his and he couldn't bear the thought of anyone else touching him.

As if things could not get any better, he was assigned the duty of bringing Lord Okimoto and his wife's meals to them in their own private dining room. It had just been a stroke of luck that he happened to be there when Sato san was looking for a servant to bring the couple their evening meal for the day. He had selected Fusao for his pale good looks and beautiful smile that made him a cut above the other servants. Fusao was overjoyed because it meant he would be able to see Okimoto sama every day until he had to return to the west wing and his old work area.

The first time he went beyond the first set of sliding doors to the samurai's private chambers was to bring them their dinner that evening. It was a surprisingly simple room with only a low table and two sets of elaborately patterned gold floor cushions and the only claim to opulence was a beautiful folding screen completely painted in real gold with almost life size pictures of white cranes splashed right across it.

Fusao felt his knees growing weak as he approached and saw Lord Okimoto sitting on a pile of floor cushions with his back to the door and he prayed that his legs would not buckle and throw him and the tray of food he was carrying off balance. Lady Sachiko sat opposite her husband and it was obvious they were trying to make polite conversation, more like acquaintances, Fusao noticed triumphantly, than a married couple who shared the same room and the same futon. He was convinced now more than ever there had been no intimacy between them. Lord Okimoto was a very passionate and expressive lover and if he had been intimate with his wife, he would not be sitting stiffly and as far away from her as he could possibly get.

"Your dinner, my Lord," Fusao said and almost dropped his tray as his lover spun round, his eyes at first widening in shock and then misting over with unconcealed joy and love. Then he saw Lady Sachiko looking at him and recovered sufficiently to say casually, "Fusao, my old personal servant when I was staying at the west wing. I didn't expect to see him here today so it is a bit of a surprise! You may put our dinner trays on this table, Fusao."

Lady Sachiko looked a little surprised her husband had bothered to explain about the presence of a servant much less notice him but she said nothing.

Fusao managed to stop his hands from trembling as he laid out the little dishes of culinary miracles Sato san had managed to whip up in the kitchens but the tension between them was so sharp it could cut like a knife. Fusao was relieved that Lady Sachiko did not seem to notice it and was busying herself with admiring Sato san's masterpieces.

"I never knew that food could be so beautiful. You must have a very good and skillful cook in this castle," she said appreciatively.

Her husband nodded and replied absently, "Yes, the best around these parts."

But Lord Okimoto's eyes followed Fusao everywhere and it was fortunate for both of them that his wife appeared too preoccupied with the food presentation to notice.

* * * * *

But they were actually both wrong in that assumption, Lady Sachiko did notice how much her husband was affected by the servant who had brought in their dinner and she couldn't make it out. What was going on between the two of them and wasn't it improper for a samurai to pay so much attention to a servant?

She was finding out each day what a strange man she had married and a week into their marriage, she was still a virgin. Although she had heard plenty of stories about how painful having sex the first time was and did not mind being left to sleep peacefully each night, Lady Sachiko knew that it was not natural or flattering to her that her husband did not seem to want her and how were they going to have children if they did not consummate their marriage?

When her mother called on her two days ago and asked briskly, as if it was a business transaction, how her wedding night had been, Lady

Sachiko was too ashamed to tell her the truth that she was still a virgin. So she spoke demurely about her wedding night based on a married sister's account and was relieved that it seemed to satisfy her mother.

"Well, you had better produce an heir for the Nobunagas soon otherwise it will dishonor our family's reputation as a good and faultless bloodline," her mother had then said plunging Lady Sachiko into greater anxiety when that night her husband again turned his back on her after a chaste kiss on the forehead.

She agonized every night whether she should try and talk to him about their lack of physical intimacy or could she initiate it? Lady Sachiko was horrified at the thought of that because she had always been taught that ladies of breeding and class did not initiate physical intimacy with their husbands, they had to approach that subject with delicacy and well-bred tolerance. But she was desperate to get it over with, this whole purpose of getting married, finish her duty of producing an heir or heirs and then be left alone to pursue her other interests and close one eye on her husband amusing himself with other concubines. That was how marriage to a samurai from a great family was supposed to be but so far, her marriage was still a non-starter!

Lady Sachiko decided she would give it two more weeks and if nothing happened she would have to think of a way to approach her husband about the matter. She had never been married or had a husband who either didn't desire her or had a physical problem and she was too ashamed to seek advice from anyone and suddenly, Lady Sachiko felt very alone and helpless. She wished she was seven years old again and all she had to do to please her family was excel in her singing, dancing and koto lessons all of which she loved anyway, so they brought her more pleasure than stress.

Tears threatened to ooze out of her eyes and, terrified of embarrassing herself by losing control and irritated at the servant still intent on hovering over her husband, the source of her grief, Lady Sachiko waved him away and said sharply, "I think that is all and you may leave us to have our dinner."

* * * * *

Fusao suddenly remembered his place and, appalled that he had forgotten himself and lingered a little longer than was acceptable in a servant. He gave a deep bow and slipped out of the room. He had better be careful next time Lady Sachiko was not as clueless as he thought and for all her demure and gentle ways, she was in fact quite sharp and was beginning to show signs of a temper.

"Better watch it next time," he told himself as he hurried back to the kitchens. "Unless you want your act with Lord Okimoto to be found out!"

"Today I saw Lord Okimoto and as soon as our eyes met, I was overjoyed because nothing has changed, the same electrifying passion and love still flows between us only now a woman, his wife, keeps us apart." Fusao wrote in his diary that night.

The next day was his last day serving the samurai and his wife as he had to return to the west wing. He would miss serving in the kitchens and helping to prepare food knowing that he was doing something for Lord Okimoto. Seeing him again that night and feeling his smoldering eyes on him made Fusao ache for his lover's touch and with the raw passion raging through his body, he wrote, "Is he feeling the same need tonight as I do? I do not understand the cruelty of a world that forces us apart and I am afraid that we will never be together again."

The next morning, Sato san called him aside and said, "You must have made quite an impression on Lord Okimoto yesterday because he has ordered me to assign you the job of serving his wife and him dinner every night, even at official functions in the castle. He must really like the way you serve food because to me, you are just a numbskull that can hardly focus on anything!"

It was obviously one of Sato san's bad days but Fusao was so overjoyed he did not have to leave the east wing and was going to see the samurai every night that not even the caustic tongue of Sato san could dampen his spirits. He felt a little bad to deprive Michio of his job in the east wing but his selfless friend didn't seem to mind.

"Be careful," he said. "You know, of course that you are playing with fire and when the fire burns out or is forcibly put out, guess whose head will be on the chopping board! It's always the peasant who is wrong and needs to be punished, never the samurai. I am your friend and I just want you to remember that."

His words made Fusao uncomfortable because they were true but he couldn't stop himself from jumping into a fire for love of the samurai so Fusao changed the subject with the only topic that would distract Michio.

"How is it going with Yuki chan?"

Michio's face lit up instantly and a happy flush stained his face as he replied, "Oh, it's going very well, I've already visited her parents and they approve of me so we just need to decide when we should get married."

Fusao nodded, happy for his friend. How nice it was to be like Michio and Yuki, happy and blessed in a relationship from the same social background and status that was approved by their families and society. For him, there would never be such contentment and uncomplicated happiness. Both he and Lord Okimoto would never be allowed to openly share their love with the world and be accepted as other lovers were. It was tragic and painful.

"Yes," Michio replied. "Until I knew that she reciprocated my feelings, you can't imagine what I went through!"

Fusao was forced to bite his tongue to keep from blurting out that he knew exactly how it felt to keep his love a himitsu, a secret, from the world because of insecurities, not knowing if his lover still wanted him and knowing everyone else would never accept how he felt for the Lord Okimoto. And now his beloved was married to a woman and they would be forced to produce an heir. *Oh my friend, Michio, you will never know the real pain of unrequited love thank goodness for that*!

They parted on the happy subject of the best way Michio should ask for his ladylove's hand in marriage and then Fusao escaped to his quarters to pack his few possessions to move to the East wing. He understood Michio's concern and appreciated his friend did not judge or turn away from him in disgust. Maybe Michio understood because he too was caught in the powerful drag net of love and Fusao was grateful for that unconditional and non-judgmental friendship.

But deep within himself, he could not find peace and Fusao's last entry that night in his diary was a passionate cry for help

"I am torn between joy that I am to move to the East wing to be near my beloved Okimoto sama and yet I am afraid of what lies ahead and how this will end for me! If only someone can help me flush out these feelings that make me a prisoner of the castle!"

161

Chapter Thirty-Four

The move to the East wing did not turn out as well as Fusao had expected The new head servant who oversaw them was a tyrant, very different from the cantankerous but soft hearted Okuno san and the two servants who shared his room did not have the warmth and kindness of Michio and the rest of the servants in the west wing. And of course, Sato san was a law unto himself in the kitchens and threw his weight shamelessly around. Fusao could see that the going would be tough but he was prepared to put up with that and more just to stay close to Lord Okimoto who had ordered personally that he be put on the staff of the east wing. That was enough for Fusao.

Night after night he brought dinner to Okimoto and his wife and stayed around for as long as he could without drawing attention to himself. He knew by the way the samurai looked at him and the desire that flowed between them when their hands accidentally touched one night that they still wanted each other. If anything, their enforced sexual deprivation had heightened that desire which would, sooner or later, have to find release.

One night, Fusao went into Lord Okimoto's dining room and found him alone.

In answer to his silent query, the samurai whispered, "Lady Sachiko has gone back to her family's home for a few days because her father is not well."

"Then you will be dining alone here until she returns?" Fusao stammered, hardly able to believe the opportunities for intimacy.

"Yes," Lord Okimoto said softly and all the pent up emotions and frustration burst forward as he got up and kissed his beautiful lover hard on the mouth.

For a moment, Fusao was stunned and then he responded with all the passion that had been bottled up inside him since their last meeting at the teahouse before the wedding. When they surfaced for air, he asked anxiously, "But it's dangerous for us to get intimate here with all the bodyguards and servants outside, anyone might just come in!"

"Not when I have told my bodyguard outside that I am not to be disturbed for whatever reason," Lord Okimoto replied. "The samurai will eat very slowly tonight and I have the very pleasant feeling that I will eat more than just food."

With the urgency of weeks of deprivation, they tore off each other's clothes and sank down onto the soft floor cushions in a tangle of entwined limbs but taking care to keep their moans of pleasure down and out of earshot of the bodyguard standing barely meters away. The sense of adventure and the risk they were taking heightened their pleasure and Fusao would later find teeth marks on his hands where he had bitten them to silence his moans of sexual ecstasy.

That night he wrote in his diary, "Lady Sachiko is away and tonight for the first time in weeks, Lord Okimoto and I made love right there in his dining room with two bodyguards standing just outside. I think we were mad but oh, may this madness last forever. I am so happy and fulfilled I can hardly sleep!"

For the next three nights, they made love repeatedly, rolling away from each other only when their bodies had become satiated, but on the fifth night, Fusao entered the room to find that Lady Momoe had decided to take dinner with her son and derailed their plans for another night of passion. Fusao went to sleep feeling a sense of loss and his entry that night in his diary was a melancholic one.

"I have become a victim of my own passion and love and I don't know what will happen when Lady Sachiko comes back."

The next day, Fusao went about his duties waiting only for 6:30 p.m. when he would bring the dinner trays to Lord Okimoto's rooms, he had heard from the kitchen staff that Lady Sachiko would be back the following day and tonight would be their last night together. He prayed that Lady Momoe would not decide to have dinner with her son again and was overjoyed when he found Lord Okimoto alone and waiting for him.

Both of them were soon in the throes of passion and the knowledge that this could well be their last night together for a while, heightened their desperate need for each other. Neither of them noticed a soft commotion outside and the sliding door opening very gently until a scream pierced the evening calm in the room that had been broken only by their heavy breathing.

Fusao was the first to raise his head and the shock of what he saw struck him with the force of lightning. he stood rooted to the same spot still crouched over Lord Okimoto, unaware even that he was stark naked. Something had gone wrong, Lady Sachiko shouldn't be here but she was, cowering in a corner of the room weeping in fear and mortification at what she had just witnessed.

Fusao started to shake.

He stole a look at Lord Okimoto who had thrown a yukata on his own naked body, his face set and as white as a sheet of paper. Someone must have called Lady Momoe because she appeared within minutes followed by Shuhei, an old and trusted servant who had served the old samurai from the age of 15 and watched over Lord Okimoto from the time he was born. She dismissed the bodyguards, closed the door behind her and watched the group silently for a few minutes, not trusting herself to speak.

* * * * *

What a despicable character her son was, if he didn't look like his father she could swear that he was the spawn of some low class man from the gutters, he didn't have the dignity and nobility to even keep his penis inside his yukata for the honor of his family and heritage, she thought angrily. He was not fit to be a Nobunaga samurai and if he were not her son and the male figure she needed as a front to stay in control, she would banish him to a distant branch of the family in the extreme northern island of Hokkaido and never set eyes on him again. Then she noticed Fusao still naked trying to cover his private parts with his bare hands and threw a yukata at him in disgust.

"Put this on, you disgust me!" she spat "and go to the room outside to wait."

Fusao was only too glad to be ordered to leave the room and he crept out, his head down, not daring to look at anyone.

Then realizing that Lady Sachiko was the main player now and everything depended on what she decided to do, Lady Momoe hurried over to the weeping girl and helped her to a smaller connecting room next door, leaving the sliding partition door open so that she could keep an eye on her daughter in law. Focus, she told herself fiercely, focus on the only thing that matters right now, damage control.

"Stay here, Sachiko san and leave everything to Shuhei and me," she whispered, allowing herself one small embrace to comfort her distraught daughter in law.

After making sure that Lady Sachiko was comfortable, she hurried back to the next room and unleashed the full force of her anger on the somber couple. Fusao stood through the diatribe, prepared for the worst. Lord Okimoto was the samurai and her son and the worst he could get was a lashing and a slap across the knuckles. But Fusao was just a worthless servant who would be blamed for seducing the samurai and whipped or even killed for his "crime." Love had made them careless and they had taken a gamble and lost. Fusao braced himself for the punishment he knew for sure would be meted out to him with all the venom Lady Momoe could muster.

In the end, it was Shuhei, the old servant, who injected some calm into the situation and started the process of finding a solution. Although he was just a servant, his great age and years of devotion to the Nobunaga family gave him the privilege of speaking his mind freely and he did so now.

"Both of you were very indiscreet tonight and a lot of damage was done. Poor Lady Sachiko has the right to be furious, upset and hurt and indeed shocked as no young girl of her background or of any background for that matter should have witnessed such a bestial act. In fact, I hope she doesn't lose her mind over the shock," Shuhei began. "Whatever happens, none of this must leak out."

"I have a plan but before that I have to ask Okimoto kun here a few very direct questions and I need honest and absolutely truthful answers."

Lord Okimoto nodded, looking straight ahead. Shuhei continued.

"I've known about your condition for a long time. In fact, I saw it developing as you grew up and I hoped against hope that it was just a passing phase in your life. But over the years, I watched you consorting with young men of like mind and I knew that this disease was so deep inside you that it was there to stay. The only thing I could do was cover up for you to protect your name so that no one should know about this side of you. I swore to your father that I would never allow the Nobunaga name to be shamed by public knowledge of this secret but tonight I failed in my duty and promise to your father."

"My Lord Okimoto, can you answer very honestly whether your aversion to women is so great that you will never be able to have a physical relationship with your wife so that she can conceive and produce the heirs that are needed to carry on this line?"

"I'm afraid so." Lord Okimoto replied. "We have not consummated our marriage and every time I try, I become impotent."

"Oh God, what are we to do? Why, why, Okimoto?" Lady Momoe was visibly distraught as she paced the room, wringing her hands.

"Calm down, Lady Momoe," Shuhei said soothingly. "Just listen. You need an heir to continue the Nobunaga line and Okimoto kun will never be able to produce one so I am thinking maybe we can persuade Lady Sachiko to have a baby with another man selected by you and he is brought up as heir to continue the Nobunaga line and be the next samurai."

There was a stunned silence as the audacity of Shuhei's suggestion sank in. Then Lady Momoe cried out hysterically, "How dare you suggest such an absurd plan? Who will Sachiko have a baby with? Okimoto has no other brothers!"

"I did say that at first my plan would sound rather far-fetched but when you have had time to think it over, you will see that my suggestion is the only option available in such a situation," Shuhei replied calmly and his calmness somehow communicated itself to Lady Momoe and she sobered down considerably. "I'm thinking of selecting one of the guards and after that sending him off with a good pension to some distant part of Japan with his whole family."

"Have the baby from the blood of a bodyguard on the samurai seat of the Nobunaga clan?" Lady Momoe replied. "No, that wouldn't be right, the samurai who inherits has to be of the blood of this family! The next Samurai must have the blood of Nobunaga!"

"Yes, I know," Shuhei said quietly. "But the last pure Nobunaga is unable to father a child so what other options are we left with?"

"Well, at least he must have some of the Nobunaga blood in him," Lady Momoe said slowly. "We could select someone from another branch of the family who is a Nobunaga although a few times removed. I remember now my husband had a cousin who was sent to the north to head another branch of the family and they shared the same grandfather. They were here for the wedding and they spoke of their son, Kazuo, 17 years old and single. If we can persuade his parents to help us perpetuate

166

the Nobunaga name with a good sum of money and a big tract of land perhaps, I think our problem could be solved!"

"So you see, Lady Momoe, this plan is not so far-fetched as you thought at first!" Shuhei said, delighted. "There is only one problem left here, to persuade Lady Sachiko to agree. It won't be easy to ask a lady of great virtue who is married to sleep with another man and bear his child. I am truly sorry that we have to put her through the ordeal of such an indecent proposal."

For a moment Lady Momoe's face crumbled and she cried out in real anguish, "How can I ask this of any woman most of all, my own daughter in law? Tell me please, Shuhei, where is the justice in all this? My only son and heir turns out to be doseiai and unable to father a child and I am now left with the task of persuading my daughter in law to be impregnated by another man!"

Shuhei let her rant on for a while then he said gently, "You are a great lady from one of the finest families in Japan and you know that big sacrifices have been made in the name of honor for centuries. In fact you yourself might have also made some sacrifices as well and you know honor and the preservation of a great dynasty are worthy of any sacrifice. Lady Sachiko is now a Nobunaga too and she has a duty towards this family. Given time to think and consider, she will not refuse to make this sacrifice, I'm sure of that."

"I know it seems harsh but we have to talk to her tonight, right now, everything has to be settled by tonight and no one must leave this room until the matter has been resolved and we are sure none of this will leak out. It will never do to let the people know their samurai cannot have children and feel the instability of a feudal system without an heir," Shuhei said. "It's a very delicate issue and one I think will sit better coming from another woman so I'm afraid, Lady Momoe, you will have to talk to Lady Sachiko."

Lady Momoe nodded but her usually smooth and beautiful face was ravaged and grim, the thought of facing her daughter in law with this proposal frightened her to death and she had to tell herself repeatedly she was the only person who could persuade Lady Sachiko to at least consider the plan. It was her fault she had produced a weak and defective son for the Nobunaga family and she was the only one left who was strong enough to bring them out of this crisis.

With a deep sigh, she got up, administered a stern warning to her son not to leave until she returned and went to the next room where Lady Sachiko sat, staring listlessly out of the window, her tears spent.

From the connecting door that Lady Momoe deliberately left open, Lord Okimoto and Shuhei could see her taking Lady Sachiko's hands in hers and start talking in low, subdued tones. It was an emotion charged conversation and they could see Lady Sachiko weeping again while her mother in law looked on helplessly and waited for her sobs to subside. By the way her eyes had widened in shock and horror, they gathered Lady Momoe had told her what she had to do to produce an heir for the Nobunaga family and her sobs started up again.

In the other room, Lord Okimoto winced at the sound of his wife's sobs and he cursed himself for the pain he had inflicted on her and his mother. He was a hopeless homosexual but he still had a heart and a conscience. He had let his animal urges for pleasures of the flesh cloud his sense of duty and brought dishonor to a great family. He prayed silently that if his wife accepted Lady Momoe's proposal, he would deny himself of all carnal pleasures and never see Fusao again.

The old man Shuhei had spoken of sacrifices and Lord Okimoto vowed that the supreme sacrifice he would make was to give up Fusao, the one man he had truly loved because only this great suffering and pain would be enough to cleanse the stain of dishonor he had brought to the Nobunaga name.

Back in the other room, Lady Momoe did something she had never done before, she unlocked her heart and told Sachiko the story of her own suffering when she was forced to give up her forbidden love for Takashi, the poor tutor and honor her family with marriage to the prominent samurai, Lord Nobunaga, a man years older than her whom she did not know or love.

"I never thought I would say this but it's the fate of women of our time, to sacrifice first for the honor of our families and then for the honor of our husbands and children and it's because we are strong enough to make such sacrifices that great dynasties like the Nobunagas continue to survive," Lady Momoe continued.

Lady Sachiko looked at her elegant and confident mother in law and felt relieved that even Lady Momoe had weaknesses and flaws in her life. Suddenly Sachiko felt the terrible mess in her life could be forgiven.

Besides, which would be the greater dishonor and shame, to return to her family a virgin, married to a man who could not impregnate her because he was a doseiai or to be impregnated with the seed of another man and at least in the eyes of her family and the rest of society, she would have produced an heir for the Nobunagas and fulfilled her duty. At the moment, nothing could be worse for Lady Sachiko than having to explain to her family that she had left her husband because he was a homosexual and unable to make love to her, so she put out a hand timidly to Lady Momoe and whispered," Yes, I will do it but I have one condition."

The relief that hit Lady Momoe was so great that for a moment she could not speak and when she did, for once, her voice was hardly above a whisper, "Oh Sachiko, thank you. You've made me the happiest woman in the whole of Japan tonight. What condition do you have, please let me know and I'll make sure it's met."

Lady Sachiko hesitated for a moment, then she said firmly, "That servant, Fusao, I want him out of the castle and my husband's life. The only way I can be sure that he will stay away is if he gets married too. That's my condition, I want that servant, Fusao, who participated in my husband's shame to sacrifice himself too like all of us have done. He must marry and when he does, I will fulfill my part of the bargain."

Chapter Thirty-Five

Fusao had known he would not get off lightly. In fact, he had even expected to be thrown into prison or killed for his part in "defiling" the samurai and bringing shame to the Nobunaga family. What he did not expect was Lady Momoe's grim declaration that, fortunately for everyone, Lady Sachiko had decided to stay on at the castle and cover up the incident on condition that Fusao must get married and leave the castle immediately.

Not once had she looked at Fusao, not even when she said contemptuously, "You are lucky Lady Sachiko did not insist that you be punished. Tomorrow, two soldiers will bring you back to your parents' home and stay there until they see you married. Then you are never to come to the castle or attempt to see Lord Okimoto again. If you ever do that or any word of what happened tonight ever passes from your lips, not only you but your whole family will be severely punished. Do you hear me?"

Fusao nodded and he managed to control his face so that it did not reflect the turmoil of shame, humiliation and self-loathing that was swirling crazily inside him. What he really wanted to do was throw himself at Lady Momoe's feet to beg for another chance but he did not do that. What could he ask of her? Another chance for what? To continue his homosexual relationship with her son?

Having said her piece, Lady Momoe dismissed Fusao as nothing more significant than a rotting branch that had to be chopped off a tree and discarded. She went back to more important matters at hand. In her mind, the servant had been let off too lightly, thanks to Lady Sachiko, but beyond a fleeting resentment about that, she didn't have time for him anymore.

Like a dead man, Fusao allowed himself to be escorted by Shuhei to his room with instructions to stay there until the next morning. He did not even notice that his two roommates were nowhere in sight, probably moved to another place so they would not witness his distress and become suspicious of the two guards stood outside the door to assure he did not try to escape in the night.

It was only much later as he lay in the darkness listening to the swishing of the trees outside that the full impact of what had happened that long night came down upon him and the sobs started to wrack his body with a ferocity that knew no respite.

That night, Fusao knew with certainty that it was over between him and Lord Okimoto and their tragic forbidden love that had always hovered between joy and despair, fire and ice and living on the edge had come to an end. He would never again feel the joy and wonder of love. From now on, life would be mere existence, trapped in a loveless and forced marriage and just waiting until his lease of life expired to end this suffering at last.

They had to let go because Lady Momoe had regained absolute control of her son through emotional blackmail and threats to destroy Fusao's family and confiscate their land. Lord Okimoto did not have the making of a ruthless samurai like his forefathers who did and took what they wanted and because of this, he could not stand up to his mother and protect his lover from the fall out of living on the wrong end of society and gender. But again, wasn't that the reason in the first place why Fusao had fallen in love with him? The sensitive and gentle samurai that a young peasant boy had dared to love?

At daybreak, one of the two soldiers shook him awake and told him to get dressed, gather whatever possessions he had and leave the castle under their escort. Now that it was time to leave, Fusao wanted to go as soon as possible. There was nothing to stay for any more. Throughout the night, he had half expected a miracle, that Lord Okimoto would burst in to rescue and recognize him and tell his mother to stay out of his business because he was the samurai, the ultimate authority over all of them and he had the right to do whatever he wanted and with whomever. But no miracle happened. And yet Fusao could not hate the samurai or think less of him.

Fusao's father had just left for the rice fields when they arrived and his mother's joy at seeing him after so many months was eclipsed by her anxiety over why he was being escorted home by two soldiers.

"Is something wrong, Fusao?" she asked, her hands nervously wringing the front of her kimono."

"No, no, mother," Fusao replied. "I've left my work at the castle and they are just escorting me back and staying around for some time. You see, I've decided to come back and be the good son and obey Father's wishes that I get married to Aiko chan."

"Oh Fusao, is that so? I'm very happy you have come to your senses and decided to do the right thing," his mother said but she continued to survey the two soldiers uncertainly because they did not look as if they were going to leave any time soon. But she was in no position to question them about their motives or ask them to leave, they were soldiers of the samurai and she was just a peasant. The samurai owned them and everything they had so his soldiers could stay as long as they wanted and there was not a thing she could do about it.

So she swallowed her fears and invited them in, wincing at the way they walked into the house without taking off their heavy rush boots and spreading dirt on the old and worn tatami floor. But still she couldn't insult the samurai's soldiers by asking them to take off their boots.

Fusao went to put his things in his old room and followed his mother to the kitchen where she was preparing a pot of green tea for the soldiers.

"Are you in some kind of trouble, Fusao?" Yuko asked as soon as they were out of earshot of the soldiers. "Please tell me what is happening. Whatever it is, I promise not to tell your father."

"It's really ok, mother," Fusao replied. "There was some trouble but it has been settled." He paused for a moment, wanting to tell his mother about his secret tryst with the samurai Lord Okimoto. Could her fear over her husband's disapproval be eclipsed and overcome by her love for her son? "I don't know how to tell you this," he continued, "but I am in love with the samurai Lord Okimoto. When they discovered us, they forced me to leave the castle and come back here."

Yuko's eyes widened with horror and disbelief. She nearly dropped the tea pot.

"What did you just say?" she whispered and then before Fusao knew it, he felt a stinging blow across his face. His mother had slapped him hard across the face with all her might. "How dare you insult our samurai with such filthy words? Do you know everything we have, this house, the rice fields and even the food we eat is provided by him?"

"I'm sorry, mother, but I speak the truth. No matter how many times you hit me, it'll still be the truth," Fusao whispered, trying hard to hold back his tears. "But it's over and I am back to marry any girl you and my father choose for me and I will be nothing but a good son to both of you from now on. I'm sorry for all the trouble I have brought upon this family."

Yuko started to cry and she said in between bewildered sobs, "I don't know how or why two men, a peasant and a samurai, as far apart as the sky is from the sea, can say they love each other but you are my son. I just want to believe it when you say that whatever that was, it's over and done with."

When she was done with crying, Yuko wiped away her tears with the sleeve of her kimono, straightened her shoulders and said with the stoicism of a lifetime of enduring, "We will never speak of it again. Whatever happens, I'm glad you are safely home. As soon as your father gets back tonight, we'll discuss your marriage with him."

Towards nightfall, the two soldiers left for the castle with the unwelcome promise to be back the following day. At home, both Fusao and his mother waited anxiously for Naoki to return. Yuko had cooked all his favorite dishes for dinner to start him off on a happy note and prepared a hot scented bath in their own bathtub sohe would not have to go down to the public bath that night. Steam was rising out of the cracks of the thick rush mat she had used to cover up the bath so that the heat would not escape.

Naoki was late that night because he met a friend on the way back and the two men decided to drop by a bar to share a bottle of hot sake. This proved to be fortunate for his family because by the time he got home, he was in good spirits and prepared to accept Fusao's presence at his dining table with greater enthusiasm than he would otherwise have done.

"And are you home for a visit or to stay?" Naoki asked absently as he joined them at the dining table, his eyes sweeping appreciatively over the spread of his favorite food before him.

"He has left the castle and has come home to stay," Yuko replied quickly before Fusao could answer. "Naoki, our son has decided to do the dutiful thing and get married to a girl of our choice."

Naoki's face crinkled into a rare smile of delight. He got up and embraced his son in an unusual display of affection, helped obviously by the sake still creating warm responses in him.

"Good, my son, I'm happy my prodigal son has come home," he said. "Come, let's eat and drink to our good fortune tonight. Tomorrow

I'll send word out to Aiko chan's father that Fusao is ready to honor his father's promise at last!'

For the first time in a very long while, the family had a happy dinner together, eating and drinking late into the night. Naoki even entertained them with a couple of folk songs in his rich baritone. Although Fusao tried to join in this rare burst of family fun, his heart was not in it because he knew they were singing under false pretenses and in reality a cloud hung over them darker than any the family would ever see.

Later, when he lay in the futon in his old room, the sobering thought of how he was going to explain the two soldiers' presence to his father the following day hit Fusao and the pain of his last day at the castle that had sat in his heart like a stone intensified, making sleep impossible.

The muffled sounds of his parents making love in the next room separated only by thin walls not designed for privacy served only to heighten his own loneliness and sense of loss and Fusao started to cry into his hard pillow of rice and bean husks. Even his parents, a couple of aging peasants condemned to a life of agricultural toil and submission to the forces that be, had found love and warmth because they followed the rules and didn't try to break out of the system of correct social and moral behavior.

When he could bear it no longer, Fusao did the only thing he knew could ease his pain, he took out his wooden file of papers and started to write.

Chapter Thirty-Six

Fusao need not have worried because in the course of the night, after giving him his conjugal rights with special and an unusual attention to details, his mother had explained to her husband the next day, there would be two soldiers at the house who were sent by the samurai to protect Fusao until he got married.

Fortunately, Naoki saw the wisdom of his wife's reasoning and kept his peace when the two soldiers appeared the next day at the crack of dawn with an imperative message from Lady Momoe, how was the marriage of Fusao progressing? If Naoki wondered why the samurai's mother would take a sudden interest in the marital affairs of a peasant and at best an ex servant at the castle, he kept his thoughts to himself.

Naoki sent back a message he would make a trip to Matsumoto to formalize the initiation of marriage plans for Aiko and Fusao but it would take several days of travel on foot. One of the soldiers ran back to the castle to inform Lady Momoe of this and within the hour a carriage bearing the emblem of the Nobunaga samurai appeared in front of the house, accompanied by hordes of curious children gawking from a safe distance.

"Our Lady Momoe decrees that you should go to Matsumoto this very minute by her carriage and return by nightfall today. I am to accompany you to make sure all goes well," one of the soldiers said. "The samurai orders that your son's marriage must take place this weekend so we had better make haste and leave now."

Although the nagging question of why the samurai and his mother were so interested and involved in Fusao's marriage was growing more disturbing, Naoki did not dare question their motives. The samurai owned all of them and that alone gave him leave to do whatever he wanted with them. Without a word, Naoki followed the soldiers into the carriage, glad that at least he would not have to make the three-day walk to Matsumoto and back.

For Fusao, it was the longest day he had ever known in his life. His mother seemed to be avoiding him, disturbed by the many unanswered questions that lay between them. To take his mind off the harrowing days ahead and forbidden thoughts of Lord Okimoto, Fusao took a hoe and went out to tend to their vegetable field behind the house. His hands had become soft from the easy life at the castle and protested against this sudden assault of hard physical labor by breaking out in red angry welts almost immediately.

But Fusao welcomed every pain, every bruise he was inflicting upon himself. He didn't stop even when his hands became raw and bleeding. Did he hear the soldier say that the samurai had ordered that he was to marry by the weekend? No, those had to be Lady Momoe's words spoken in the name of the samurai, Lord Okimoto could not possibly want him to marry, they had been forced apart to follow very painful paths by circumstances beyond their control.

And yet Lord Okimoto had not said a word to protect him that night. He had allowed his mother to take control of his life and had not acted like a samurai but more like a little boy hiding behind his powerful mother's skirt. He had taken a young impressionable peasant boy and introduced him to forbidden pleasures of unforgettable intensity and then he had calmly walked away and let others deal with his indiscretions.

As yet more tears fell to mingle with the dark fertile soil he was attacking, Fusao knew he should hate Lord Okimoto and forget him but it was impossible, love didn't come and go at the snap of a finger or upon command, it just lingered on until one was destroyed by it or grew too old to care.

At noon, his mother called him into the house for a simple lunch of rice, pickles and hot seaweed soup and they ate in near silence, very different from the almost festive atmosphere of warmth and laughter at the previous night's dinner.

"I hope everything is going well at Matsumoto," was the only thing Yuko said throughout the lunch and Fusao nodded, not knowing what else to reply.

As the sun went down, the tension in the house increased and Yuko did not even have the mood to potter around the kitchen to get the evening meal ready as she usually did around sunset. What was taking Naoki so long? Had he been taken by the samurai's soldiers somewhere else and never coming back? Naoki could be hot tempered and what if he got into an argument with the soldiers and insulted the samurai? Yuko was beside herself with worry by the time the sound of a carriage brought her and Fusao racing to the front door.

The samurai's carriage dropped Naoki at the house and sped off to the castle with the two soldiers. They could see by his stooped shoulders and slow gait that it had been a long day.

Without a word, he changed out of his dusty clothes into a comfortable loose yukata and sat down for the simple dinner his wife had kept for him. It was only then that he started to speak of the day's events.

"I arrived in Matsumoto to find out that Aiko chan has been married off to another family and Uncle Joji is not very happy about the way you refused her, Fusao. But he is still family and when he heard of your plight, he arranged for Tomoko, the daughter of another family, to marry you. Today I visited her family and her father accepted my proposal on your behalf. She is 15 years old and she will arrive this weekend for the wedding, it's all very sudden and not very proper but you know we cannot disobey any decree of the samurai, no matter how unfair or abrupt it is."

"I am not even going to ask why this is happening, I just hope that with you safely married, we will be left to continue with our lives peacefully."

Fusao went over to his father to kneel at his feet and apologize, "I'm truly sorry, father, for all the trouble I have brought to this family. If I had accepted marriage with Aiko in the first place, none of this would have happened. Please forgive me, father."

Naoki sighed deeply and replied, "I don't really know what happened at the castle although I do have some ideas that I prefer not to think about, but I hope that chapter of your life is closed forever, Fusao, and I mean, forever. Once you're married to Tomoko, I expect you to behave like a married man and think about starting a family as soon as possible."

Fusao nodded. At that moment he would have agreed to anything to make amends with his father and it didn't matter who he married really, Aiko or Tomoko, what was the difference, they were all the same to him, strangers he would never love.

Fusao joined his parents to discuss plans for his wedding but throughout the discussion, he felt detached. As if they were all talking about someone else.

He went to bed that night, physically and mentally drained. Not even the sight of his wooden file of papers could arouse his interest. There was an unbearable ache in him, to see Lord Okimoto even though he knew how impossible that was. When the ache became so intense and he couldn't bear it any longer, he knew what he had to do. His parents were spreading out their futons and Fusao waited until the lull of their voices stopped completely and he was sure they were asleep. Then he got up and crept out of the house.

He had forgotten to put on anything over his thin yukata and the cold night air chilled his body but Fusao did not feel anything. His feet were taking him up the road toward the castle. He felt and saw nothing as he continued to walk as if in a trance and it was only when the distant lights of the first sentry post of the castle appeared that he slowed down. Fusao knew this sentry post had at least six soldiers standing guard at any one time, all heavily armed to fight and kill any intruders. If he got too near, he would be challenged and the commotion would land him in trouble with Lady Momoe and his family would surely bear the brunt of her displeasure.

Sanity returned and for a long moment, Fusao stood against a tree by the side of the road staring blindly at the castle with its tiny pinpoints of lights that held his samurai lover within. With a heavy heart, he turned round and walked slowly back to his house but somehow, the sight of the castle and its warm yellow glow of lights brought a small measure of comfort to Fusao because it reminded him that his time at the castle with Lord Okimoto had been real and not just a dream and in the coming days, that was the only thing he would have to hold on to.

Yes, those yellow pin-points of lights had attracted him like insects were drawn to the light traps set for them in summer only to be snapped up and killed even before they reached their forbidden fruits. With a deep sigh Fusao turned and retraced his steps back to his father's house. Later, he got out a flimsy piece of paper and wrote on it "My love for Okimoto sama is not over yet."

The next day was Wednesday and his wedding was just three days away. The marriage preparation of their only child they had planned for years had to be compressed into three days under the watchful eyes of the two soldiers from the castle. Fusao watched it all dispassionately as if it was happening to someone else and he was an outsider looking in. Not even when he was fitted for his formal wedding kimono with all the elaborate headdress and accessories did Fusao feel that he was a part of this ceremony not until Saturday when a carriage arrived bearing his bride to be and Fusao was forced to meet the sad faced young girl who was obviously as unwilling to get married as her bridegroom was.

When Fusao looked into a pair of the most innocent and trusting eyes he had ever seen, he felt a pang of guilt. It was all wrong, every one of those people who were forcing this beautiful young and completely untouched girl into marriage with a man who had been defiled in ways that would shock even Miyoshi san, generally considered philanderous in the village. But like his lover, Lord Okimoto, Fusao's life seemed to have been taken over by more powerful forces with their own agendas and both he and poor Tomoko were just pawns.

They had a traditional ceremony in the smaller local temple the peasants used for such events, followed by a wedding feast attended by almost everyone in the village. There were only two events in a peasant's life that were considered significant and memorable, one was when he got married and the other when he died, so customs revolving round weddings and funerals were fiercely adhered to, no expenses spared.

The only people who did not celebrate were the bride who clung red eyed and tearful to her mother and the bridegroom who was starting to dread nightfall when he would be left alone with his bride on their wedding night.

In a way, Fusao felt he was reliving what Lord Okimoto must have gone through on his own wedding day, the only relief he had was that Tomoko was only 15 years old and would be more than happy to be left alone by her husband on their wedding night.

Sensing his new wife's understandable fear of being alone with a man whom she didn't even know, although he had just become her husband, Fusao was more than willing to leave her alone to sleep on her own futon beyond a chaste kiss on her forehead. Exhausted by the turbulent emotions of the last few days, he fell asleep almost immediately, his last thought was that if Lady Momoe wanted to punish him with this marriage for "defiling" her son, she wasn't going to succeed. Given Tomoko's apparent aversion to physical intimacy of any sort, it wasn't going to be difficult for him to shirk his conjugal responsibilities!

The two soldiers left as soon as the wedding ceremony was over, no doubt to report to Lady Momoe that Fusao was safely married and for everyone else, the departure of the two guards took away the nervous tension of being watched. But to Fusao the last link with the castle was gone and he felt a sudden depression, wondering if their report would reach Lord Okimoto as well and whether he would feel anything.

Chapter Thirty-Seven

It had been a very long journey from the castle to Sendai in the north where a third removed Nobunaga cousin had his family seat and it was there that the daring plan of Shuhei endorsed by Lady Momoe was going to be played out. Lord Okimoto hadn't wanted to go but his mother had insisted that it would be improper for him not to accompany his wife on a mission that was very difficult on her and all of them.

They traveled in a convoy of six carriages, one for Lady Momoe, Lady Sachiko and two of their most personal servants, another for Lord Okimoto, his bodyguard and a servant, the third for Shuhei and four other servants who would be serving the whole party and the last three carriages bore gifts for the family of the young man Takushi and their luggage and supplies for the trip.

The journey took four days and each night the party stopped to rest at the samurai guest houses along the way, hikyaku, or foot messengers, had earlier been dispatched to inform the caretakers and guards of their impending arrival and nothing was spared to make the stay of an important samurai, his family and their appendages as comfortable as possible.

For the young samurai, this was a journey of humiliation, it was bad enough that a man was delivering his wife to be impregnated by another man but when that man was a samurai, traditionally a figure of power and authority, the humiliation was a thousand fold. In fact, Lord Okimoto didn't feel like a samurai at all. He felt like a freak show having his life, lover and even his wife controlled by his mother, and yet he was too weak to fight back and regain control.

Maybe he did not have what it took to be a strong and fearless samurai like his father and forefathers had been. They took what they wanted without excuses and accountability but Okimoto Nobunaga just could not do that. More frequently than ever, his sleep was plagued with nightmares of himself as the knife that severed the long line of blue blooded Nobunagas and he would go down in history as the weak ineffective samurai whose only claim to fame was being a homosexual with a penchant for young peasant boys.

He knew he had betrayed Fusao and the love they shared, he hadn't protected him and Lord Okimoto was haunted by the look of disappointment and disbelief on Fusao's face the night they had been caught and he had allowed his mother and Shuhei to bully his lover into agreeing to leave the castle and get married. He had been unable to face Fusao and averted his face as he left the room. Later that night, Lord Okimoto had justified his actions by telling himself that Fusao was just a peasant and should not expect a samurai to stand up for him. Just because they had become intimate, it did not mean Fusao could forget his station in life and make demands on a samurai, his feudal lord and master who owned him and his whole family.

Okimoto didn't expect peasants to understand the duties and responsibilities of great families like the Nobunagas and how sometimes, family honor and duty had to take precedence over self-gratification and even a love as great as theirs had been. Lord Okimoto was a samurai from a prominent family and his mother would never allow him to weaken his family's grip on power and survival in the feudal hierarchy over a peasant boy.

But he knew he had hurt his beautiful lover irrevocably as if he had plunged a knife hard and deep into his heart and he would have to live with that forever. But did it have to be forever? Maybe, just maybe, there could still be another chance for them?

And as day turned into yet another night and night became day and their convoy of carriages continued its journey northwards, Lord Okimoto sat in the bumpy carriage plagued by images of a fresh faced peasant boy whom he had turned into an animal of passion and love to match his own and then discarded in the name of duty and class distinctions. His every waking thought centered around how to repair the damage and pain he saw in his lover's eyes. Daily he hated himself a little bit more for deserting his only love when he was most needed.

Lady Sachiko had refused to sleep with him since that traumatic night and Lord Okimoto was glad to be spared the agony of being alone with her. In fact, the only condition he had imposed on his mother's daring plan for the continuation of the Nobunaga family was that he would not need to share a room with his wife anymore and she had readily agreed.

Takushi's family welcomed their Nobunaga cousins a few days later with guarded enthusiasm.

The boy's mother had initially objected to the proposal but her husband had broken down her resistance with both family loyalty reasoning and exertion of pressure as the head of the family and she had to submit to him in the end. He saw it as an opportunity to forge a strong alliance with the reigning Nobunaga samurai that would be further enhanced because his grandson would be the next samurai. It was an opportunity not to be passed over lightly.

But Miyuki was a good wife and a gracious and dignified hostess so she hid her misgivings and received her guests with great warmth, introducing the shy Takushi to the prospective mother of his child as if it was the most natural thing to do and she put everyone at ease with her graciousness.

That night, a big feast was prepared for the guests and sake flowed freely. For a solemn occasion, the atmosphere was almost festive and it seemed that everyone was determined to get drunk. They had earlier discussed the best way to enact their plan was to get Takushi drunk and "allow" him a beautiful woman to "break him in." This was tolerated and even encouraged in most noble families, to "break in" a son when he reached marriageable age to ensure his interest in women would be stimulated and aroused. Only in Takushi's case, the girl who would "break him in" would not be some easy servant girl but Lady Sachiko, a samurai's wife and herself still a virgin.

Lady Momoe was remembering an incident years ago when she had brought a servant girl to "break in " Lord Okimoto and stayed outside his room to listen. But she had heard nothing, not a sound and next morning, the girl had come out of the room and told Lady Momoe that Lord Okimoto was "special" but although she was thoroughly grilled about that remark, the girl gave nothing away.

It was only much later when Lady Momoe began to have suspicions about her son's sexual orientation that she understood the servant girl's words. She didn't know why she should be making a comparison between tonight's event and the incident involving her son years ago but perhaps she was guilty about the distasteful deed she had encouraged or in fact ordered and was worried about the poetic justice she believed in if

Takushi turned out to be as "inept" as Lord Okimoto had been around a woman.

Lady Momoe sighed and asked herself what was happening that young men couldn't even be trusted to like women anymore! She had ordered Shuhei to arrange for Lady Sachiko to spend the night in Takushi's room and had gone to bed as soon as it was polite for her to do so. The thought of what she hoped was happening in Takushi's room was suddenly so nauseating and vile it reminded her of the horses and cattle breeding in the farms. Lady Momoe rushed to the bathhouse and threw up, retching violently until all the self-disgust had been purged from her.

And then, right there on the floor of a strange bath house, the steel in Lady Momoe crumbled and she started to cry, sobbing out years of having to be strong even as she watched her husband take on one woman after another and her son dishonoring the family with his secret trysts with young boys. And now the survival of the Nobunaga dynasty was on her shoulders and she had no one stronger than her to share this burden with. There was only one person she pitied more than herself tonight and that was Lady Sachiko. Should she put a stop to this ridiculous plan and let Lord Okimoto take responsibility for his own follies?

Then she heard voices outside the door of the bathhouse and a gentle knock before Miyuki's anxious voice called out from the other side of the door.

"Momoe sama, are you all right? One of the maids said she heard you being sick."

Lady Momoe straightened her shoulders and composed her voice before she replied, "I'm fine, just the exhaustion of the last few days' traveling and overdoing the sake tonight! I'll be out in a minute!"

"All right, just ring the bell if you need anything," Miyuki said and Lady Momoe waited until her footsteps had disappeared before venturing out of the bathhouse and making a dash for her room. But the interruption had broken her moment of weakness and she was glad she had not relented. What they had started needed to be finished and that night, standing at the window and looking up at a star studded sky, Lady Momoe prayed that Lady Sachiko would become pregnant.

The next morning, the chambermaid reported Takushi's futon spotted the virginal stain. Lady Momoe was relieved, their mission had been vile but at least it had not been in vain. They had scored their first success, it was a good start and somehow, she felt it in her bones that

Lady Sachiko would become pregnant. She was, after all, a healthy young woman in the prime of her reproductive life and the castle physician had made all the tests and worked out her most fertile part of the month and she had been given herbs to stimulate her fertility so everything had to go right.

"Yes, everything has to be all right because I can't hold on much longer!" Lady Momoe cried.

The couple took their breakfasts separately and were not encouraged to interact beyond their nightly couplings for the next three days, this was supposed to be an intimacy purely for reproduction purposes and there was no room for emotional entanglements especially as the young and impressionable Takushi appeared each morning, obviously finding his "breaking in" becoming more pleasurable.

"I almost feel sorry for poor Takushi kun and I hope this does not leave any long term scar on his mind," Lady Momoe confided in Shuhei as she watched the love lorn young man hanging around the guest rooms hoping for a glimpse of Lady Sachiko outside their nocturnal interactions.

"No, don't worry, my lady," Shuhei replied. "These young pups mope around for a while but they recover very fast and move on as soon as they find another pretty girl to be infatuated with so Takushi kun will be all right."

Fortunately, Lady Sachiko merely tolerated the nightly invasions of her body to honor what she had agreed to do and was visibly relieved when the three days and nights were over and they prepared to return home to the castle.

Lord Okimoto cloistered himself in his rooms the whole three days and hardly made any appearance. His mother wisely left him alone because she could understand how he felt and had in fact questioned the wisdom of her decision to insist he came along. But she had been angry with him for the trouble and burden he was putting on her and wanted to punish him but in the end, she had punished herself for the pain she felt at his humiliation. Such was the curse of a mother that she should love her son no matter what he was and had done.

A big tract of land was given to Takushi's family for the favor they had done, for the samurai Nobunaga and for keeping the secret they would all carry to their graves. Lady Sachiko did not look at Takushi or anyone but walked straight to the carriage and no one reprimanded her for her lack of manners. The past three days had taken a lot out of her and she wanted only to be left alone.

In the carriage, Lady Momoe embraced her briefly but did not engage her daughter in law in conversation as she sat, stony faced and dried eyed for almost the entire journey. They would never speak of the event again, not even a month later when it was announced Lady Sachiko was pregnant and congratulations to the Nobunaga family and Lord Okimoto poured in from feudal lords all over the country.

Almost every day for the next nine months, Lady Momoe went to the bigger temple reserved for the feudal lords and their families to pray for a healthy baby boy and for Lady Sachiko to recover from the depression which clouded their happiness. But if there was retribution for the unholy act Lady Momoe had initiated, it was her daughter in law's mental condition. She never smiled again and spent her days and some nights praying at a small shrine on the castle grounds.

"Another life destroyed," Lady Momoe thought sadly and a message that arrived later in the day did nothing to cheer her up. Lady Miyuki had sent a tearful message to inform the samurai and his family that her son Takushi never recovered from his infatuation with Lady Sachiko and was insistent on going to the monastery to become a monk. But he was only 17 so his family hoped he would have a change of heart and that his state of mind was only a passing phase of unfulfilled first love.

Shuhei had been wrong about Takushi and Lady Momoe was so distraught by the news that she stayed in bed the whole day.

"One more life affected and maybe destroyed," she whispered into her futon. "How many more lives, dear Kami, will this curse on my son claim?"

Chapter Thirty-Eight

"Do you know the latest news that the whole village is talking about?" Naoki arrived home one evening to announce. "In the bar, in the bath house, everywhere!"

"No, of course not," his wife answered. "Quick, tell us!"

"The samurai's wife, Lady Sachiko is pregnant and the baby will be born in early autumn! They have started selling amulets down at the temple to pray for a boy for the samurai."

Fusao who had been half listening to this conversation sat up and felt a cold clammy wave wash over him. His hands were so tightly clenched that the nails bit into his skin leaving red angry welts but he could not feel any pain because the pain in his heart was so great. Lord Okimoto's wife was pregnant! How? When?

Did this mean they were having a normal sexual relationship all the time?

"No," his heart whispered. "Lord Okimoto cannot have sex with a woman, he promised me that. He said he becomes impotent when he sleeps with a woman."

"So he lied! So he lied!" the wind whistling through the cracks on the walls mocked him. "How then do you explain the baby, you fool?"

Fusao felt the room spinning and closing in on him and he got up and walked out of the house. He was sure his father had made that dramatic announcement to test his feelings for Lord Okimoto and what had he done? He had failed, became emotional and had given the game away! But how was a person supposed to feel when he lay, night after night, filled with longing and memories of a lost passion, memories that just would not go away, no matter how hard he tried to erase them.

One night the longing and the loneliness had been so great that Fusao tried to make love to his wife.

"Try, Fusao, try," he told himself. "Maybe tonight you can cross over and become normal again."

187

Fusao was thinking of the night he had tried to touch Tomoko and the image of Lord Okimoto appeared, angry at his betrayal. His whole body had become limp. Fusao rolled away from his wife, barely able to stifle the sobs of frustration and humiliation. Perhaps that was what Lord Okimoto had done, tried to cross over but in his case he had succeeded and now Lady Sachiko was pregnant.

Fusao knew he ought to accept his relationship with the samurai was over, hadn't Lord Okimoto himself made it clear? That night he did the only thing that could calm him down, Fusao took out his wooden file of papers and began to write.

"Today father told us that Lady Sachiko is pregnant and I am beside myself thinking of how Lord Okimoto, my love and my partner in passion, has betrayed me. I cannot believe that his love is so shallow that he now sleeps with another, a woman, but she is pregnant and I cannot fool myself and deny the truth anymore."

"There is a demon in me, I cannot rest until I go to the castle and exorcise this demon. Tomorrow I will go to the castle even though I risk getting my family punished for I must see Lord Okimoto again."

"I know I will see the love in his eyes again, I must understand that a samurai needs heirs so my love did what he had to do but I must see the love shining out of his eyes again, the love that changed the life of a peasant boy forever."

The next day turned out bitterly cold and bleary. The sky was dark and heavy with snow clouds. It was so cold that even the roaring fire in the main living area could not warm the house as it usually did.

Tomoko had come down with a chill and was snuffling away in the kitchen. she was homesick and had asked permission to return to see her family in Matsumoto. Naoki had agreed but only for a few days because the neighbors would think that Tomoko had left her husband and it would be an insult to Naoki's authority if she stayed away too long.

Fusao was relieved to have some space from his wife because since the night he had tried to make love to her, it had broken the easy friendship between them that had sprung from the understanding that neither of them wanted sex in their marriage and they would be friends and it had worked very well. When Tomoko did not become pregnant month after month, her parents in law simply presumed she needed to take more time than other women and being only 15 years old, they reckoned she had plenty of reproductive life left and were not unduly worried.

But since that night, things had changed, Tomoko distanced herself from Fusao and each night, she pretended to be asleep when her husband came to join her in their room. It was almost as if she was afraid of him. Certainly she lost some of her respect for him and Fusao missed the friendship they had before that humiliating night. It was the samurai's destructive curse again. Fusao tried to hate Lord Okimoto but it was impossible.

"Where are you going, Fusao?" his mother called out from the kitchen when she saw him putting on his thick warm outer clothes. "It's a very nasty morning and certainly much better to stay in, look, it has just started to snow!"

"I know, mother and I won't be long. Michio, my good friend from the castle has asked me to meet him at the outer guardhouse," Fusao lied. "He's getting married soon and needs some advice from a married man like me.

"Don't go to the castle, Fusao," his mother snapped. "Our lives are peaceful now and it's better you stay away from that place. Besides, your father won't like it if you go there again."

"It's ok, mother, I'm not going into the castle. they wouldn't let me in anyway," Fusao replied. "I'm just meeting Michio outside the castle in one of the outer guard houses where the servants are allowed to meet their families. I won't be long and please don't tell father."

With a final promise to return within the hour, he slipped out of the house, his thick fur lined straw boots sinking softly into the freshly fallen snow on the road. He knew in a way his mother was right, he shouldn't go near the castle, even the weather had turned ugly to discourage him from going out of the house but a greater force was pushing him forward and Fusao couldn't have stopped himself even if he wanted to.

He had told the truth when he said he was going to the outer guard house to wait but not for Michio. He was going to wait there in the empty guard house to catch Lord Okimoto on his daily carriage ride to the administrative offices of the samurai a few miles away, come rain, snow or hail. Fusao had worked at the castle long enough to know the young samurai's schedule and that he was a stickler for a planned agenda and never allowed inclement weather conditions to stop him from following it.

Fusao felt strangely light hearted as he plodded slowly along the familiar road leading to the castle, feeling the soft flurry of tiny snowflakes on his face. He could already see Lord Okimoto's smoldering eyes slanting his way. By the time he reached the outer guardhouse, his knees were already shaking, not from the cold but from the fact that every step brought him closer to the place where it had all started.

He noticed with great relief that the outer guardhouse was empty. This was good because he didn't want anyone to recognize him. Fusao could hear the rumble of voices of the guards in the next guardhouse and he quickly slipped into the shadows of the empty outer guardhouse. Fusao could not tell what time it was because the sky was overcast and dark but he knew Lord Okimoto would not have left the castle yet because the big heavy front gate was still open, waiting for his carriage to pass through.

The lack of sleep of the previous night was catching up with Fusao. As he sat waiting on the single hard wooden bench he struggled to stay awake, straining his ears for the familiar sounds of the carriage wheels squeaking and creaking as they rolled over the wooden bridge spanning the moat that surrounded the castle. But today these sounds were muffled by the thick layer of snow on the bridge and Fusao almost missed Lord Okimoto's carriage. It was only the sounds of the horses snorting in the cold that roused him. He sprang to his feet and ran out to the road waving just as the carriage glided towards him.

He saw the curtains of the carriage move and Lord Okimoto's face appeared for a split second. Then the curtains dropped and the carriage moved on, leaving the desolate figure of Fusao behind with the snow raining down on him as he cried out blindly, "He saw me but he moved on as if he didn't know me!"

* * * * *

In the distance, the carriage slowed down as if hesitating and then took off. Inside its dim, protected interior, the young samurai closed his eyes to hold back his tears because he had denied and betrayed his lover again. Frantically, he shouted to his two horsemen to stop but then as the carriage slowed down and prepared to stop, he came to his senses and ordered them to move on.

No, he could not see Fusao because if he did, he would lose himself again and forget that he was first and foremost a samurai and second but no less, a Nobunaga. He had asked himself over and over again how he could have found love in two such ill-fated and impossible places, a man and a peasant. But Lord Okimoto was no ordinary man. He was a samurai and had sworn to uphold an honor that superseded all earthly feelings and desires so he had done the right thing, turned his back on Fusao and moved on..

Chapter Thirty-Nine

The air had grown very still as Lord Okimoto's carriage thundered off and disappeared into the distance, only the lines of hoof and wheel marks remained on the snow to remind Fusao of Lord Okimoto's final rejection. For a long moment, he stood there in the snow, hoping that another carriage would appear and run him down so he could end his life. But there was nothing, only the deafening silence and the tiny snowflakes raining gently down on him. Fusao turned away from the castle and ran blindly down the road towards his home. There was only one thing that could ease the pain in his heart, the precious stack of papers that the old samurai had given him a long time ago He needed to write.

When Fusao reached home, he stood for a long while outside to compose himself. He had promised his mother there would be no trouble today and he couldn't let her see him with tears on his face. Fortunately, the wetness on his face could be passed off as melting snowflakes and his eyes red from sobbing the result of the biting cold and driving winds outside. His mother saw nothing amiss as she came out to help him shake the snow off his outer garments.

"So you met Michio and everything is all right?" she asked scanning his face for any signs of distress.

"Yes, I met him and it was nothing, just a panic attack of nerves before the wedding." Fusao replied and he was amazed at how calm he sounded.

As soon as he could escape from his mother, Fusao went to his room, took out two pieces from his precious stack of papers and began to write.

"Today Lord Okimoto drove past me as if he didn't know me. He has broken my heart and I should hate him. But I can't. I still love him beyond life itself and I have decided that if I can't have him, no one else can."

He reached over to Tomoko's sewing box and took out a needle to prick his finger till a little drop of blood began to ooze out. Fusao smeared the tiny drop of blood on the paper and wrote. "His blood shall be my blood and tonight I will go to the castle and end it all."

The sliding door of the room opened slightly and Fusao hurriedly shoved the papers back into its wooden case. It was Tomoko and she was smiling for the first time in weeks

"Father has allowed me to go back to see my family in Matsumoto," she said happily. "I was supposed to leave today but the weather is so bad he said I should wait until the snow clears so I will leave in three days' time. You don't mind, do you, Fusao?"

"No, of course I don't," Fusao replied. "I know things haven't been easy for you here and spending some time with your family in Matsumoto will lift up your spirits and when you come back, we'll be friends and start all over again."

Tomoko's face cleared and she laid a hand timidly on her husband's yukata sleeve ,still damp from the snow outside.

"Thank you, Fusao," she said. "Yes, I know things haven't been good between us since… since… you know… but as you said, when I return, we will forget about everything and start afresh."

On an impulse, Fusao went over and hugged his wife. This time she didn't resist or flinch away. Tomoko felt so fresh and young, filled with innocence and goodness as he had once been and Fusao vowed that he would protect her so that sweet innocence could never be sullied as his had been.

Yuko, who had come to call them for hot tea and the red bean paste cakes she had just made, saw their embrace through the open sliding door and smiled.

* * * * *

Towards nightfall, it stopped snowing and a shivery moon appeared in the sky, throwing slivers of silver light across the snow covered roads and fields. Fusao had never seen such a beautiful night.

It was a night for lovers that reminded Fusao of another similar beautiful moonlit night when he had run across the castle grounds with wings on his feet to the teahouse to meet Lord Okimoto and his eyes filled with tears.

A tiny sparrow flew across and landed on the branch of a tree just outside his window, its head cocked to one side and looking at him whimsically as if to ask whether he was doing the right thing.

"Go away, bird," Fusao said, trying to wave the sparrow off but the plucky little creature strangely stood its ground and continued to stare at him and, uncomfortable under its ridiculous scrutiny, Fusao slammed the paper screen shut and went back to the room where Tomoko had fallen into a deep sleep after taking a herbal remedy for her cold.

He did not go to his futon because he could not risk falling asleep so he sat in the corner of the room, huddled under a blanket and waiting until he was sure his mother was fast asleep. Thank God, his father was away at an agricultural event in the next village because he was a very light sleeper and got up at the slightest noise. From the paper screen doors of his room, Fusao saw his mother snuffing out the oil lamps and going into her room. His heart began to race. He knew that she fell asleep quickly and was a sound sleeper, hardly moving in her futon until the magic hour of six in the morning when she got up like clockwork every single day, even when she was sick. He wouldn't have to wait long to creep out of the house and take one last walk to the castle. He heard the familiar sounds of his mother's gentle snores, Fusao knew it was time.

With a final glance at his sleeping wife, Fusao left the room and made his way to the kitchen where his mother kept her hochos, her knives, in a big wooden pail.

Selecting a long hocho with the deceptively thin but lethally sharp blade that was necessary to slice raw fish to perfection, Fusao hid it under his yukata and softly left the house, throwing on the same outer garment he had used that morning.

It was already past midnight and there was not a soul in the dead quiet and empty streets, only the hazy moon sailing across the sky. It gave him light and showed him the way to the castle. The chilly air bit into his skin and he stumbled several times on the slippery ice covered road but Fusao kept on going, wincing as the sharp tip of the knife hidden under his clothes grazed his stomach. Tonight he would end it all and free himself of this torture that had gripped him for so long.

If only Lord Okimoto had shown him any sign of compassion, recognition and love that morning, he would still be able to take more suffering but he had rejected Fusao, swept him away as if he was nothing more significant than a pesky insect in summer and this was on the heels of the devastating news that Lady Sachiko was pregnant. Yes, Lord Okimoto had coldly cut him off and as Fusao thought about that, the anger built up in him again, strengthening his resolve to finish off first his samurai lover and then himself.

Fusao knew that he could not gain admission to the castle through the normal way because most of the guards knew he had been driven out of the castle by Lady Momoe so if he failed to get in, the only other way was through a secret passage Lord Okimoto had shown him once. If he was turned away, he would wait until the guards stationed nearest to the entrance were distracted by the changing of shifts and slip in through a side door and make straight for the door of the secret passage.

For a moment Fusao felt a pang of remorse. No one, not even the guards, knew about the secret passage. Lord Okimoto had trusted him enough to show it to him and now Fusao might have to use this trust against him.

"No, I cannot stop now," he told himself. "If I can't have him, no one else must have him, Lord Okimoto belongs to me!"

The weather was on his side tonight and because it was so cold, the guards were huddled around the stove inside the guardhouses and not patrolling much. Fusao was able to reach the main entrance without any incident.

The two soldiers standing guard there looked familiar and Fusao prayed they would remember him and let him in.

There was a rush of footsteps as the chief guard appeared and signaled to the soldiers to let him in, informing them that it was Fusao, the samurai's personal servant.

He had a moment of anxiety as one of the soldiers started to protest that he thought Fusao had been dismissed from the castle and how they should check with the samurai before letting him inside the castle.

But it was a bitterly cold night and the chief guard was in a foul mood and took offence at being talked back by a minor soldier under his command so he growled, "I said let him in, or there will be hell to pay if we insult one of Lord Okimoto's protégés."

"Yes sir," the soldier replied and waved Fusao reluctantly past the check-point.

Fusao's heart was thudding wildly against his rib cage as he crept down the dark courtyard, stumbling over the uneven stone surface as he headed towards the east wing and Lord Okimoto's chambers. He negotiated the complicated maze of passages with ease. He remembered that to get to Lord Okimoto's bedroom, he would have to pass through at least two bodyguards but Fusao knew the bodyguards, lured by the confidence that they were inside the castle and didn't have much danger, were always slumped into various stages of falling asleep. He was right. Lord Okimoto's bodyguards were asleep and so Fusao managed to slip by them and into Lord Okimoto's room without much difficulty.

It was dark but he could see from the moonlight streaming into a corner of the room, the peacefully sleeping form of Lord Okimoto and a deep anger rose in Fusao again. How dare he sleep so soundly while Fusao himself lay night after night tortured by the pain of their impossible love? Lord Okimoto moved and stretched out his hand, for his wife, Fusao thought, and with a cry of pain like a wounded animal, he lifted the knife and drove it deep into the chest of the sleeping samurai. It was only when he had struck a second blow that Fusao realized that there was no one else in the room, Lord Okimoto had been sleeping alone and the words on his lips before he cried out in pain was "Fusao... Fusao, you have come!"

In deep anguish, Fusao threw down the hocho and whispered, "What have I done? What have I done?" as Lord Okimoto lay, writhing in pain, the pool of blood slowly spreading across the tatami floor of the room.

The screams and moans of pain had alerted the bodyguards and they charged in, swords drawn, shouting out in horror at the sight of the samurai they were supposed to protect covered in his own blood and the man they recognized as his former personal servant, cradling his head and moaning like a half crazed animal.

"Get away from Lord Okimoto, you filthy animal!" one of the guards shouted, kicking Fusao away from the bleeding samurai. "Call the physician, hurry, he is losing a lot of blood!"

"Take this man away and lock him up in the holding room. We'll inform Lady Momoe of what has happened and decide what to do with him later," the chief bodyguard ordered and Fusao felt himself pulled up and dragged away by two heavily armed guards.

His last glimpse was of Lord Okimoto's deadly white face and what sounded like "No... no... no..." coming from the young Samurai's gaping mouth.

Chapter Forty

In her chambers, Lady Momoe was near collapse, hyperventilating from the news that her son had been stabbed by his former personal servant, Fusao and was in a critical condition. Her first thought was Lady Sachiko and the baby she could lose in what had proved to be a difficult pregnancy if she received such shocking news. If anything happened to Lord Okimoto, it was all the more vital that the baby survived, especially if it was a boy. Summoning all her strength, Lady Momoe called the chief guard and ordered that no news of what had happened should get to Lady Sachiko and anyone leaking information of her son's stabbing would be severely punished.

The physicians were attending to the severely wounded young samurai and there was nothing much she could do but wait. Earlier, the guards had come to ask for permission to kill the peasant who had dared to stab Lord Okimoto but Lady Momoe had stopped them. She didn't think that death was enough punishment for Fusao because that was probably what he wanted. No, death would not come to the servant boy so soon.

"Do you want us to execute the peasant for the crime he committed against our Lord Okimoto?" Jiro asked, his head bowed low for his unpardonable failure of duty to protect the young samurai.

"No, I don't want him killed. He should live to suffer for what he did to the samurai," Lady Momoe replied.

"I beg to offer my opinion but Fusao committed the most serious crime of all, harming our great lord samurai with intention to kill him so he deserves death," Jiro replied, surprised that Lady Momoe had chosen to spare the life of her son's attacker.

"Oh yes, I have a punishment all prepared for him," Lady Momoe replied and her lips were set in a thin, hard line giving her the steely, almost cruel look that those who crossed her feared most.

* * * * *

Fusao was dragged along several dark passages to a remote part of the castle where servants were locked up and punished for all kinds of misbehavior. He had heard about the dark cold cells when one of the servants who served in the kitchens had been locked up there for weeks and flogged for stealing. when the servant was released, his pale and gaunt face told the others what he had gone through and, certainly, he never stole again.

But Fusao did not care what happened to him. He thought of Lord Okimoto's face as he saw Fusao's hocho coming for him. Images of red rivers of blood flowing out of his lover's body flashed in front of him as he was kicked into a damp cold room and a heavy wooden bar was pushed into place to lock him in. Fusao lay where he was thrown in a stupor and waited for them to come back to kill him. He wanted to die, what he had done deserved nothing less than death. If they didn't execute him, he would kill himself, use the hocho that still had Lord Okimoto's blood on it to commit hara kiri.

Fusao reached inside his yukata and started to cry. There was no hocho because they had taken it from him.

Desperate, he banged and shook the door shouting, "Give me back my hocho! I want to commit hara kiri, I want to die with my Lord Okimoto… give me back my hocho… please… please…"

But there was no answer, only his own voice echoing down the long empty corridor and although he continued to shake the door, the sturdy wooden bar held fast Eventually Fusao passed out in a heap and slumped against the door.

When he awoke, he could see the tiny pin pricks of light through the tiny hairpin cracks in the roof high above the icy damp and dark cell and knew it was morning. His mouth felt cracked and dry and the cold floor had seeped through his thin clothes throughout the night to turn his body into an icy block that moved automatically but couldn't seem to feel anything.

Fusao was disappointed he was still alive. He had dreamed that night that both Okimoto sama and he had passed on to another world where their love was accepted and they didn't have to hide from anyone or be forced into marriages just to please society. In that dream, they had lived openly together, held hands and embraced publicly and no one respected them less for being doseiai but now facing the cold, unfriendly walls of the holding cell, Fusao realized that it had been just that, a dream and nothing more..

The hours passed and it seemed as if everyone had forgotten about him. Fusao drifted in and out of sleep, his tongue so dry that it practically filled his whole mouth. As his stomach growled and churned with hunger, it occurred to him that maybe this was the punishment Lady Momoe had ordered for him, slow death by starvation. But it did not bother him. In his feverish brain, death was his ultimate goal and how it was achieved did not matter. The more he suffered, the better.

Whenever he thought of Lord Okimoto, he would get a panic attack, screaming for someone to let him out so that he could find out whether the samurai was still alive. He had been so wrong. Lord Okimoto had never stopped loving him and even as he lay there bleeding, he had tried to stop the guards from kicking the peasant who had stabbed him.

Needing to inflict pain on himself, Fusao started to bang his head on the floor until he tasted blood and only then did he stop.

At around noon, he heard footsteps and voices along the corridor and he started to tremble. Someone was coming to get him and he would learn soon enough his fate. The heavy wooden bar was pulled out and four guards entered the room.

"Get up, peasant," one of them said. "We're taking you home."

"Home?" Fusao cried." Have I been allowed to return home?"

"You will see," another said and pulled him roughly to his feet, wrinkling his nose and twitching disgustedly at the faint stench of urine from the far corner of the room where Fusao had relieved himself when he could not hold back any more.

No one bothered to give him water or warm outer clothing. Fusao walked all the way back to his house hunched between two guards shivering in the cold. He noticed one of the guards, a young man he had briefly met while working at the castle, nervously wetting his lips almost the entire journey.

Desperate for news about Lord Okimoto, Fusao pressed the guard he was acquainted with to ask what had happened to him.

"He is still critical but according to the physicians, he will live," the young guard replied, looking straight ahead.

"Don't talk to him," the other guard replied giving Fusao a rough push. "He's owed no answers!"

Fusao slipped on the snow covered road from the push and was flung against a roadside tree but he hardly felt anything, not even humiliation at being treated like an animal. All he cared about was that Lord Okimoto wasn't going to die. He had no idea why he was being brought home without any apparent punishment for his unpardonable crime and it wasn't like Lady Momoe to leave such a serious attempt on her son's life unpunished. Something was wrong here but Fusao was beyond caring.

As they approached the house, his stomach dropped. He began to worry about his parents and how they were going to accept what he had done. Like everyone else in the village, they put the samurai and his family on a pedestal and idolized them for being in control of all the things they could never have such as unconditional power, vast lands and immense wealth. Naoki and Yuko would never be able to live down that their only son had attempted to kill the young samurai, especially if word got around the village.

Even before they arrived, his mother had opened the front door and ran out to Fusao, crying. When she saw his soiled clothes and bloodied face, "What happened to you? Was there an accident? We are sick with worry over you because you went out last night and never returned! Oh, Fusao, what are we going to do with you? When are you going to stop making us worry like this? Thank Goodness your father is still away! "

The bigger of the guards brushed past her and demanded, "Where is your wife, peasant?"

"My wife? You mean Tomoko?" Fusao stammered.

"Yes, your wife. Where is she?"

"What do you want Tomoko for? Please don't hurt her, I committed the crime and I should suffer any punishment that has been ordered, take me, take my life but please leave Tomoko alone!" Fusao cried. "She had nothing to do with all this!"

Tomoko came into the room, and Fusao saw the guard looking her up and down, a strange light in his eyes.

Without a word, he caught hold of her arm and pushed her into another room sliding the door shut behind him so hard it shook.

Fusao and his mother sprang into action as the horror of what he intended to do to Tomoko dawned on them but the younger guard barred the way, his sharp lethal katana drawn.

As they heard Tomoko's pleas and then screams in the next room,

Fusao and Yuko threw themselves at the guard clawing at him to get to the other room to help poor Tomoko, but the guard was too strong and easily held them back with his muscular arms and katana.

"Please stop him, stop this crime against a defenseless girl," Fusao screamed. "I was the one who did wrong, punish me, cut up all my organs, dig out my eyes, anything, but don't hurt my poor innocent wife! Please, let her go!"

"Stay back, Fusao," the guard replied pushing Fusao back with the tip of his sword. "This is the punishment Lady Momoe has ordered for you."

The screams and sobs from the next room became louder and more hysterical.

"Lady Momoe ordered this?" Fusao shouted. "No, let me in! Let me in!" He lurched forward but the guard's katana slashed him across the arm and he fell to the floor, writhing with pain.

"Curse, I am a curse for everyone, even Tomoko," he screamed and he was still screaming the words over and over again when the door opened and the guard emerged, smirking as he adjusted his clothes.

Strolling over to Fusao, he spat contemptuously and said, "What a little tigress, your woman is, peasant!"

Laughing, he rubbed his loins appreciatively and nodded to the other guard to follow as he left the house.

When they had gone, Yuko hurried over to Fusao stemming the flow of blood with her yukata sash and whispered, "What have you done to us? It's your obsession with the samurai that has brought this on all of us."

"Why did you go to the castle? Why didn't you listen to us?"

* * * * *

She got up and stumbled to the next room where Tomoko lay weeping softly on the tatami floor. There were blood stains on the rumpled futon and Yuko gasped as she realized that Tomoko had been a virgin after five months of marriage with her son! Poor child, what pain she must have suffered being ravaged like that by that big burly guard. Worst of all, Lady Momoe had ordered this bestial deed to be done. What kind of woman could cause something like that to happen to another woman and one so young and innocent just to punish a man? At that point, she didn't even think of the implications of Tomoko still being a virgin, her grief for what had happened was so great.

Yuko gathered her dazed daughter in law into her arms and the two women wept silently together. If there was any moment in her life that Yuko could bring herself to hate her son, it was now. It was all his fault, his obsession with the samurai and the castle that had brought this down on them, how many times had they warned him that, for peasants, samurai were to be worshipped from afar? How many times had they told him to stay away from the castle and let go?

"How many times?" Yuko wept.

Then she softened, actually it had been the old samurai who had come looking for the peasant boy who could write and his son had later taken their relationship to more sinister heights so it wasn't entirely Fusao's fault. He hadn't been able to resist the glamorous lure of the castle and the attentions of someone like Lord Okimoto but then which poor peasant boy born into a Spartan life of toil and making ends meet could?

* * * * *

Long after the guards had left and his mother and Tomoko remained cloistered in the next room, Fusao stood rooted to the same spot. If Lady Momoe wanted to humiliate him and make him look small and totally ineffective, she had succeeded. Fusao didn't know how he was going to face his mother and his wife who had been brutally ravaged because of him. Would they ever forgive him?

And suddenly Fusao realized that it was truly over, the special relationship between him and the samurai. He didn't know whether this was the end of his punishment or there was more to come but he could never again go to the castle or see Lord Okimoto. The peasant and the samurai had a beautiful dream but now it was over and they had been defeated in the end. As they always knew they would be…

Fusao decided that he would leave society behind, go to the monastery in the mountains and become a monk, it was the only way he could face life. Death was no longer an option because it was a coward's way out and he needed to live and suffer.

Chapter Forty-One

Mayumi was finding it more difficult to decipher the characters on the latter half of the bundle of Edo period papers she had come to call simply "the diary" because they were now written haphazardly often with blotches of what looked like drops of water or perhaps teardrops. She couldn't be sure but the patches blotched up the characters and made them difficult to decipher.

But the untidy, disjointed characters and sentences threw some light to the very disturbed and disorientated state of mind of the writer and his desperation and distress reached out across hundreds of years to touch Mayumi immensely.

"Poor guy," she told her cat, Miki. "All this suffering in the name of love!"

What she had managed to translate into modern language told a very tragic story of an old Edo period struggle with forbidden homosexual love across another forbidden zone, the mixing of strictly defined social and class lines. Although she had not reached the end of the whole stack of papers, she knew that the end would be merciless and cruel and it was not difficult to guess who would receive the brunt of that cruel end.

Her thoughts drifted idly to the proprietor of the teahouse she and Toyoki had visited a couple of weeks ago. Was there a link between him and one of the players of this Edo period drama? Mayumi remembered he had mentioned something about the teahouse being acquired by one of his ancestors and cursed herself for not asking any questions. she had been too excited about being in the very teahouse where Fusao and his samurai lover had arranged their secret trysts, to focus properly. She would have to return to the teahouse again to find out any possible link if nothing turned up in the diary.

Mayumi was casually shifting through the next few pieces of paper when her eyes caught one particular piece which had brown stains smeared right across and upon closer scrutiny, she realized with a shock that the stains looked suspiciously like dried blood. Was it possible that she was looking at the blood stains of someone who lived centuries ago?

The beeping of the alarm clock reminded her that she had to get ready for her monthly dinner date with Sayuri.

"I know what," she said. "I'll bring this to show Sayuri and let's see whether she agrees with me that it's dried blood."

For the first time Mayumi was actually reluctant to leave the apartment to meet her closest friend, Sayuri, because she wanted to start deciphering the page with the stains straight away. Even Miki, her cat, expressed displeasure when he saw her dressing to go out, by sulking in a corner and swishing his long tail in obvious protest. Poor Miki, she was always neglecting him when a new case took a lot out of her as this one was.

"I'll make it up to you soon, Miki chan," Mayumi called out to the cat but he ignored her and grunted as if to say "Promises, promises!" and she smiled, despite herself, dear Miki, he could be so human sometimes!

On an impulse, she went over and picked him up, rubbing his belly and smothering him with kisses until he thawed a little.

"I need you so much to love me, you little imp," she said as she set her cat down and handed him a piece of his favorite snack and another few pieces hidden around the apartment for him to find later. That was the game they played sometimes when she had to go out and Miki cooperated fully, starting the treasure hunt only after she had left.

But as soon as she stepped out of the apartment, Mayumi was glad she was out, and away from old diaries and a time machine that was playing havoc with her imagination. It was already well into spring and still light at six in the evening and the sight of housewives hurrying home with shopping carts from nearby supermarkets made her feel strangely happy and comfortable.

They had decided to go suburban this time and arranged to meet at a nearby family restaurant called "The Royal Host." Sayuri had dressed to suit the environment in a simple light sweater over denim jeans and hair held back in a pony tail with a blue scrunchie and minimal makeup.

"I know, I know," she said sheepishly to Mayumi's raised eyebrows. "But the truth is that my latest boyfriend is Spanish and he says Japanese girls put on too much make up even to nip across to the supermarket and European men are uncomfortable with that so I'm trying to tone down just to make him happy."

"Look at me," she rolled her eyes. "I feel like a frump and kind of naked without my make up! Well, I guess when the romance wears off, the make-up will come right back on!"

"But actually, you do look quite sweet without all that make up, you know, fresh and younger," Mayumi replied and she meant it, Sayuri did look really fresh faced and pretty without her trade mark dyed hair and heavy eye shadow.

After they had placed their orders and exchanged the latest news about each other and mutual friends, Mayumi took out the precious piece of paper and showed it to Sayuri.

"Look at this," she said. "Would you say they are blood stains?"

Her friend became serious immediately and took the paper from Mayumi, handling it with reverent care and wonder at having such an authentic piece of history in her hands.

"Wow, this is really something," she whispered and peered closely at the stains Mayumi had pointed out, even putting the paper to her nose as if by doing that, she could smell blood that had been spilled hundreds of years ago.

"So what do you think?" Mayumi asked again. "I haven't deciphered the contents yet but my gut feeling is that the writer wrote this entry in deep distress over a traumatic event and cut himself as an expression of his pain and sorrow."

Sayuri examined the stains again and nodded, "Yes, I think you're right, I'm sure it's blood."

"It's amazing, isn't it, that we are touching blood spilled from a man who lived hundreds of years ago," Mayumi said. "This is the most awesome thing about history and being a historian!"

Mayumi told Sayuri about the teahouse and her feeling that the proprietor was somehow related to Fusao, the writer of the diary.

"Don't ask me why and how," she said. "I just get this feeling about people sometimes, call it the sixth sense if you want."

"But that's kind of impossible that he could be a direct descendant because remember Fusao was gay and presumably couldn't have children." Sayuri reminded her.

"Yes, I know but I just have this hunch so I guess I will find out as I continue deciphering these old scripts," Mayumi replied. "I'll probably go back to the teahouse to talk to that proprietor to trace the ancestor he said acquired the place."

Both of them had been so caught up in the script that they practically spent the entire night analyzing it and it was almost 11 p.m. by the time they left the restaurant. The two friends parted at the station with Mayumi's promise to keep Sayuri informed of the events surrounding the blood stained page when she had got it done.

Chapter Forty-Two

"I forbid you to go to the monastery and become a monk," Naoki thundered, banging his fist so hard on the table that the little plates of pickles shook. "You will not escape your responsibilities to your wife or have you forgotten you have one? She is with child, your child, and how can you think of leaving her to join the monastery?"

His wife sat across the table, her face ashen as she prayed that he would never find out the truth about Tomoko's pregnancy and what had happened that day he was away. She shuddered as she remembered that terrible day when a guard had been sent by Lady Momoe to rape Tomoko and she and Fusao had begged her not to tell Naoki anything when he returned.

For a while Tomoko had been traumatized by the incident and withdrawn into herself, sometimes weeping silently in her room until the weather cleared and she was able to make the trip back to Matsumoto to see her family. Fusao had cried when she left. If only Tomoko had gone back on the day she planned and hadn't been held back by the snow, none of this would have happened. And with time, Lady Momoe would have calmed down and realized the inhumanity of her plan and opted to take Fusao's life instead or inflict extreme pain on him in some other way.

With Tomoko back in her family home, Fusao and his mother tried to put the terrible day of the rape behind but nothing was ever the same between them again. Fusao went back to the rice fields with his father but he could not focus, he had the strange premonition that they had all not seen the end of the incident, and in some way he would still have to pay for his sins.

And despite everything, he could not stop thinking about Lord Okimoto and every night he poured out his sorrows on a new sheet of paper from his wooden file.

"If I love him, I should forget him and pretend that I killed him that night in the castle but it's so hard when there is still so much longing in this heart."

"Why am I this way? Why can't I forget or hate someone who has brought me so much pain?"

"I have decided to join the monastery in the mountains in Niigata and live the rest of my life in religious seclusion to atone for my sins. It's the only way I can get Lord Okimoto out of my head and soon I must speak to father about it."

But the days passed into weeks and still Fusao could not pluck up enough courage to speak to his father about his decision to become a monk, not even when they worked side by side in the rice fields. Then fate stepped in one Sunday morning when Naoki brought up the subject that Fusao should go to Matsumoto to fetch his wife back because she had been away too long and the neighbors would be talking soon about her prolonged absence.

Fusao's heart sank because Tomoko's absence had enabled him and Yuko to live with what had happened the previous month and he knew that he had to discuss his desire to become a monk that day or let it go forever.

He was about to broach the subject when there was a loud banging on the door and Naoki opened it to a foot messenger who said he had a message from Matsumoto. As they spoke, Naoki's eyes widened in disbelief and then his face broke into a beautiful smile. Fusao's father seldom smiled but when he did, he brought sunshine into the darkest of rooms and after the messenger had gone, he literally danced to the table in a very rare moment of jubilation to break the news for his happiness to his wife and son.

"The messenger came from Tomoko's family in Matsumoto and we have some good news in this family at last. Tomoko is pregnant!"

The silence that followed was so resounding that they could hear the sharp intake of breath from Fusao and his mother's chopsticks sliding slowly to the floor. "Oh Naoki, do you really mean that? Tomoko is pregnant?" His mother cried.

"Of course I mean that! One cannot make any mistake about such news," Naoki replied happily and looked at Fusao, "For the first time in a long while, this is something you have done right by this family!"

Fusao said nothing because he couldn't trust himself to speak and because he was stunned by the form his "punishment" had taken. Lady Momoe had won after all, she had ensured there would be a specter to haunt him for life and he would never escape the scar of that night. Now there would always be a living reminder of their night of shame and dishonor. A kind of panic seized him and he started to laugh and the harder he tried to stop himself, the more hysterical his laughter got.

Alarmed his mother went over and shook him whispering, "Pull yourself together or your father will suspect something is up!"

Her words of caution pierced through the fumes of bitter confusion and Fusao recovered his composure sufficiently to say, "I am overjoyed, father, at the news. Can you see how I can't stop laughing with joy?"

Yuko looked at her husband's smiling face and was relieved that he hadn't noticed Fusao's strange response. She knew how lost and confused her son had to be feeling because she too felt faint and unprepared to cope with this new twist in their misfortunes. In the days and nights to come, Yuko asked herself, could she ever accept and love a "grandchild" who was conceived not of the blood of her son but from the brutal rape of Tomoko by a nameless, faceless guard? Tomoko has asked whether she can stay on with her family for another month and in view of her pregnancy, I have agreed. It's probably wiser, anyway, for her not to travel until the pregnancy has stabilized," Naoki went on, blissfully unaware of the undercurrents flowing between his son and wife.

And suddenly, before he could stop himself, Fusao found himself blurting out, "Father, I want to ask your permission to join the monastery in Niigata."

His father was silent for a moment and then he spoke, "Are you out of your mind? Did you not hear what I just said, that you are going to be a father? And is this your response, that you prefer to shake off all responsibilities of fatherhood and escape to a monastery? Why, Fusao, why must you spoil even this moment of great joy for your family?"

"Don't be too harsh on him, please, Naoki," Yuko interceded. "I think the news was just a great shock to us and he's saying things on impulse."

"Don't be stupid, woman!" Naoki retorted. "I really don't see what is so shocking about the news, a young man gets married and before long, his wife is pregnant, it's a very normal and expected cycle of life! I forbid you to join the monastery, Fusao, you are to stay here and take your responsibilities seriously like a man. If you go against my wishes, you are no longer my son."

"And instead of spending your time thinking of how to escape, you should start thinking about building an extra room at the back of the house now that we will have a new addition to the family," he added.

For a long moment Fusao was silent and his mother held her breath, oh God, was he going to rebel and blurt out everything and irrevocably destroy Naoki's spirit and faith in his family? He had never directly discussed their son's homosexual tendencies with her because it was a subject he was thoroughly ashamed of but Yuko knew that it was always there, a shadow over all of them and Tomoko's pregnancy meant more than just acquiring a grandchild. It meant that there was hope Fusao was growing out of his unnatural and socially unacceptable sexual orientations and becoming normal.

She looked at Fusao beseechingly, her eyes telling him not to go against his father, at least not yet because he didn't know the full circumstances of Tomoko's pregnancy or that she had been a virgin when she was raped.

It was on the tip of Fusao's tongue to defy his father and press on ahead but he saw the pleas on his mother's terrified face and he relented. In the end, he just couldn't do it because he had already caused Yuko so much pain and it wasn't fair to leave her to Naoki's wrath and live with their dreadful secret alone if he just walked off and did what he wanted.

So he swallowed hard and replied, "I'm sorry, father, I don't know what came over me. You're right. Of course, I should stay here and be with Tomoko and the baby, this monastery thing was an idea I was toying with before but now that Tomoko is pregnant, everything has to change."

Naoki's face cleared and he smiled, "Good! That's exactly what I want to hear from you. Tomorrow we start making plans to build that extra room at the back. Just imagine, a grandchild in this house at last!"

Fusao let his father talk on about his plans to extend the house, hardly listening to what was going on except that his mother was distracting herself with unnecessary chores, obviously relieved that a major crisis had been averted. Beyond that, neither of them wanted to think about anything else.

It was only much later when his parents had retired to their room for the night that all the angry thoughts came crowding into his mind. Lady Momoe had succeeded in trapping him in a lifetime of suffering and guilt worse than death itself and there was no escape. She hadn't wanted him to die and now Fusao knew why, she had planned a far worse fate for him that had robbed him of the chance to find peace in a monastery.

How would he live with the pain of his unrequited love for Lord Okimoto and having to accept a child from the rape of his wife as a punishment for his sins?

Chapter Forty-Three

The castle was alive with excitement again, one that was far greater even than Lord Okimoto's wedding more than a year ago because in a matter of weeks, his first child was to be born and the temples had seen more worshippers recently, all praying for a boy and heir for the Nobunaga family. Certainly Lady Momoe who had a very big stake here prayed harder than anyone else.

For quite a few months, the young samurai had not been seen in public and rumors had it that he had been badly injured in a horse riding accident and was recuperating. When he did finally appear, apart from a dramatic weight loss, Lord Okimoto didn't look any worse off physically but the servants who served him closely noticed a change in him. The young outgoing and confident samurai had become quiet and withdrawn and wasn't interested in anything around him, not even the forthcoming birth of his child brought him any joy. Instead he seemed to have developed a strange obsession with sword fighting and spoke frequently about traveling to the north to join a very prominent school there.

"After the baby is born, please," Lady Momoe pleaded with him and he reluctantly agreed but he wasn't happy. Lady Momoe's maids gossiped in the kitchens that the young couple didn't share the same room but perhaps it was understandable because Lady Sachiko was very heavily pregnant and needed all the rest she could get. It had not been an easy pregnancy and Lady Sachiko had been depressed and weepy for most of it although no one could understand why.

Lord Okimoto eventually ordered a private bathroom to be built for himself because he hated to show anyone the deep scar that ran right across his stomach, legacy of the night Fusao had crept into his room and stabbed him. At first he had felt deep anger against Fusao for this betrayal of his love and trust and as he lay there writhing in pain and high fever from the wounds, often slipping in and out of consciousness, his lover's face haunted him, pleading with him for forgiveness and understanding of the insane pain that had driven him to this. But it was only later when the messenger he sent out frequently to obtain news of Fusao came back with the information that Fusao's wife too was pregnant that Lord Okimoto understood at last the pain that could drive a person desperately in love to insanity.

As he hovered between life and death, the physicians worked day and night to keep the infection from the hocho wounds under control and it was during this period of heavy sedation from the pain relieving herbs that were forced down his throat in great quantities that Lord Okimoto saw images of his life passing by him, a weak ineffective samurai who could not assert his absolute authority to take what he wanted and wrench the control of his life back from his mother.

And suddenly Lord Okimoto realized that he had never wanted to be grand samurai and didn't have the capacity to make great sacrifices the way his mother had. He was doseiai, an incurable homosexual that his family was ashamed of and he was better off fading into some obscure place with no remarkable future demanded or expected of him. Or he could stop wallowing in self-pity and use whatever energy he had into turning the Nobunaga family and the samurai legacy into even greater heights to pass the torch on to the son he hoped Lady Sachiko was carrying. Either way, he could never see Fusao again. That love was forbidden, even to a samurai, and would exist only in their hearts and memories. But there was one thing he could do. He could reopen their teahouse. The haunting beauty of the place should not be kept hidden, like his love for Fusao but stand, proud and noble, a monument to their forbidden love.

On the seventh day, the physicians finally drained out all the poisons from Lord Okimoto's body and his fever subsided. He was declared on the road to physical recovery but the soul of the most powerful and important man in the prefecture who had been almost fatally stabbed by the man he loved more than anyone else, would stay wounded for a long time.

True to a half conscious decision made while he was still burning up with fever, Lord Okimoto ordered the re-opening of the teahouse that had hosted his many trysts with Fusao. As soon as he was well enough, and much to his mother's surprise, Lord Okimoto led a team of builders and carpenters to the abandoned building and personally saw to a complete overhaul of the teahouse. Within a matter of weeks, all the cracks were repaired, the dried up pond filled with water and colorful carp once again and the weeds and undergrowth in the garden replaced with azalea shrubs which would burst into a stunning glory of blood red flowers in summer.

It was sometimes used by Lady Momoe and her guests for small tea parties that were filled with music and songs, but Lord Okimoto himself seldom joined these happy occasions, preferring to wander there at night to sit by the pond, a solitary figure watching the fishes fussing around in the water.

On a blistery autumn afternoon, Lady Sachiko went into labor and the whole castle waited with abated breath for the baby's sex to be known. Numerous bets had already been placed all the way from the snooty personal staff of the Nobunaga family right down to the most minor of kitchen hands and a lot of money was at stake, to be won or lost in a matter of hours.

Just as the pregnancy had been difficult, the birth was no less easier and Lady Momoe spent almost the entire time in the castle shrine praying for safe delivery of the child and that it would be a healthy boy. If it was a girl, she didn't know what she was going to do to get Lady Sachiko pregnant again.

It was a nightmare situation and a time of great stress for Lady Momoe and deep inside the decent part of her, there was a gnawing guilt for what she had done to the peasant boy and his family. Perhaps she had been wrong because after all, it was her son, the samurai who had made the first move in this illicit liaison. But the deed was done and Lady Momoe tried to put it behind her and prayed that her wickedness would not be punished by the birth of a granddaughter instead of the heir she had sold her soul to the devil for.

"How," she had asked herself a thousand times in the quiet lonely hours of the night, "is it possible that any woman, least of all me, will ever find herself in a situation where she has to arrange for her daughter in law to get pregnant by another man to secure an heir for her husband's dynasty?"

"And how," was another question she agonized over day after day, week after week, year after year and never got an answer, "did I produce a homosexual son? Please Kami, is it something I did that I must be punished for?"

Right now as she knelt before the shrine, she was asking the same questions again, this time adding a new plea that after years of living with the agony of that day when Okimoto was 16 years old and she caught him intimately touching the body of a 15 year old messenger boy whom he had invited into his room, she deserved to have her prayers answered. Thankfully the boy was a messenger from a distant province and did not need to be bribed or intimidated into silence.

Lady Momoe had gone to her room and became sick but eventually she decided not to share her discovery with her husband knowing how devastated he would be so she bore that terrible knowledge in silence, her blood rising every time she saw her son with a man, no matter how innocent the encounter.

She was still at the shrine placing joss sticks on the big copper urn in front and letting the fragrant fumes wash all over her when rushing footsteps announced the arrival of Yumi, her personal maid and the only person allowed to disturb her with urgent news during her sessions at the shrine.

"My Lady, my lady, the baby is born!" she announced breathlessly.

Lady Momoe leapt up and grabbed the maid by the shoulders almost shaking her in her excitement.

"Tell me, quick! Is it a boy?" she asked and her voice was shaking.

"Yes, my lady! It's a boy! A fine boy and crying so loudly everyone is amazed!"

Even before the maid had finished speaking, Lady Momoe had rushed from the shrine to the room specially prepared for Lady Sachiko's labor. Her heart was singing with a relief that was overwhelming, her plan had worked and they had their heir and what mattered even more than that was she did not need to go through the despicable circumstances surrounding the baby's conception again.

"Thank you, Kami-sama, thank you," she whispered as she reached Lady Sachiko's room where a group of excited servants were gathered but they quickly dispersed as soon as they saw her.

Lord Okimoto was no way in sight and for a moment her joy was tempered with irritation at her son. He could at least stick around and give them some face, after all she had gone through to the extent of taking over his reproductive responsibilities so he could continue to be a homosexual and turn his back on women.

But her anger evaporated at once when she saw the tiny red wailing baby who would be the next samurai and as the midwife placed the infant in her arms, a powerful energy flowed into her and she knew this samurai was going to be all right. He would be a complete man as Lord Okimoto had never been and the vitality of the house of Nobunaga would be restored at last.

Although the baby would have to go through a name selection ceremony, Lady Momoe already knew what his name would be.

"Shintaro Nobunaga," she whispered. "My grandson, the next samurai, you must never be like your father!"

Chapter Forty-Four

The day Fusao dreaded finally arrived when Tomoko's family sent a messenger to announce that she would be returning home at the end of the week. He was very unhappy about that message because as long as she was away, he could erase all the bad memories from his mind and pretend that none of it had happened.

In the daily routine of going to the rice fields with his father, Fusao sometimes forgot he was even married and simply dismissed Naoki's frequent conversation about the baby as referring to someone else. He could detach himself from reality and turn back the pages of his life to the time before Lord Okimoto came into his world and for a few years he was caught in a world of glamour, love and a passion he didn't know he was capable of feeling. These days he could get by a whole day without thinking of that life and it was only in the still of night that he would pour his heart out in his writings.

The previous night, there had been a full moon and the silvery world it created had been so achingly beautiful that Fusao's heart had again wandered to a forbidden zone, a similar moon lit night and two lovers kissing in a teahouse. The aching and longing had become so unbearable that he had released it in a poem.

"The same moon casting its silver magic over us
So far apart we have grown
But for one moment in time, we came together
And we were filled with love and passion
But now I am alone
And will always be
For I can never love another."

And now the days of peace and detachment were ebbing away because Tomoko was coming back to haunt him with the fall out of that

216

awful night, the baby growing within her. That was the punishment Lady Momoe wanted for her son's lover, a grim lifelong reminder of that day of reckoning.

He could tell that his mother too was nervous about Tomoko's return because she lived in fear that the young simple girl would unwittingly let slip to Naoki the circumstances of her pregnancy. How was she going to cope with the daily fear of leaving Tomoko alone with her father in law just in case that happened? Was she going to have to keep an eye on them forever? There were days when she felt she simply couldn't take the stress of living on edge every day any longer and considered ending her life but the thought that Fusao and the baby would need her always held her back. She was spending more time at the small shrine she had erected at the back of the house praying Tomoko would take her pregnancy in her stride and not crack up and that peace and contentment would someday soon return to her family again.

Like her more powerful compatriot, Lady Momoe, Yuko spent many a night questioning herself where she and Naoki had gone wrong to produce a son who was socially so sick. She used to look around at all the sons of her neighbors and friends, none of them were like Fusao and she would go to the temple and ask why Kami-sama had chosen her son to mess around with. In fact, before she was forced to confront the problem in her own family, Yuko didn't even know there were homosexuals in Japan!

And now Tomoko was coming home and not a single day would pass without Yuko living in fear that Naoki would find out about the rape and Fusao's part in it. She knew her husband well enough to foresee that he would never be able to take this insult and dishonor to the family and someone's blood would shed for it..

She had seen plenty of it when she was a child in their fishing village in Shimoda. When her father got drunk on sake, he would beat them up and although he would be very remorse about it when he sobered up, the kids especially were scarred for life. Noaki wasn't a violent man but he could lose control if he knew the extent of shame and dishonor Fusao had brought to the family. And who could blame him after the way his patience and tolerance had been tested again and again by his son?

According to the foot messenger, Tomoko had just started out on her journey and given the slow pace they had to travel because of her condition, she would arrive in three days' time. Yuko decided she should intercept her daughter in law before she reached the house to remind her of their pact not to tell Naoki anything. Tomoko was such a simple and guileless girl that if Naoki had any suspicions at all, he could break her down easily to disclose everything to him.

When Yuko was mad at her son, she toyed with the idea of confessing everything to Naoki to lift up this terrible cloud of secrecy and deceit that was getting heavier and harder to bear each day and let Fusao face the brunt of his father's anger. Perhaps if that happened, it would finally make a man of him but she did not because she knew Naoki's formidable temper when his family's honor was challenged.

Blissfully unaware of the undercurrents that were going on in his home, Naoki spent all his free time building the outhouse extension. On top of being an excellent rice farmer, he was also a talented carpenter and builder and by the time Tomoko was due to arrive, the walls of the extra room were up.

He had cleared part of his precious spring onion field to build the extension and even added a small wooden rocking horse to it. Naoki was a serious man and never did anything frivolous or unnecessary or extra unless he was overwhelmed with joy. It broke Fusao's heart to see his father so excited about a baby that wasn't even related to him and he recognized this and every pain he would feel for the rest of his life as the punishing sentence Lady Momoe had passed on him.

That night Fusao's heart strayed once more to Lord Okimoto, and once again, the pain was passed over him in powerful, overwhelming waves and could not be quelled. It became so terrible he struggled with an overwhelming desire to run to the castle just for anything that would be an antidote for this all-consuming pain that came night after night to attack him.

He did the only thing that could help. He took out his wooden file and began to write, feeling the pain slowly ebbing away and giving him relief.

"I wonder what you are doing, my Lord Okimoto? Are you suffering as I do? Are you living with the same pain as I do?"

A few days later, Tomoko arrived home and Fusao noticed at once that she had put on weight and her slim girlish waist had thickened to support a small protrusion in front.

"My baby," he thought. "I've got to start thinking of it as my baby and purge my mind of that thick set guard who fathered the child in such a terrible way."

He rushed out to help Tomoko with her things, carefully avoiding looking at her expanding stomach. Her face was expressionless and the only emotion she showed was exhaustion but when Fusao went over to hug her, Tomoko's face carefully composed crumbled and she started to cry.

"I'm sorry, Fusao," she whispered. "I got pregnant and made everything difficult for everyone here."

A lump rose in Fusao's throat. For a moment he could not speak. What a lovely selfless girl his wife was, apologizing for a condition that she was in no way to be blamed and thinking of him and the family first, above herself. He felt the tears welling up in his eyes too as he thought about how wrong it was for Tomoko to be married to a man like him who could never love her in the way she deserved.

He swallowed hard and replied, keeping his voice low so that his father could not hear.

"Don't cry, Tomoko, it's not your fault,. I should be the one kneeling right before you to ask for forgiveness. The child is innocent so we must all love it as if it was conceived in love and happiness. Look at father, how happy he is. He has even built an extension for us now that the baby is coming! And Tomoko, father doesn't know anything about that day so mother and me are asking you to please don't tell him anything. If he knows the truth, it will just kill him."

Tomoko nodded," Don't worry, Fusao, I will never speak of that day to anyone."

Fusao took her hand and led her to the back of the house saying, "Come, let me show you the extension father has built for us."

They spent a pleasant half hour in "the new wing" of the house with Tomoko clapping her hands in delight at all the extra space they were getting and the amazing workmanship right from the thickly thatched roof down to the tatami mats on the floor.

Yuko prepared a big dinner for them and they even enjoyed meat which was usually reserved for grand occasions. Everyone drank steadily that night except Tomoko because they had their own reasons for wanting to get drunk. Naoki simply because he was happy, Yuko because she wanted to get over the first difficult night by falling asleep in drunken oblivion and Fusao because he wanted to pass out to avoid the awkwardness of sleeping with his wife again.

Life settled into a normal routine with Fusao and his father going off to the rice fields every morning and Yuko and Tomoko tending to the house. As each day passed without incident, Fusao and his mother relaxed. They had done up the extension and Fusao and Tomoko moved there ostensibly to have some privacy. Still, each night they slept on separate futons and made no physical contact. But they did have very companionable conversations and were comfortable with each other as friends. To Fusao's relief, that seemed enough for Tomoko and it certainly made having to sleep with her much more tolerable.

Sometimes Fusao went to a local sake bar to drink and listen to gossip about the samurai and his family. Recently, the men had started to place bets on the sex of the child Lady Sachiko was carrying and sitting there listening to the gossip made Fusao feel that he was back at the castle, working in the kitchens with the buzz of the servants' gossip all around him.

One night, there was great excitement at the bar because Lady Sachiko had gone into labor and those who had wagered on whether the child would be a boy or girl waited for news of the birth and a declaration on the sex of the baby. Fusao knew he should get home as the hours wore on but he had an even better and more intimate reason than the men and their bets to stay and wait for news of the baby's birth.

At around midnight, someone who had a servant working at the castle rushed in screaming, "It's a boy! The samurai has a son and heir!" followed by loud cheers from those who had won their bets and groans from those who had lost.

Fusao weaved through the surging crowds drinking to the health of the new baby boy or collecting their winnings, he had got the information he had waited the whole night for the news and now it was time to go home. After the last few nights of waiting, he felt strangely deflated as he walked slowly home to his own pregnant wife, depressed by how their great love had ended, the samurai back to his position, powerful family and now with a son and heir to have made the sacrifice worthwhile and he back to his peasant family and a wife pregnant with the seed of a castle guard conceived in hatred and revenge and all of them living with this shame for the rest of their lives. Ashes, their great love had become ashes all around them.

The leaves of the trees lining the dusty road whispered taunting words at him.

"Where now is that great love you still can't let go? Where is he who lodges in your heart and refuses to go away?"

"Be quiet, I don't feel anything anymore!" Fusao replied.

"Liar! Liar!" they whispered back. "This will not be the end, there is more to come!"

Fusao shivered and quickened his steps. The dark road with its canopy of trees, usually so beautiful and serene, was giving him the creeps and he wanted to get home as soon as possible.

Even before he arrived home, Fusao had felt the feeling of an oppressive aura looming over him in the distance. when he reached the house, his intuition turned to dread. There was a light in the living area. By now, usually, the lights were off and Fusao's family was asleep.

He ran the few meters to the front door and as soon as he entered the house, his heart sank instinctively. It had happened then, the thing his mother and him feared most.

Naoki was pacing the room, his face as white as a sheet and his eyes were staring at nothing in particular. On the tatami floor, Tomoko lay crouching and weeping silently into her kimono sleeve and Yuko sat stony faced and dried eyed.

Fusao considered fleeing from the house but his father was too quick for him. With lightning speed, Naoki leapt across the room and his grip on Fusao's arm was so strong he could almost feel his bone cracking.

"How could all of you lie to me about something so important?" he shouted. "Have you no respect for me? You have watched me bursting with pride and joy every day because I believed I was going to have a grandson and none of you said anything!"

He lifted his hand and struck Fusao right across the face.

"You have single handedly caused all this. I don't know of any son who has brought so much shame and dishonor to his family as you have done! Do you know, you have broken my spirit and killed my soul?"

"Please, father," Fusao pleaded. "We didn't tell you because we thought it was better for you not to know the truth."

"Don't talk to me!" Naoki thundered. "How dare you decide what is better for me! You have saddled this family with a baby fathered by a criminal. Do you think you can live with that? Get out of my sight, you are no son of mine but a disgusting doseiai that society should spit on."

He raised his hand to strike Fusao again and spat on the floor contemptuously, but Yuko sprang to her feet and stood between her husband and her son.

"Please, Naoki," she pleaded. "Fusao did a lot of wrong but he is still your son."

Turning to Fusao, she gave him a push and said, "Take Tomoko and go to the room at the back, your father needs time to cool down."

In a daze, Fusao followed his mother's order and went to the extension room Naoki had built with so much joy and pride just weeks ago. Tomoko followed suit, still sobbing quietly.

When they were in the room, Tomoko flung herself at Fusao and said tearfully, "I'm sorry, Fusao, I was the one who told him by mistake. I don't know how it happened or what he said to make me believe he knew about it and had forgiven us but all of a sudden I found myself confessing everything to him."

"I have betrayed your trust and that of mother and now father will not accept this baby and we will always have anger and hatred in this family. I feel like killing myself, it's no point living a life that has no future and only a long road of loneliness, hatred and mistrust."

She started sobbing again, great deep sobs of despair. Despite his own distress and depression, Fusao took her into his arms and consoled her. There was nothing else he could offer her to right a very grave wrong, nothing else but weak words of consolation.

After a long while, her sobs subsided and, exhausted, both of them fell into a deep sleep right there on the tatami floor without even bothering to spread out the futon. They didn't even stir when the door opened a crack and Naoki peeped in to have a look at them. His heart was heavy with the weight of what he was going to do but he couldn't carry on any more with this life long reminder of an irrevocable dishonor to his name and his family. He would wait Until Yuko was asleep and then he would go out of the house and end it all.

* * * * *

The next morning, Fusao woke up with a very bad headache and a very bad taste in his mouth and as memories of what had happened the previous night came floating back to him, his head pounded and throbbed even more. For a moment he contemplated lying there and not getting up to face the world and another bad day but then he saw that Tomoko had left the room and he needed to make sure she was all right.

Reluctantly, he got up and went outside and was relieved that his father was not there, only his mother listlessly laying out some breakfast for Tomoko.

"Eat your breakfast first with Tomoko," Yuko said. "I'll prepare your father's breakfast later because it's better you don't eat together today."

Fusao nodded and sat down without a word, there just didn't seem to be anything he could say to make things better. The hot green tea helped to clear away some of his headache As the refreshing liquid coursed down his throat, he began to feel better and more able to think about how he was going to work with Naoki in the fields today. Maybe he should carry his mother's advice even further and stay off work for a few days until Naoki had cooled down and they could have a conversation to try and resolve the matter.

He saw his mother disappearing to the back of the house and then a piercing scream and a crashing of crockery shattered the quietness of the air. Yuko rushed into the room covering her face with her hands as she screamed over and over again, "No! No! No!"

Alarmed, Fusao sprang to his feet and asked, "What is it, mother? What is it?"

"It's your father! He's... he's..." she said almost incoherently pointing a shaking finger to the back of the house.

Fusao didn't wait for more as he ran out to the back of the house and then it was his turn to scream, "Father! Father, no, no..."

Hanging from a length of rope looped onto one of the sturdy branches of a tree was Naoki, eyes protruding and his tongue hanging out in a death mask. Fusao felt his legs giving way as he sank into a heap at the feet dangling above him, his father had hanged himself

Sobbing wildly, Fusao hung onto his father's feet as if by doing so he could bring life back to Naoki and was hardly aware when the strong arms of Hiroki, their neighbor carried him away from that ghastly sight.

Naoki's funeral was a typical peasant's, simple and unpretentious and he was buried in the small cemetery next to the village temple. Although generally a man of few words and not known to be very sociable, he had been highly respected and well liked for his kindness and generosity and the turn out at his funeral in the driving rain was good.

* * * * *

Yuko was inconsolable, she cried right through and didn't stop even when it was over. They went home to a house that felt suddenly lost without the strong presence and authority of Naoki. She couldn't understand how it had all happened so suddenly. It was only a few short weeks ago, Naoki had broken his reticence to chatter incessantly about his grandchild and the house had been filled with precarious but welcomed laughter. Although she tried not to blame Tomoko, it was hard when she realized that she was left all alone now with a pregnant daughter in law and a son whom she could not rely on. Why had that wretched girl not followed her orders and kept quiet?

But no, when she was rational to think dispassionately, it was not Tomoko's fault, but her own son who had brought this upon them. a religious woman, Yuko believed it was in some way retribution and punishment for living his life with the sin of going against nature and Kami-sama's rules for the people she helped to create. He had brought the curse of rape and death to his family and yet he was her son, born out of her body and she could not hate him. From now on, her days would be even harder and her nights would be lonely and cold.

From the time she had married Naoki at the age of 15, Yuko had always relied on him and had never made a serious decision in her life. Now, suddenly without warning, he had left her to head a family that was so dysfunctional. What could and what would she do without him after decades of dependency? Yuko never admitted to being courageous enough to take up the challenge her husband had left her and her first instinct was to join him or flee to her family in the south. But something stopped her, the thought of that innocent little life who was in many ways also a victim of her son's deviations even before he was born. That little life that the world saw as her grandchild was about to be born to a doseiai father and a young simple-minded mother who didn't have a clue about being a mother and was in many ways a child herself. Yuko knew she had to be around to protect that innocent life so no, she couldn't join Naoki, not just yet.

Chapter Forty-Five

For five days after his father's death, Fusao stayed in his room punishing himself by pouring out abusive self-condemnations in the remaining sheets of papers in his wooden file. He hardly touched the trays of food his mother left outside his door and only memories of what his last visit to the castle had brought prevented him from going to Lady Momoe and running a hocho through her heart. She was a cruel woman who didn't know the meaning of love and Fusao was sure she hated him because Lord Okimoto, her son, still loved the peasant boy he had fallen in love with all those years ago and nothing Lady Momoe did could break that love.

"It is powerful, this love," he wrote. "Ever since that last time we made love in his room at the castle, I have not desired any other man and the next time I make love, if ever, it will be with him, in this life time or another but until then, I desire no other man."

* * * * *

Fusao eventually recovered from his father's death and took over his work in the rice fields but because he was no farmer, their harvest fell each year and Yuko had to supplement their income by taking up sewing. To her delight, she discovered she had a great talent with the needle and soon became quite a name in the village. And for the first time in her life, Yuko discovered that she didn't have to depend on a man for a living but could sew and earn an income in her own right. This discovery was exhilarating and helped her cope with the great void her husband's death had left in her life.

Eventually, although Naoki's death still weighed heavily on them, there was a kind of peace. Fusao realized how quiet the house had become without his father to boss them around. Yuko was always at her sewing, Tomoko went about the household chores with a quiet

225

contentment and Fusao himself was still struggling with his ineptitude at farming that he found himself helping his mother out at her sewing more and more and becoming better at it!

In the autumn of that year, Tomoko gave birth to a baby girl and the infant was so big that she almost didn't make it. They called her Hoshi for the stars that lit up the sky the night she was born. She had a big round face and even at birth they could see that she didn't look like any of them but to the world, she was Yuko's granddaughter and Fusao's daughter and that was enough for them to love and accept her as their own.

Yuko had become such a household name for making and repairing clothes that even the servants of the castle started to come to the house with their orders. She was not particularly comfortable to have reminders of the castle, no matter how indirect, in her home but it was not proper to refuse anyone from the castle. But she made sure that Fusao didn't see or speak to any of them. Afterall, they were just starting to have some peace in the house.

One day a familiar face appeared and Fusao, who usually didn't interact with any of his mother's customers ran out to meet the visitor.

"Michio? Is it really you?" he shouted, beside himself with excitement.

Although he looked different, somehow, taller and bigger and more confident, it was Michio, the young friend of his castle days indeed. All the sweetness and innocence of youth was gone and he was very clearly a man now. With him was a pretty woman whom Fusao recognized immediately as Yuki the kitchen maid he had been courting when they first met. Apart from a slightly fuller figure and a more matured and subdued giggling habit, she hadn't changed much.

"Yes, it's me, Fusao! I came because I wanted to see you and of course because we do need your mother's services to sew some new clothes for Yuki. But to be honest I mostly wanted to see you here," Michio replied. "It's been quite some time since we last met and we were both so young then! You know Yuki of course? We got married a couple of years after you left and we have three children now, twin girls and a boy. Can you believe it, Fusao, I am the father of three children!"

Fusao saw his mother hovering anxiously in the background and he remembered her condition for continuing to give him a home, that he should never interact with anyone from the castle, whatever the circumstances.

"It's all right, mother," he assured her. "This is Michio, my best friend when I was working at the castle and we have some things to catch up."

Yuko did not look convinced but there was nothing she could do and while she was fitting Yuki out with some clothes, Fusao took his old friend out to the backyard and they sat down on a rough wooden work bench to talk.

"Are you still working at the castle in the same job? And Okuno san, is he still there?" Fusao asked, knowing that he was shooting random questions at his friend to stop himself from asking about a forbidden subject he had sworn would never cross his lips again.

Michio nodded, "Yes and no. I'm now assistant head housekeeper at the castle and Okuno san is still there too. But Yuki left after the twins came."

There was a silence then Michio looked his friend in the eye and said, "You want to know about him, right?"

When Fusao did not answer, he continued, "Lord Okimoto is not a happy person despite being the grand samurai and the wealthiest and most powerful man in the prefecture. Although he now has a son and heir and little Lord Shintaro is a very beautiful child, none of us have ever seen him spend any time with his wife and child

"He spends most of his time on sword fighting in a field next to the old tea house at the far end of the castle grounds. I am sure you remember the teahouse which Lady Momoe I think ordered reopened and now they actually use it for tea ceremonies and as a general teahouse."

"They opened up the teahouse and he's always going there?" Fusao asked, his eyes flashing with excitement at the first news about the castle and Lord Okimoto he had received in years and he did not bother to pretend with Michio any more.

His friend nodded and said, "And in case you want to know, he is never seen with any man other than in his capacity as samurai and lord of this region."

There was a long silence as Fusao absorbed all the precious information Michio had passed to him with mixed feelings. On the one hand he was elated because it was obvious that Lord Okimoto still carried a torch for him, on the other hand, he was upset because the young vibrant samurai filled with passion, laughter and swaggering arrogance who had driven him insane with love was gone and now a brooding young man with a dark past and a bleak future took his place.

"I've always known about you and Lord Okimoto, you know,"

Michio continued. "It wasn't any improper behavior or anything like that, but just a look here and there and the magnetic force that seemed to flow between the two of you was so strong that sometimes even I was intrigued by it."

"I'm sorry things didn't work out, but I guess our society is not ready to accept it but for me, your love is no less than that of Yuki and me, only different."

"He seems to live only for the many sword fighting competitions he attends all over the country and sometimes he participates in those fights. Lady Momoe is always at him to give up the sport as being reckless to risk not only his life but that of the samurai who belongs to the people. But he doesn't listen to her and carries on with the ferocity of someone who no longer values his life."

"Even worse, there's a crisis at the castle right now because there is a grand sword fighting match next week and Lord Okimoto is determined to participate. His mother cries every day and tells him not to go but has given up because he agrees that this will be his last match and like everyone else, she's just praying he will get through this match safely and never go again."

There was a little scuffle as Hoshi, who had just turned four, appeared. Michio, the natural father figure and never able to resist a child, bent down to scoop her up.

"This is your little girl, isn't it?" he said as he swung the child up onto his shoulders and galloped like a horse bringing out peals of delighted laughter from the normally solemn toddler.

Fusao watched them and sighed. He could never be so normal and so comfortably entrenched in society like Michio. Both he and Lord Okimoto were suspended in a lost world and could not connect with real life but for the young samurai, it was worse because he was constantly under public scrutiny while he, Fusao, could hide under the cloak of anonymity.

"It's strange, isn't it, how things turned out, look at Lord Okimoto with a son and you with a daughter, born just a year apart. I don't know how that happened but I never thought you especially would be a father so soon!" Michio said as he set Hoshi down and watched the child scamper away. "I still can't get over the fact that you have a daughter!"

"Sometimes I can't believe it myself," Fusao smiled and was disappointed when Yuki appeared to cut short their conversation.

"Promise me, Michio, that if anything ever happens to Lord Okimoto, you will tell me about it because I can't expect information from anyone else," he whispered to his friend. "Especially about this sword fighting match he's going to participate in, what if something happens to him and I never get to know about it?"

"Don't worry, Fusao," Michio said. "I'll make sure you get all the information you need but we are still hoping he'll change his mind"

* * * * *

That night after the lights in the house had gone out and Fusao and the rest of the family retired to their rooms, a dark shadowy figure leading a magnificent horse walked slowly past the house, stopping for a moment in front of its little gate of rush matting and bamboo. As the moon emerged slowly from the dusky clouds, the figure jumped onto his horse and rode quickly away, disappearing without a trace into the dark, impenetrable night.

Chapter Forty-Six

In the little house with the extension attached neatly to its back like a mother carrying her baby, a young girl was packing her father's things into a big piece of cloth that she then folded up and tied into a tidy knot at the top. Her heart was heavy with mixed feelings, happiness because her father was fulfilling his heart's desire to join the monastery to live out the rest of his days in peace and prayers now that she was all grown up and he could leave her with her mother and sadness, because she would miss him and his quiet strength and wisdom around the house.

Although they had not been close when she was a child, in later years, they had formed a bond and he would tell her stories of a servant who fell in love with a samurai but their love was doomed right from the start. Hoshi figured her father always looked sad when he told her this story and she wondered whether he had known this servant or maybe had been in love with her himself.

Her mother had nearly gone berserk the day her father, Fusao, announced to the family he was leaving to join the monastery in Niigata and although she first ranted and then tried to persuade him to change his mind, he remained firm.

"It's time I find my own way," he said. "For years I wanted to do this but because of you and Hoshi I stayed back to look after you both but now you have managed to take over the business from Mother and it's very successful, serving even Lady Momoe and her family Besides, Hoshi chan is all grown up. You don't need me anymore and it's time I move on to do what I wanted to do for a long time."

Eventually, Tomoko relented because her own passion with her tailoring business and the fulfillment she got from it made her understand her husband's own need to seek fulfillment and release from a life and marriage he had never been happy in. They shared only one thing and that was their love for their lovely sunny young daughter, the rest had just been staying together until Hoshi was big enough for Fusao to go.

"But we will still be able to go to Niigata to see you, right, Father?" Hoshi asked tearfully. They were sitting in the extension of the house she had been told her grandfather, Naoki, had built for them with his bare hands when he learnt that her mother was pregnant. Hoshi loved this room best because it was very quiet and right outside the window was a beautiful tree with extraordinary curved branches and the birds who built their nests there sang to her every morning.

"I love that tree, father," she used to say. "The branches wrap around the room like they are protecting me."

Fusao thought sadly at the time about what his daughter would say or feel if she knew that tree was where her grandfather had hanged himself before she was born because of her but perhaps Hoshi was right, perhaps Naoki was there on those branches always keeping an eye on his granddaughter and that made her feel safe and protected. Fusao hoped that wherever Naoki was, he had accepted Hoshi as his granddaughter at last!

And now on the day he was to leave for Niigata, he hugged his daughter and said, "Of course you can always come and see me in Niigata and bring me my favorite food because I'm sure the food at the monastery is very bad!"

"Remember, Mother's cooking is no better!" Hoshi laughed and the heavy moment passed.

His last view of his wife and daughter were two tiny figures running along the road waving until his carriage had disappeared into the distance. Inside the carriage, Fusao's eyes were filled with tears as he set out on a journey he had delayed for 16 years and as the carriage rounded a familiar corner and rode past the castle, memories of another time, another moment in his life, came flooding into his mind. He was approaching middle age and his hair was thinning and graying but his heart could still feel and hurt, it was the last time he would see the castle and all it stood for in his life.

His mind went back to that day when his friend Michio had knocked on his door and said, "Remember, Fusao, you told me to let you know if anything ever happens to Lord Okimoto?"

Fusao nodded, unable to speak because his heart was hammering with fear and a terrible premonition. He knew it was Lord Okimoto and something had happened to him.

Then an ice cold finger gripped his heart as a horrifying thought occurred to Fusao and he whispered hoarsely, "It was the sword fighting match, wasn't it... he's not...?"

Michio hung his head and when he spoke, his voice was barely audible.

"Yes... Lord Okimoto was badly injured in the competition and he died two days ago, the amazing thing is that his personal servant who attended him said he thought he heard Lord Okimoto mumble a name over and over again before he died but the servant couldn't make out what name. I'm sure it was your name, Fusao."

Fusao didn't hear anything, only the words "Lord Okimoto is dead! He is dead!" kept beating a rhythm in his head. It was finally over, he would never again see the light shining out of those eyes and feel the strength and warmth of those arms around him. Death had stepped in to end the suffering of one of them but for the other, the suffering would continue.

After Michio left, Fusao packed a small bundle of clothes and fled to Matsumoto to spend a week with his uncle. He could not bear to be in the village to witness the official mourning and funeral for Lord Okimoto and would return when it was all over and he could pretend that his samurai lover was still alive.

Fusao was thinking now of the agony of continuing to live and accepting the death of the samurai before the passing years blurred the pain as he watched the castle disappearing in the distance. This would be the last time he could think of Lord Okimoto and the passion they had once shared because soon he would be ordained a monk in the monastery and be asked to denounce all earthly possessions and desires. But just for a few more hours he could think of the handsome face of the samurai who never lived to grow old and how much they had loved each other and the nights spent at the old teahouse. Just for a few more hours, he could think and remember the fire of that love before he had to flush it out of his life forever.

The night before he left, he arranged all his years of writing neatly in his wooden folder, each bundle tied with a red string and written across the front of the folder, were the words "The Samurai and I." With all the love he felt for his long dead samurai lover, Fusao hid the wooden file of papers under a loose piece of tatami in his room.

Then he changed his mind and retrieved the wooden file and slipped it into his cloth bundle. No, the writings should stay with him until it was time to pass them to Hoshi. Someday he would tell his daughter about his diary but not right now, she was still too young to accept a doseiai father who was not really her father but someday she should know.

The castle faded into a small black dot and finally disappeared and along with it a turbulent chapter of Fusao's life had finally closed. All that remained was a wooden folder of papers tied up in red strings and hidden in the nondescript cloth bundle of a monk.

Chapter Forty-Seven

Mayumi folded the last of the papers and put them very carefully back into their old original wooden folder, her thoughts in a turmoil. She had just finished explaining the last of her translations to the elderly couple who sat, straight backed and unsmiling before her, trying to come to terms with the findings they had just received of a centuries old family mystery. Their grandson, Toyoki, leaned against a steel file cabinet, his eyes alight with a strange luminous light.

Mayumi shivered as she looked at the young man, he looked like a ghost and if she put a dark heavy samurai yukata and samurai head piece on him, she could imagine him to be the resurrection of Lord Okimoto who had started this whole legacy of Edo period scandal, intrigue and mystery and left behind a string of broken hearts, broken lives and a few deaths. It was as if the ghost of the long dead samurai was hanging around them listening to her exposing his tortured life to his descendants. But he didn't seem to mind. It was as if he was relieved that it was all out in the open at last.

"So our ancestor, the grand samurai Lord Okimoto Nobunaga was a homosexual?" Harumi san said. Her stilted voice brought Mayumi back to the present and she could see a hint of tears in her client's eyes.

Even though she didn't approve of gays in any period be it the 17th or 21st century, Harumi san could not help being touched by the poignant and ill-fated love story of two young men sucked into a vortex of passion and pain from the day their eyes first met, a story that had been preserved and kept alive in those age worn flimsy papers her grandson had discovered.

"Yes, "Mayumi replied. "He fell in love with Fusao, a young man from the village whom his father had taken an interest in because he could write unusually well. Some say that in his final years, the old samurai became senile and took a passing but extraordinary fancy to Fusao and

234

his writing. One day he took his son, Lord Okimoto with him to the peasant's house, their eyes met and the rest is well, history as you know it now through Fusao's writings."

"Yes, to be honest, at first it was hard trying to accept that there was a social outcast like a homosexual in what we always thought was a perfect and unblemished line of samurai ancestry in our family but I guess in retrospect, it's better a homosexual in those writings than some vile serial murderer"

There was a stirring in the steel cabinet corner. Toyoki straightened his lounging frame and said in a voice so soft they could hardly hear him.

"Do you really mean that, O bachan, that you can accept a homosexual in our family?"

And with a quickening of her pulse rate, Mayumi knew what Toyoki was going to say even before he came out with it. It had all made sense now, his deep intrigue into Fusao and Lord Okimoto's secret love.

"O bachan, I have been meaning to share this with you a long time but just didn't know when was a good time to start," Toyoki went on. "But I don't want to live like our ancestor, scared, alone, and miserable and unable to be who I want to be. To be who I want to be. O bachan, I am also gay. "

The cup of green tea slipped from Harumi san's lips and shattered on the ground Her pale elegant face had gone even whiter and she tensed up for a moment before letting out a sigh that came out in a tiny moan.

Mayumi prayed that she would handle it right. It was as if history was repeating itself to give the family a second chance.

There was a long silence and Mayumi held her breath as she saw the myriad of expressions flowing and ebbing on Harumi san's face until the one she was hoping for settled on it, one of acceptance and recognition.

The young historian sighed with relief as her client held out her arms and silently embraced her grandson. The tragic young samurai who had died for his forbidden love in the 17th century had finally found acceptance in his family 400 years later.

"O'bachan, thank you for accepting me as I am. Now I am free to find my Fusao and live openly in-love as our ancestor had wanted to do. We can make right and dispel the curse our family has lived under for so long."

Toyoki and his grandmother smiled and shared a deep understanding of what had just happened. They both knew the past horrors their family had suffered for generations was over." By the way, there's a teahouse which was given to Fusao's family by the samurai and is now run by his descendants, it was the place where Lord Okimoto and Fusao often met to spend some time together," Mayumi ventured. "Perhaps you would like to see it someday."

Harumi nodded and said after a brief hesitation, "There's just one last thing I'd like to ask. If the papers were written by Fusao and kept with him all the time, how did they get to the castle and finally passed down to us?"

"I've been asking that question myself," Mayumi admitted. "Maybe Fusao left instructions for his descendants to pass them to someone at the castle or maybe the samurai's family discovered their existence and ordered them to be confiscated or stolen to prevent any scandal from leaking out or maybe not. I guess we might never know! They were very careful to keep the samurai's himitsu."

Epilogue

The dusty and travel weary carriage finally came to a stop at its final destination in the carriage terminal of the Minamimoto village square and Hoshi and her mother tumbled out and started the short walk home. They had just returned from a one week trip to Niigata to see Fusao and both of them knew that it could very well be the last time they would see him alive.

For Tomoko a painful chapter of her life that had started when she was barely 15 years old was about to close and she was eager to return to the only love left in her life apart from her daughter. After her patient and much loved mother in law, Yuko died, the exquisite sewing and tailoring business that had gained, and was continuing to gain fame and reputation in the whole region, had passed to her. It had saved her life at a time when she had lost all hope after becoming pregnant from a rape and discovering that her husband had been a homosexual lover of their samurai. Few, if any women, had seen the humiliations that she had suffered and she had lived through it all and emerged a successful business woman in Edo period Japan and today, Tomoko had every reason to be proud of herself.

When they reached home, Hoshi removed a much handled flat wooden box from inside her kimono and opened it, making sure first that her mother had gone into the kitchen to prepare their evening meal and was not likely to come out any time soon.

She thought about her father and how, as they were leaving the monastery in Niigata, he had placed the box in her hands and told her to do something for him.

"This box belongs to the castle and someday I want you to deliver it to the future samurai, Lord Shintaro," Fusao said, and, choking back her tears at leaving her father for the last time, Hoshi nodded her head and promised to do just that. At that moment she would have promised him anything.

But now as she put the flat wooden box away, safely hidden deep in her oshire, Hoshi wondered how and when she would have the chance to meet the Lord Shintaro to pass the box to him. Her father had made it sound so easy but the reality was that she wouldn't be able to get past even the first outer gates of the castle, let alone see Lord Shintaro.

Since her father hadn't told her she couldn't open it, before she put it carefully away, Hoshi had taken a look inside and been disappointed that there was nothing more sinister than a big package of papers filled with writings she couldn't read.

It had grown dark and the stars for whom she had been named were twinkling their brightest in the clear night sky. Hoshi sighed as she gazed at the distant lights. someday, somehow she would find a way to keep her promise to her father and deliver that brown wooden file to Lord Shintaro Nobunaga. But until then, she had to keep it safe for her father.

With another deep sigh, the most beautiful young girl in the village with the twinkling deep brown eyes looked whimsically out of the window at the night sky at a patch of sparkling stars, she sighed, then started to lay out the futons.

In the distance, a neighbor's dog howled and the moon slowly glided out of its hiding place among the few clouds to light up another clear night in Minamimoto village.

Not too far in the distance in the castle a young samurai lay on his silken soft futon looking at the same stars and wondered what it felt like to fall in love.

About the Author

Rei Kimura is a lawyer with a passion for writing about unique events and personalities. She has adopted an interesting style of creating stories around true events and the lives of real people in a number of her books, believing that is the best way of making hidden historical events and people come alive for 21st century readers.

With this objective in mind, Rei has touched on historical events like the horrific sinking of the Awa Maru and the Kamikaze pilots of World War II and woven them into touching stories of the people who lived and died through these events.

Then there are stories of courage, love and rejection beautifully portrayed in "Butterfly In the Wind" a story of the concubine of Townsend Harris, first American consul to Japan, set against the colorful and turbulent era of the Black Ships. This book has touched the hearts of many and been translated into languages from Spanish, Polish, Russian, Dutch to Thai, Hindi, Indonesian, Marathi.

Rei's writing also touches on interesting issues like that raised in "Japanese Magnolia" a book based on the true story of two men, a samurai and a peasant who dared to cross two forbidden areas in feudal Japan, that of homosexuality and a class society "so sharply defined it cut like a knife."

Other controversial stories she has written include "Japanese Rose" a book which asked the question was there ever a Japanese female kamikaze pilot in the Second World War?

But it's not all history and culture, she also writes on contemporary events like "Aum Shinrikyo-Japan's Unholy Sect" an expose of the 1995 sarin gas attack on the Tokyo subway. Occasionally, her love for animals and sense of humor surfaces in this very heart warming and delightful story of a rogue Pomeranian dog, "My Name is Eric," a complete departure from Rei's normal story lines but nevertheless, a refreshing one!

Kimura considers her writing as part of the perennial quest for truth, challenge and fulfillment. Her books have been translated into various Asian and European languages and widely read all over the world.

Apart from being a lawyer, Rei Kimura is also a qualified freelance journalist and is associated with the Australian News Syndicate.

Also by the Author: *Butterfly In The Wind, Alberto Fujimori-The President Who Dared to Dream, Awa Maru-Titanic of Japan, Japanese Orchid, Japanese Rose, Aum Shinrikyo-Japan's Unholy Sect, My Name is Eric, Japanese Peony, Soulmates In Tokyo*

If You Liked This Riverdale Avenue Books Novel, You Might Also Like:

Silk Threads - Three Tales of Passionate Japan
by Cecilia Tan, Laura Antoniou, Midori

The Virgin King
By John Michael Curlovich

The Tattered Heiress
By Debra Hyde

Made in the USA
Middletown, DE
06 April 2024

52482687R00139